*Author's Note*

*Dances with the Daffodils* is a work of fiction. Some characters are based on real people, in Grasmere and elsewhere in the Nineteenth Century, and others are inspired by the subjects of Wordsworth poems – especially the principal character Luke, who features in the poem *Michael*. The rest are purely imagined. A number of scenes in the novel track real events in the lives of Dorothy and William Wordsworth in 1802 – as chronicled in Dorothy's Grasmere journal – but the actual characters of Dorothy and William in *Dances with the Daffodils* are fictional. One of my aims in writing this book was to recreate for the reader the everyday world of Grasmere life so vividly described in Dorothy Wordsworth's journals. I tried to do this by portraying the forgotten 'ordinary' people – the farmers, shepherds, wallers, war widows, housewives, servants, labourers and beggars – as well as the extraordinary. Indeed, it was one of Wordsworth's original (and revolutionary) poetic aims to show that "men who do not wear fine clothes can feel deeply".

*MVC*
*April 2013*

# DANCES WITH THE DAFFODILS

## A NOVEL

By Matthew Connolly

NOVEL-DNA BOOKS

NOVEL-DNA BOOKS LTD
www.noveldna.co.uk

This edition first published in 2013
Copyright © Matthew Connolly 2013

The Author asserts the moral right to be identified as
the author of this work

Set in Garamond by MTP-Media

Printed and bound in Great Britain by
Clay's Ltd, St Ives plc

ISBN 978-0-9575740-0-7

*For Felicity, James and Catherine*

# Part One

Part One

# 1

# Father Nature

*March 21st, 1802*
First day of spring. Luke inched his way to the lip of Westminster
Bridge and peered down into London's great tide of misery. It
looked strangely purifying as it surged a hundred feet below,
glistening in the sunshine, inviting him in. Had it really come
to this? It seemed only yesterday that Greenhead Ghyll in
Grasmere had mixed its song with his mother's lullabies, and
Michael had gazed down on him, an infant in arms, with the
full might of a father's love. Yet here he stood, astride the grave
of all those other submerged suicides, poised for the sorry drama
of self-destruction.

What wild beast had hunted him to this cliff edge, consuming
everything in its path, not only all the love and gladness he'd ever

had in his heart, but even the blind, desperate will to survive that had got him through Alexandria a year before, hauling him out from beneath soldiers and horses spattered across a crimson field? What force had broken his spirit so completely that, although his belly was as empty as an old wolf, he could no longer bear to beg strangers for food?

He thought about Alice, and her dignity that morning, not ranting away with the gin-drunk syphilitics of Newgate's female quarter, but stooping almost elegantly to nurse her bleeding ankles as she was led across the yard in leg-irons – her final steps, neck bowed, lips grey as a corpse's. There she'd stood, a rosy-lipped girl of sixteen, noosed, pinioned, a white nightcap over her head. 'Hats off!' the crowd had cried, not out of respect but to clear the view. To rowdy applause and the braying of urchins, dogs and pie-hawkers, Alice had fallen a full eighteen inches into taut rope. For two tortuous minutes he'd watched her writhe before he'd barged his way to the scaffold, scrambled up the steps, grabbed her ankles and pulled. He could see her now through his closed his eyes, the poor, snapped doll, swinging lifeless.

He dared not even think about what he'd done afterwards, but he now knew he was no longer merely worthless – that was too innocent a word. He glanced down again at the river, and fancied he saw his own reflection. His breath quickened. The fiend had hounded him here, and it begged his presence below. He looked up into the sky and groped in his pockets for the rocks that would sink him to the riverbed. 'Do it now!' he roared, and out of the celestial blue came an unexpected feeling of calm. He was ready.

He placed a foot forward and fell. It was less of a jump than a tumble through the air at a terrifying and accelerating speed. And then the gigantic smack against the granite of running water, knocking him half-unconscious. The Thames gulped him down and dragged him a mile eastwards round a bend in the river, replacing the balmy air of spring in his lungs with all the filth from London's dunghills, factories and slaughter-houses. He came to near Blackfriars Bridge, his limbs wrapped round each other and something hooked onto his arm, reeling him in like a dead fish.

'I have you! Hold on to my cane!' he heard a man shout, and he felt himself being heaved out of the water. It turned out, by a stroke of ill luck, to be a wretched do-gooder who'd spotted him in the sludge and come to the unwise decision that he was better off alive. A doctor was sent for, and he arrived with experimental apparatus for reviving the near-drowned – tobacco smoke to the lungs, applied from the rear by means of a pipe. The suicide breathed again and, in immediate possession of the worst headache of his life, fainted in his rescuer's arms.

He later found himself in the George and Blue Boar Inn at Holborn, his limp limbs being cajoled into the frock-coat, waistcoat, silk cravat and leather shoes of a gentleman. The good Samaritan had acquired them for him at a second-hand stall, and afterwards bought him a hearty meal. The man finally left him, thrusting a few coins in his hand and telling him a mailcoach was leaving London from outside the inn at half-past nine that same evening – in one hour.

He stood in a daze on Holborn corner opposite Red Lion Street, watching the usual pageant of drunken beggars and vagrants, pickpockets and swindlers, pimps and ogling jades. His people. He'd been drawn to them soon after he'd arrived in London as a lad of only eighteen, in a flush of excitement at earning a wage running errands between coffee houses for a new club of rich men called stockbrokers. The stock they broke, he seemed to recollect, was negro slaves, but he'd had money in his pocket for the first time, and could begin tasting the pleasures hidden within London's honeycomb of thoroughfares.

'Here!' called a voice, and the sallow hand of a gypsy pushed a withered flower into his own. 'Shall I tell yer fortune, sir?' she added with a leer.

He told her to go to hell, and she treated him to a free, public fortune-telling, saying he could look forward to a 'royt good scraggin' himself one day, 'just like that little twang I saw you tendin' to at Newgate this morning'. Luke shook a weary fist at her and she backed off.

'Surgeons' Hall at the Owd Bailey,' she shouted. 'That's where they took your friend after in that cart, you know? Public dissection!' She cackled as she walked away, and he watched her propositioning some other unfortunate further along the street.

St Sepulchre's clock struck the hour.

He couldn't possibly go now. How many other wasted beggars and worn-out soldiers were drifting back to where they'd once had homes, to villages preyed on by want, worklessness and failed harvests? But he couldn't stay any longer. Not after this day. He retreated back inside the inn and sat down by a candle-lit table in the corner. He watched the candle's shadow dance on the wall behind. There'd been no flame in him for years beyond count. He pinched the wick and watched the smoke rise. He'd tried to snuff out his whole existence, but the shadow had lingered.

A barrel-organ outside was playing a mournful air about unrequited love, and some long-forgotten words suddenly came back to him. 'In whatever fate befalls thee, Luke, I will love thee till the end.' Michael's valediction. Could there really still be a home there for him, and even love?

He emerged again from the inn to discover the coach loading the mail and the passengers in feverish preparation for departure. He looked up into the clear evening sky at a pool of stars, and felt in his pockets for the coins his rescuer had given him. A small, undead ember of hope flickered inside him to think that something – someone – might await him right back where he'd started out half a lifetime ago.

St Sepulchre's struck the half hour.

'Three hundred miles in three days!' the coachman yelled as the Flying Machine hurtled northwards, jolting Luke straight into his fellow rooftop traveller and triggering a duel-like fusillade of recrimination between the two of them. The only way to stay on board at this insane pace, they soon realised, was by overcoming their mutual antipathy and hugging each other tight.

'Fast as the wind!' shrieked the coachman again, glancing round and grinning at the two grown men in reluctant embrace behind him on the roof. 'An' you know whoy my friends? Cos in that wind there's sammit else blowing. A new age, me boss says, of strange contraptions called steam-locomotives!' He thrashed the creatures in front of him harder, howling, 'I tell ya, if we ain't quick enough to beat that lot, the end o' the horse-drawn coach is noigh.' The steeds whinnied at the news and the Flying Machine rattled ever faster out of London.

At around ten o'clock, Luke let go of his companion and craned his neck forward to observe a menacing figure on horseback galloping past, and fell off the side of the coach. He began chasing after the vehicle, but it halted less than a furlong further, thanks to the lone equestrian, who'd crossed the heads of the horses, stood up in his stirrups and brandished a pistol.

'Give me your money or I'll blow out your brains,' Luke heard the horseman demand as, unseen, he edged closer to the Flying Machine from behind. Coins and timepieces emerged from a hand inside the carriage, the passenger to whom the hand belonged calling out, 'I warn you, my good man, I duel often and win every time.' The highwayman responded with a smile that seemed like a prelude to casual murder.

Luke flew recklessly through the air and dragged the highwayman off his horse to the ground. The villain was subdued, with the help of the coachman and his former roof-mate, while the passenger in the carriage, though mute in his gratitude, at least provided the few extra thruppences Luke needed to get a little further north, seated inside this time not on top.

As the Flying Machine careered onwards he scrutinised his new companion, a puce-faced toff in the coat, boots and breeches of a classic English country gentleman – just the type not to think twice about stepping over half-dead peasants at Alexandria, soldiers like him weeping in the mud and the blood for a cause no more noble than the nobility's endless tyranny over them. The gentleman, clearly unsettled by his scowl, sought refuge in polite conversation.

'They say the iron-edge railway is coming,' he declared. 'But I say good old-fashioned horse breath will see off the rash assault of steam, what?'

Luke made his response in the form of cold silence.

'I say, did you see the hanging at Newgate?' the nobleman tried again. 'A fine one first thing this morning, so I believe. I was on my way but, infuriatingly, so was the rest of London. Not even the pounding we gave Bonaparte in Egypt last year sparked such a blasted orgy of fraternity!'

A more irate version of silence greeted the speaker, but he pressed on.

'Some blackguard in a scarlet coat stood gawping into my cab. "May I suggest your driver turns the horses round, sir," the rascal bleated, claiming he was a Captain of the Guards or something. "The mob is heading your way. There could be a riot. You know how excited they get when a pretty young woman hangs – especially a child murderer." Well I never got to see it, thanks to the confounded 'Captain of the Guards', but it was one of the best hangings in years, so I hear. A long, drawn-out agony, the obstinate little harlot!'

It would have been a suicide bid too far to cut the throat of an aristocrat and then end up back at Newgate gallows swinging from the end of his second-hand cravat. 'Stop the horses!' he bawled to the coachman. 'Let me out.'

He tramped northwards over many days, hitching a ride in a dung cart at one stage but getting in an argument with a drunken cattle-walloper who accused him of looking to steal one of his cows. His only lift of distance was at the front of another mailcoach, thanks to a mislaid postilion.

At length he reached the gloomy city of Manchester and managed to wind up outside a large cotton mill, half-dead and begging for food. He'd learnt hand-loom-weaving at home as a boy, spinning and carding wool all hours of the night with his mother, but most old-style cottage weavers were no more than jobless loiterers outside the factories and mills these days. He was amazed, however, to find the mill-owners took him on, to work night and day on spinning and carding machines powered by huge, noisy monsters called steam engines. He soon discovered they took anybody on – black slaves, white slaves, pauper children, monkeys if they could. The toil and heat were killing, and he earned nothing but the odd stale crust. He stuck it for a week and was spewed out with all the other human husks they'd driven to that point in the road between exhaustion and death.

He finally arrived at the grubby market-town of Penrith thirty miles from the Scotch border, where he slept in a gutter, his feet putrid and his head throbbing with fever and fatigue. He pushed south-west the following day and fell asleep in a ditch that night. The next morning he woke up with the damp scent of lake air in his nostrils and, like a stray dog returned, he tracked down the tail of Ullswater and planted his first steps on Lakeland soil in twenty years.

basked on the ground; but most – and now there were thousands upon thousands – danced in the breeze seemingly with sheer joy as blossom scattered over them like butterflies.

He fell to his knees, drank in the daffodils' perfumes and felt a great cascade of sorrow gush through him to have misspent so much of his life. The sky turned charcoal with raincloud. Out of nowhere appeared a woman, a thin, gypsy-tanned thing in cloak and shawl, hopping and tumbling along the lane like a chaffinch turned over by the wind, the gusts playing havoc with her poke bonnet. Luke shrank behind an oak.

'Look, William!' she shrieked as eyes blue-grey as Snowdonia slate beheld the daffodils and she knelt down among them as if in worship. 'So wild and full of glee! I shan't forget a single feature. Might they make a poem?'

The gentleman – a tall and ugly mantis of a creature, presumably her husband – was veering along picking his way through the bramble, his greatcoat flapping like a mad, flightless bird. His muttering lips reminded Luke of a Herdwick going at couch grass. He had a Roman nose and a mouth whose architecture was in the style of mean-spirited amusement. His voice, however, was a mirthless growl.

'Yes, Dolly. But please don't do all that nervous blubbering. Put it in your journal.' With that the gentleman struck off diagonally along the path, scowling, head tucked in against the wind, legs yards ahead of body.

Luke watched from behind the oak tree as the birdlike woman flew off in his wake. She was no Lady Hamilton and would surely never be painted among Grecian-style drapery, but her eyes were fervid, even wild. And although he was clearly not in possession of his senses, she'd looked to him – if only for a flash of a moment as she'd knelt among the daffodils – like some kind of pagan goddess.

The wind dropped once the couple had disappeared and the flowers drooped as though into a mope. Luke emerged from his hiding-place and crouched among the daffodils, ripping a handful out of the ground with such force that they came bulbs and all. As he stood up the clouds burst open and rain sobbed all over the landscape. Trees seethed, becks turned to torrents, Herdwicks congregated beside stone walls and all of Lakeland cowered beneath a pitiless April storm as he resumed his journey home to Grasmere.

He stopped several hours later, beaten numb by a wind flinging rain like shards of flint at his face. He raised his head insolently to the black, cold sky. As he lowered his eyes a light glimmered, maybe a quarter of a mile on the road ahead. Within minutes he was standing beneath the sign 'Nell House'. He knocked, and saw flames from a hearth through a window, and ached for it to singe the hairs on his shins. He spotted a tall, stooping figure shuffling around the room. It was William from Ullswater. And if he was in there then presumably ... He squinted so tight his forehead blanched.

'Yes, there she is,' he whispered as he saw Dolly pacing around the room with the light from the fire crackling in her ardent eyes. The front door opened and two drooling setters set upon him, knocking him to the ground.

'Cum here you stinking hounds or I'll skelp thy backsides,' trilled a woman's voice. The dogs leapt back inside and the door closed again. Yelps of canine self-pity ensued, and the door re-opened to reveal a short, wide dame, owning inside her apron a bosom ample enough to do damage to a barn door. 'Full up, offcomer,' she said, her smile more sour than a lemon in vinegar. Then, contradicting herself as quickly as Lakeland weather, she added, 'Yuv got ten minutes to dry off byt fire,' upon which she glided back inside, cursing her dogs continuously. The name 'Hannah!' echoed off the walls and a set-upon-looking young maid emerged.

'Wait in here,' Hannah said, bustling him into a cavernously cold room. 'When tuther guests go up you can shift next door and stand byt fire. I'll fetch a drink.' He knew it was an over-reaction but his gratitude for her felt like love. Minutes later his arms were reaching out, not to Hannah or – even better – to Dolly, but to flames so inviting that he would willingly have stepped into the hearth had the fire asked him.

Hannah eventually reappeared bearing rum, water and haverbread, which he accepted with grasping thanks. The rum boiled him within while the fire cooked him without, and as he stood with his back to the flames his coat emitted clouds of steam making him feel like a heretic simmering at the stake. The coat had all but evaporated when the door opened and Dolly scuttled in.

'I... I... I... can see you're warming up,' she stammered, venturing a chuckle.

'I... I...' he spluttered, by no means intentionally in imitation of her.

'Forgive my intrusion,' she said. 'I left a book here.' She picked up a small volume, entitled *Lyrical Ballads with a few other poems*, from a table and backed away to the door. She was so polite – quite a gentlewoman. Surely he hadn't fooled her into thinking him a gentleman?

'You must forgive me,' he blurted. 'I intruded on you and your husband. At Ullswater.'

Her eyes contracted with befuddlement, then darted across the floor as if looking for an explanation in the wainscoting.

'The daffodils?' he added by way of an extra clue.

'Ah!' she said, then paused. 'But I don't remember seeing you.'

'You were too affected by the flowers to notice anything else,' he said, beginning to feel too affected by the rum. She fired her reply at him like grapeshot.

'I was so very deeply moved. At first we fancied the lake had carried the seeds ashore and that a little colony had sprung up, but as we went along there were more and more of them, under the boughs of the trees along the lakeshore, among the mossy stones about them – they were everywhere! They looked so gay in the wind, ever glancing, ever changing!'

She blushed.

'Yes,' he perspired, 'like girls at a country dance.'

'That's it exactly!'

'Here,' he said, opening with a sense of conquest his waistcoat and, like a clown-magician, revealing a sopping wet bunch of wilted daffodils. Dolly looked horrified.

'No, I really can't,' she said, thrusting them straight back.

Feet shuffled into the room.

'You're gunna have to go,' said Hannah. 'Mistress says time's up.'

Dolly withdrew and Hannah led him to the front door, peering into his barbed visage. 'Me alfella looked like you. Went tut war. I can hardly remember him now. Not you is it, Fadder?' she asked, a forlorn forefinger touching his arm.

He racked his brains. 'No, not me.'

She eased him out of the door. 'Where yeh heading now?'

'Kirkstone Pass over to Ambleside. Even if it kills me.' His heart wasn't as brave as his words but the rum, or whatever it was, would make the ordeal less painful.

'Ower't Pass?' she said. 'Tha's bluddy barmy.'

With gratitude less than love this time he thanked her and stepped out into a howling hell. A window broke open.

'*Narcissus pseudonarcissus*!' sang the wild-eyed chaffinch.

'I beg your pardon?' he yelled back, as if insulted.

'It's the Latin name for wild daffodils. And so good luck to you!'

'And to you!' he bawled as he strode away from her headlong into the storm, suspecting it resembled the infernal abyss into which men who coveted their neighbours' wives all sooner or later found their way.

Night flung its greatcoat over evening, transforming the dainty beck at his feet into a silver snake. The pass stiffened, vapours rose off the rain and rock-shadows crept alongside him. He could hear Michael's voice again. 'Tek care, son. Winds in them fells can knock a yowe off her feet, and mist can coax a farmer off a cliff. Watch out for them ghosts an all – howls, cries and moans in the wind. Turn a plucky shepherd into a gibbering bairn, they can.'

Eventually he reached Broad Water, and beyond that a fork in the road. He spied through the mist a long, ruined building by the roadside. He reached it, climbed inside the shell of its walls, looked up through its lack of a roof, then sank to the ground, arms round his knees, rain plopping off his nose. When he heard the distant sound of hooves he knew he might be delirious to think it, but he was sure the ghosts of the fells had come for him. He stood up and saw the vague shape of a vehicle fronted by a shattered-looking beast. The apparition clattered nearer and he marvelled at the silhouette of an elegant arm thrashing an ancient horse in the moonlight. A cart flagged to a halt yards from him and he recognised the outline of the horse-walloper.

'Stupid old nag!' barked Hannah. 'Gettin. I'll tek thee o'er to Ambleside with these here gentlefowks I picked up in Patterdale.'

He climbed in and sat opposite a bedraggled gentleman and his wife. After ten terrifying minutes in the cart, careering downhill in the pitch dark at the mercy of Hannah and her horse, Luke remembered why the road over to Ambleside was known as the Struggle.

'This excursion,' the lady bawled out, 'was supposed to be an inexpensive way of seeing the Alps in spring, not a sightseeing tour round the outskirts of hell.'

'My dear,' hollered the gentleman, 'Lakeland is most definitively not the Alps. It is like a squashed version. But these are difficult times and we are all squashed versions of ourselves, so do try to make the most of the inferior countryside and be cheerful.'

'How inconvenient!' she clipped. 'Well, I do hope the weather will not disappoint, despite this insane storm.'

'The weather? If you are expecting a fine spring you will be dismayed by the wet Lakeland climate. Perhaps we should turn back and walk through our own gardens for a week instead?'

'No, no, I have suffered enough already. But how are we going to find a good picture to paint if the sky is full of rain and black cloud? Where will all those colours be that Gilpin harps on about in his book on the picturesque?'

'The whole point of being an artist, my darling, is that you paint what you want to see anyway. Just make it up. If you wish to see a tree glistening in the sunshine in the background of your painting, why then put one in for goodness sake. If you wish to see a cart-horse drooping its head poignantly in the rain, then paint one.'

'Well I intend to sit by a lake or in some grove or other, preferably with a blanket on my lap, sketching a spring flower or two. You will not catch me scrambling up mountains for some sublime experience.'

Hannah, sensing the discomfort among her passengers, embarked upon a local tale presumably to cheer them all up.

'You know fowks don't call it Broad Water anymore, but Brotherswater,' she bellowed.

'Why?' Luke asked.

'It all happened on New Year's Day. Two young bairns, brothers they was, went out to skate on the ice while their mudder was busy back at home nearby. They were full of high spirits as they ran off, skates in hand and coats buttoned up to necks against the icy cold. A few hours passed and the mudder wondered why they weren't back, then a farmer came running shouting for her to come quickly to Broad Water, saying he'd heard screams. She dropped what she was doing and ran. When she got to the edge of the lake she saw what no mudder should. Under the cracked and shattered ice was two dark shapes, her two bairns floating face-down. The poor mites were holding hands.'

With that, all chit-chat was rendered defunct, and Hannah fell silent as her nag galloped on. Around two in the morning Ambleside chapel came into view. Luke thanked his driver, jumped off, and the cart rumbled away.

As he approached the chapel the wind died down and the rain petered out. He opened the door, crept in and lay down face upwards on a back pew. For many hours he tried to sleep, but he ended up watching the slow tide of dawn wash away the darkness and leave pools of sunlight in the chapel's corners. Morning had come, and the final five miles to Grasmere begged.

# 3

## Glow-Worm

---

The storm over eastern Lakeland the night of April the Fifteenth – she'd logged the date in her journal – had gnashed itself hoarse outside Nell House by early morning, and Dorothy Wordsworth lay staring at a curtain whose hems were ablaze with sunshine. She could stand no longer to lie in bed in stillness, neither hearing nor seeing anything as she dwelt on the prospect of all their time together being over. The thought would send her mad. She flung off the blankets, sprang out of her bed, wrenched open the window and sniffed the dewy air.

'Wake up, William. Look what a fine day it is! We must make our way home.'

William didn't even have time to complete a yawn before she was on at him again.

'Come, William!' she cried.

'You're in a hurry,' he croaked.

'I am,' she shot back. 'Have your shave and let's be done with breakfast.'

William climbed out of his bed, stumbled around in dizzy urgency and began attending to his shaving rite.

'How did you sleep?' Dorothy asked him as he brandished the razor drunkenly, gazed at himself, swashbuckled the blade in water and began the grins and grimaces into the mirror required for extracting stubble.

'I didn't,' he said through puckered lips.

'Why? The storm?' she asked, suspecting it wasn't as straightforward as that, knowing William's interminable wrestles with words.

'I wish it were that simple,' he confirmed, inspecting a half-shaven upper lip.

'Brooding?' she suggested.

'Tormented,' he said, pausing and permitting a long self-gaze. 'Not by illness but by unmanageable thoughts.'

'Slacken them, then, William, and lie down for a while. Breakfast can wait.'

William appeared to ignore her and retreat into inaccessibly severe thought. 'I felt a breath of breeze,' he soliloquised, 'through the window during the night, and it stirred the creative breeze within me. It became a storm, just like the one that raged all night outside, and I felt a sense of great power, that brought great promise.' The blade plunged inward and tiny bubbles of blood inflated on his neck. He dabbed the red spot with the tip of his forefinger and the blood clotted. He sat down on his bed, shave unfinished, and slackened his shoulders, even if not his thoughts, then lay down. 'So many feelings, Dolly,' he sighed. Dorothy tested the temperature of his brow.

'Then there was a flash,' he cried, bolting up straight, 'of the daffodils yesterday. A visionary gleam.'

Dorothy's spine straightened to attention at the words, and then William's drooped.

'But it mocked me.'

'Why?' she asked in synchronised dismay.

'Because that flash of light didn't bring a sky that ripened into a steady morning.'

'This is a fine, tranquil morning,' she said, knowing he was speaking figuratively but reluctant to soothe his anguish when she was plagued with her own.

'Outside, maybe.'

Dorothy put a hand on his arm. 'Can you not be at peace?'

William answered in a voice baritoned by melancholy. 'Less quiet instincts haunt me. I have all I need – a vital soul, wisdom, nature – but I want to write about my own heart, my own passions and thoughts, yet it all seems so insubstantial, so vain.'

'Do you have a vision of the poem you truly want to write, William?'

'I do,' he cried. 'A song of truth, verse that people will cherish forever.'

'Then do it, William. What's stopping you?'

'The thought. It terrifies me. So I tell myself I must wait, and let time ripen my mind, and do it in mellower years. And this brings infinite delay, and I hide in indolence, travelling towards the grave, given so much but giving nothing. Was it all for this, Dorothy? To lack courage? To fail?'

'But you have extraordinary powers, William,' she said, putting a hand on his shoulder and trying to ignore her own petty sorrows. 'What is it you fear?'

'Their loss,' he grunted.

Dorothy paused, and thought about this great poem yet to be written, with its prelude longer even than the Derwent itself, and, like that river, in an endless state of flux, subjected to unceasing revision. She wondered what else was on his mind, or heart, when she heard him, now standing erect and shaving, whisper to himself lines of freshly baked verse in front of the mirror, seeming to taste the words, smell them, certainly see how they looked in the glass.

*Among all lovely things my love had been;*
*Had noted well the stars, all flowers that grew*
*About her home; but she'd never seen*
*A glow-worm, never one, and this I knew.*

'The glow-worm,' she gasped, her knuckle wiping something tear-like from her eye. 'It must be seven years.'

William's eyebrows gathered like drapes. 'I didn't know you were listening. Oh well, now you know.'

Dorothy turned on him. 'Tell me, what is it about?'

'When you saw your first glow-worm, Dolly. Remember? By the tree in the orchard? You were spellbound, like a child. I composed it the other day on horseback. My hands got so cold I couldn't hold the reins and I fell off. In fact, the horse fell over too!'

They looked at each other glumly for a second, then laughed, then were struck glum again. 'What is the poem really about?' Dorothy persisted.

'It's about how I can never forget the years we've spent together.'

'Why on earth should you want to?' she cried out as if he'd thrust his razor down her throat. William made no reply but carried on with his shave, scraping over the final stubblesome corners in silence.

After breakfast, and weathering the overcast face of the landlady, who still didn't brighten when they handed over seven extortionate shillings, they headed for the Kirkstone Pass. A rainbow of primroses, celandines, violets and strawberries lit up the path as they passed along. Dogs yapped, cattle lowed and leather-skinned farmers ploughed, harrowed and sowed. Girls with muscular arms and sullen faces spread dung with spades and pitchforks, releasing insolent sniggers as Dorothy and William went by. By Broad Water William sat on a rainbow-shaped packhorse bridge and began trotting out a ditty to himself, seeming lighter and happier than before, as though relieved of some burden.

Dorothy wandered round the side of Broad Water, following a narrow path into a flower-carpeted grove. She stopped at a gate, rested her arms on the top of it and looked up into the fells. She thought about the glow-worm poem, and was furious with William for not having the courage to tell her what it was about. She felt an overwhelming urge to climb over the gate and run away from him, and – it was a silly idea and she had no idea where it came from – throw herself at the mercy of that curious man with the green eyes who'd been watching her at Ullswater. At least he'd showed an interest in her; at least he didn't just march on ahead. It was as if William had no time for her anymore. He had time enough to be cosseted by her, she thought bitterly, but no time to attend to her – for herself. But how would she cope if she were cut adrift?

She wouldn't think of it – it was too awful. She would regain her self-control right that moment. Unbidden and unwelcome the stranger re-entered her thoughts, as if the very attempt to banish him from her mind had made his image rebel, turn on its heel and come back, and she could now hear again the delightful way he'd described the daffodils dancing in the breeze. 'William isn't the only poet in Grasmere,' she muttered to herself. She hadn't said anything at the time but she'd been most hurt by the way her brother had censured her at Ullswater for what he called nervous blubbering.

She drew a heavy sigh.

Nature! She'd immersed her senses in the daffodils, drawn them into herself, reached out to pluck a few, then decided against it. She vowed then, and she renewed that vow now, that in the tranquillity of Dove Cottage she would recollect the passionate emotion of it all by writing about it in her journal. But she couldn't help composing the journal entry immediately. It had been sitting impatiently in the back of her mind, and extemporaneous inspiration must not be kept waiting – William had taught her that.

*I never saw daffodils so beautiful* … she composed, wishing she had the resources to fashion an impromptu quill from the nearest goose … *they grew among the mossy stones about and about them, some rested their heads upon these stones as on a pillow for weariness and the rest tossed and reeled and danced and seemed as if they verily laughed with the wind that blew upon them over the lake.*

'Goodness me!' she gasped, thinking again about the ginger-haired vagrant, who'd appeared to be quite taken by her – not William, not William's poetry, but *her*. 'Yes, little me,' she chuckled, her eyes darting about like a bird on high alert for cats. She remembered something William had said recently about one of his poems, that he wanted to show in the poem that even men who didn't wear fine clothes could feel deeply. Quite cheered up, and with a furtive second smile to think that she quite liked this fellow in return, and that it didn't matter what he looked like, she gazed out on the fells again and was struck with the most exciting thought. 'Gracious!' she declared. 'I feel like writing a poem.'

She came to suddenly, and morbid sadness clouded over her. It was gone, that intimate time they'd shared. Nothing – nothing! – could bring it back. And she squashed it in her mind, as if it were a pathetic, wriggling insect underfoot, the whole past five minutes of pleasure to think that something – anything! – might possibly offset that irreparable heartbreak.

When she returned within sight of William his scowl was inverted into a rare smile.

'So, how have you faired?' she hallooed, suppressing the cracks in her voice brought about by sorrow.

'The lines are nothing unforgettable. Would you like to hear them?'

Dorothy nodded.

*The cock is crowing,*

*The stream is flowing,*
*The small birds twitter,*
*The lake doth glitter...*

She agreed heartily that the lines were nothing unforgettable and they set off towards the Pass. When they reached the derelict inn at the junction with the Struggle, they stopped. William walked some yards away to take in the view of Winandermere.

'William!' she cried.

He turned, looking shocked by the emotion in her voice. 'What is it?'

'For the love of God, don't torment me! When is it to be?'

He hesitated, then his eyes lowered from her face. 'In the autumn.'

'I'm so happy for you both,' she said through fresh tears. 'I give you all the blessings of my heart. I shall find somewhere.'

'My dear Dolly, what do you mean?'

'There's no place for me at Dove Cottage.'

'How could you think that? Look at me, Dorothy. Could I possibly live without you by my side? You are my second self. In the lights of your eyes I see all the delight I've ever had in nature. My dear, dear friend, you are my eyes. And my ears. In your voice I catch the language of my own heart.'

'Then what's to be done?' she said, her mouth riven with the suppression of tears.

'Nature never did betray the heart that loved her, Dorothy. Let the sun shine on you now, and let moon shine on you then; let the mountain winds be free to blow against you, and if loneliness and pain ever be yours henceforth, think of yesterday, and the daffodils, when we were together still, and where we will always be.'

'Stop, William!' she sobbed. 'I can't bear it!'

They set off westwards down the Struggle in the direction of Ambleside. William allowed his mouth to slip back from an anguished smile to its habitual frown-scowl. Dorothy wiped her eyes. Within, impassioned entreaties raced along the ghylls and becks that carried her blood, but she said nothing more, and inanely counted cattle feeding in the pasture along the way. The number was forty-two. She was, after a while, softened in her heartbreak by the sight of birth-wet lambs, their umbilical cords waggling like tails. William withdrew into what Dorothy imagined to be not the soothing contemplation of spring lambs but an ongoing internal struggle with springing iambs.

Many hours later, when the silver-white surface of Grasmere lake greeted them, Dorothy felt the blackness of the sky exaggerated by the brightness of the moon, which swung like a lantern over the lake, setting a whiteness that looked like snow on the tiny island in the middle. On the island stood a stone hut, like a little house, half-hidden beneath fir trees agitated by the wing beats of herons battling for supremacy of the upper branches. As the moon decorated the tiny island house into the miniature version of a classic whitewashed Grasmere cottage, Dorothy's heart leapt with the sweet hope of home, the hems of her eyelashes ablaze with moonlight. At last they reached Dove Cottage, and she could look forward to throwing herself on her bed and sobbing through several layers of bed linen.

# 4

# Cornerstone

---

By the stone pillars of a gateway to a mansion marked 'Unthank Hall', a castle by any other name, Luke sat on a guidestone like an old man too shallow of breath to move and resigned to the aimless contemplation of whatever happened to be in front of him. He spotted a bird of prey above to the north-east, a golden eagle it could be, gliding so high as almost to scuff the top of Helvellyn on its westward excursion between the North and Irish seas. It would be able to see all Lakeland's vales beneath, swirling like a giant petal whorl round Helvellyn. Each vale nursed its own fells, tarns, ghylls and becks, and many held lakes in broad, flat cradles of ice-gouged rock. To the south lay Winandermere, above whose oceanic waters mist rose as if from an overwrought horse; to the west was Wastwater, its screes glaring at Great Gavel and Scawfell; to the north the sleepy crib of Derwentwater and to the east Ullswater, a princess whose seams were embroidered with dancing daffodils.

How could he share it all with those vile tourists, those genteel predators of the picturesque with their heads in their guide books, anaemic fingers flicking through the pages in search of the correct sentiment? If they felt what he could feel now – a yearning stronger than anything they'd ever known! And yet. It was as if nature had snagged on his heart again, and the whole thing was torn open and seeping.

From half a mile high the golden eagle swooped down into the forest side of the vale. As its prey lowered its head to the grass on a stony plot of rising ground, two clawed boots planted themselves in its back and yanked it off into the sky. The lamb's body arched, and its bleats rang across the vale of Grasmere.

He rose and started the final mile into the vale. Alongside him stood the tranquil, cat's-bowl lake of Grasmere, ruffled only by the dramas reflected on its surface by the setting clouds. He noticed the little island and stone hut, coddled by soft young moonlight. Across the lake Helm Crag knelt like a cowled monk. He reached the bottom of the village, Town End, and saw that the lake almost lapped onto a cluster of dwellings, one of which had a small oaken sign on its front wall bearing the name 'Dove Cottage'.

A lazy warmth hung in the air as he entered the village. The remnants of a spring picnic lay cluttering the green: plucked primroses, dandelions and daisies, bread and oatcake crusts and crumbs. A few mothers were clucking round their more dogged offspring to get them indoors, to sup and finally to bed.

He came to a pond, at the edge of which stood what he thought at first was a tree, but was in fact the oldest, thinnest and tallest man he'd ever seen. Thrown over the man's shoulders was a coat, and underneath the coat he clutched a glass bottle. Age – or perhaps some accident beneath a turning cartwheel – had bent the old man double, but he was still twice the height of the average Lakelander. He propped himself up on a long, knobbly grey staff that resembled his own dimensions, and from time to time he swished it in the pond, nearly toppling in each time.

'What are you looking for?' Luke asked, imagining the spectre had lost a clog in the water. The man looked round with dark, fiery eyes and swished his staff through the water again.

'Leeches,' he hissed. 'Time was there wus lots in this watter. Now it teks all day to get one or two.' He turned his gaze back to the pond and resumed his stony stillness.

Luke now remembered he'd seen the ancient many years before, at a time when his frame had been bent not double but to an angle of maybe half that. He was called Jinnyspinner, the daddy-long-legs man. He'd garlanded Luke with gloomy prayers the day he'd left Grasmere, warning no good would come of it. Rather than give the wretched leech-gatherer the pleasure of knowing he was right Luke pressed on, past St Oswald's church and towards the top of the village. Near the Swan Inn he climbed eastwards into the forest side of the vale, along Greenhead Ghyll. He recognised every twist of its melody over stone and pebble, and recalled the drone of bees and dangle of flies by the ghyll in summer, the stir of its breezes, the woodsmoke smell of Michael, the old man's arms as knotty as boughs. He remembered that last time they'd been together, the night before he left Grasmere. Michael had taken him into the Greenhead fields, dug his boot in the ground and picked up a clod of stony soil.

'Tek this, Luke,' he'd said. 'Smell the soil, taste it. One day you'll feed your own flock on these fields. But love the land, son, and protect it.' Luke felt like a man, and proud. Michael then took him uphill to a heap of unhewn stones. 'Son,' he said, 'this sheepfold was work for both of us, but now it's work just for me.' The old shepherd stood up. 'But lay this first stone of the sheepfold, Luke,' he said, lifting a large boulder. 'Let this cornerstone be a symbol of our love – an anchor and a shield when

# 5

# Nettleslacks

---

'Cum-by! Awaay! Getoffim Nance, you nosy ole bugger!' A grizzled collie was poking her snout into his neck as he lay on the ground wincing at the daylight. She looked too old to round up her own tail yet she rummaged around between his legs with quite some enthusiasm. When her tongue lolloped over his mouth he decided enough was enough; luckily the collie received a bash on the nose from a ram's-horn-and-hazel crook. Luke looked up. Above him loomed hair whitewashed by antiquity, a barley-stubble beard and the heart-shaped face of a barn-owl. A shepherd it was, wearing a hodden grey fleece that looked as if it had been transplanted straight from a Herdwick's back without any attempt to turn it into a garment. The old man was crowned with a rabbit-skin hat.

'Hoo'doo! Still alive, then?' the shepherd shouted. Nance approached Luke again. He enjoyed the dog's rank intimacy and ran his hand over her back to return the compliment. As he sat up the shepherd and his collie froze, both staring at something. He looked round and saw an old mountain hare standing motionless, head up, staring back at them. Its fixed look flashed from shepherd to dog. The shepherd growled quietly to Nance not to rush the hare, and slowly approached it. The hare's eyes became so fixed on Nance that it didn't notice the shepherd. Finally he got close enough behind it to raise his crook and, with a sudden brutal swipe, he knocked it to the ground.

'Mek a nice pie for Easter Sunday, will that. Poor ole thing couldn't run. Hurt his leg somehow,' said the shepherd, turning to Luke and booting his foot. 'By yeck, 'stha bin out all night, lad? Nowt but sheep and fells round here. Nance, gaa an' get our Sally, gaa on girl! Away! Gaa on you daf' cur! GAA!' He brandished his crook over Nance's head with such intent that the dog shrank off down the hill intoning an affronted whine. 'Bluddeeyell, I can't get the damn thing to move an inch for me these days,' he complained. 'Shoulda seen her when she were young though. By God, she were't best sheep-dog I've ever had, I tell thee, a right lish cur, and I've bin through ten or more. But she's a sulker. By yeck I can't say a dambluddy word without her gurnin and tekkin offence and gettin her own back later.'

The heart-faced shepherd hoisted Luke on his feet with the skill of a man familiar with slinging expectant ewes across his shoulders, and they staggered downhill and out through the gate.

They came to a long, low-roofed stone-and-slate farmhouse and were greeted by a woman with Viking-blue eyes and a fresh, lightly speckled face. Her hair seemed to have been fought and subdued beneath a rabbit-skin bonnet.

'Sally luv, stop gawpin and give me an 'and. Found im in the field up yonder.' Sally helped steer Luke through the porch. Nance sneaked between everyone's legs to the fire.

'Looks bowt same age our Jackie would've bin,' said the shepherd as he swung Luke down onto the hearth the way a Lakeland wrestler might.

'Same look an all,' said Sally.

'Ay, big ginger-nut, tall n' broad as a blinkin oak.' Luke looked up at Sally; she took off her bonnet to release wind-entangled hair on fire with auburn, its winter bracken curls pouring like lava down her shoulders.

'What'll we do with 'im, Fadder?'

'Lettim sleep it off, lass, dinnae fash! Nowt else wican do.'

That day fever gripped the offcomer, and while he busied himself with bouts of thrashing about Sally got on with a little light housework, boiling four weeks' worth of filthy clothes in large pots, rubbing them with stones soaked in tallow and wood-ash lye, which made them stink worse than if she hadn't bothered washing them in the first place, and dragging the leaden garments outside to drape them over bushes and rocks as though she were clothing the landscape. When the daytime had faded, and a rushlight breathed smoke but no light through the farmhouse, she eased herself onto a stool lit by the glow of the peat fire, gathered thunder across her brow and fumbled with the task of running the heel of a stocking.

Unlike women for whom the constant demands of needlework were at war with their desire for intellectual improvement, Sally's needlework was in a state of war with itself. Her hands, those of a husbandman's daughter, could purchase potatoes out of rock and lambs out of kicking ewes, and she could spin as well as any spinster in the vale, but as for running, tacking, hemming and all that governess-style needlework, she didn't have the temperament. Even the washed-out offcomer on the settle could do better. She looked up from her sword-fight with a packing needle – better suited for stitching mattresses than stockings and smock-frocks – and noticed Luke watching her. He did remind her of her long-lost brother – especially with that hair the colour of generously ovened gingerbread – but Jackie would never have looked at her in that way. 'Howdyeh sleep?' she asked.

Luke considered for a moment. He'd been up on the fells in a storm, naked, cowering under a rock. He'd fallen off a cliff. He knew he would die but he kept on falling. In this state of imminent death he'd remained for some time, not twigging that he was embroiled in the time-honoured melodrama of a bad dream. He was back at King's Cross, the old stamping ground he'd headed for straight after the hanging. The name Alice had mentioned in the cell – Kears – was met with shakes of the head and shrugs from all the people he knew. At last a link-boy on a street corner held out his palm for a coin, and Luke handed over his last halfpenny. The urchin led him through a maze of iniquitous alleyways to a door, and then disappeared. Luke rapped, waited, rapped again, and it opened. 'Mrs Kears?' He reached out his hand, not to shake hers but to stop her slamming the door in his face. He used his foot to deal with her second attempt to bar him entry, and she impolitely invited him in. He then met Mr Kears and a loud argument ensued, and Luke re-emerged, wiping the blood off his fist on the inside of his coat. Then he'd realised it was all a terrible dream but he was still trapped inside it. After a huge wrestle to wake up his unconscious self by means of shaking his head violently, he'd emerged from the nightmare gasping like a drowned man brought back to life.

'I slept fine,' he lied, his top lip glistening with the reliving of the ordeal.

'You look like death,' she sweet-talked. 'Sounded like you was having a baddun. Kept shouting out "fugive meh!"' He recalled another part of the dream, in which he was thrust back to the moments before his birth, wrestling and kicking his way through the waters of Isabel's womb. But on the disuniting of their bodies he found himself cradled not in his mother's arms but in Greenhead Ghyll, which carried him out of Lakeland to sea. After many years he was swept back into the vale of Grasmere, and washed up alongside the Evening Star as a grown man. Isabel plucked him out of the water and beckoned him back into the cottage, where a lamb hung over the hearth. Michael stood with open arms. Luke fell to his father's knees and cried 'forgive me'. That was when he'd woken up, gazed at the magnificent fireworks of Sally's hair and let his eyes fall into her lap.

'Can I help you with that stocking? I used to do a bit of weaving,' he slurred, hoping to douse his lust with cold, domestic practicality. But the fever snatched him away again and, just like in the dream, many hours – or even years – passed by instantaneously.

There was a glassy clink on the door. Sally opened it to the lower body of a very tall old man who'd knocked on the door with a bottle, and in that bottle, Luke could see from where he lay, slithered leeches. Jinnyspinner bent a degree or two beyond his usual double to get through the door and offered Sally a handful. Then he left, flashing his eyes at Luke. Over the next few hours Luke lay hosting leeches on his nipples while Sally worked on a secret recipe for what she proudly declared to be 'Sally Nettleslack's Special Grasmere Gingerbread'. She manipulated the oatmeal, ground ginger, sugar, butter and other more clandestine ingredients with requiemic solemnity, then gave Luke a piece she said she'd been maturing for months.

'Hark now before you tekka bite,' she warned. 'It might not be the sweetest gingerbread you've ever set your teeth on but it'll sort your bowels out.'

Luke didn't have the strength to point out that there'd been nothing wrong with his bowels the last time he'd looked. He enjoyed listening to those misshapen Grasmerian vowels and butchered consonants tumbling out of her mouth. She harped on about her gingerbread for some time while stretching the sole of a sock over a potato and somehow darning a bigger hole into it than had existed beforehand. She divulged as though he'd interrogated her on the matter that it was her task to provide gingerbread at the village Rushbearing in August. She warned that predators came upon her by stealth and sprinkled compliments over her. As she spoke her Norse-Irish eyes remained alert to the pounce of rivals through the doorway. She insisted he take some gingerbread, so Luke dutifully filled his mouth and looked up at her with a bilious smile. Sally acknowledged that her gingerbread was inedible, arguably harmful, for some – of whom Luke might well be one. He watched her, especially that barn-owl-like, heart-shaped face that was clearly a family feature, and the last thing he remembered thinking was how ruddy and edible she looked compared with the hollow-eyed bone-bags of King's Cross.

The fever, or the gingerbread, must have knocked him out because night had passed. He wandered outside to test the strength in his legs and the cut of the smock-frock, breeches and gaiters Sally had cobbled together for him. The house, its stone walls laid with clay and what looked like centuries-old cow-dung, had above its front door the inscription 'L.N. 1660', the date presumably denoting some kind of restoration. The whole building appeared to have grown out of the ground on which it stood. The flowers around it were untamed, irregular and on the attack. He peered into the disused byre and grainstore opposite; the whole dilapidated shambles had seen better days, but he was conscious that he could say the same about himself.

Stepping back inside he let his nose follow a smell, a queasy blend of tobacco dust, tallow and vigorously stirred poddish, which led him to the downhouse. Sally had done the laundry here, he discovered, and there were also moulds, squeezers and pats lying about indicating butter-churning and its consequences. There were signs of occasional ale-brewing and turf-firing. In the firehouse the chimney fanned outwards the further inwards it descended, presenting an inglenook where he imagined Jack would sit spinning his daughter auld

Lakeland yarns while his daughter sat on the treadmill of her treadle spinning yarn more literal than literary. Along a beam the length of the inglenook hung a cured mutton ham and a few archaic utensils. He felt the farm's gloom, which was probably the effect of its small windows rather than the consequence of regular melancholy. It made him think of the Evening Star, and a lump gathered in his throat that didn't feel like gingerbread. He ran his finger along an oaken table which reeked of the meat, fruit, vegetables, bread, blood and vomit of the centuries; it was sticky, thereby not letting his finger run so far.

Built into the oaken wall between the downhouse and firehouse was a cupboard, in which was hidden a familiar smell that made him bilious. The front door opened and in pounced Sally.

'You're not an easy customer,' she said, fortunately with a smile. 'Feeling better? You've sent back up everything I've offered you – straight outta your gob.'

'Much better, thanks to you,' he said, hankering after the poddish she was dishing out.

'We've got some Good Friday fig-sue left over if you think you'll keep it down.'

The thought of sugared ale boiled with bread and figs made him retch. 'You've been so kind already,' he said. 'Do you live here alone with Jack?'

'And Nance, ay. His name's not Jack, mind, just likes being called Jack.'

'What is his name?'

Sally looked round furtively. 'Lanslot,' she hissed. 'But he hates it. Doesn't think it's a statesman's name, Lanslot Nettleslack. Sounds more like a shepherd. Spose he's right.'

'Mmm,' Luke improvised, adding after a pause, 'I thought he was a shepherd.'

'He is, just likes to call himself a statesman, same way some do round here. Statesman-farmers. Like the ring of it, they do. But Fadder's just a poor yoweman, a nusbandman, not a statesman-farmer. We've only got one cow left.' Luke nodded sagely in imitation of one who understood. Mystery was beginning to enshroud Jack – or Lanslot.

'Use to be Mudder and our Jackie here an all,' she said, handing him a bowl of poddish and setting about her own with a spoon. 'Fadder thought he and Mudder would live long lives then follow each other into the grave. Said that's what statesman-farmers do. But Mudder went early – oopincoff – then our Jackie went missing at sea. So Fadder feels sore and cheated sometimes. But Nettleslacks are strong.' Sally stood up and peered out of the tiny window at a heavy rain shower. 'Best get in there,' she said, pointing to the inglenook. 'Only dry spot in the place when it's hossing it down.' They huddled up next to the mutton, not so far from the spice cupboard. Sally turned to him with what he thought was an accusing look. 'What were you doing, then?'

'When?'

'When Fadder found you tuther day?'

'Oh, I'd arrived home the night before,' he said, trying to deal breezily with the whole agony, adding with unconvincing lightness, 'Good to see the old place hasn't changed a bit.' His home, his birthplace, razed to the ground? His parents gone? There might as well have been an earthquake.

'Not changed?' squawked Sally. 'Not stopped changing, more like. We get the tourists in the warm months as usual, wandering round in their soft-seated carriages, looking up into the trees and down their noses. But we get poor folk more and more nowadays, trudging round all seasons, all weathers. Wind's always blowing some widow through the vale, all thin and dishonoured-lookin', dragging her half-starved babbies door to door begging. Near every one of them bairns has lost a fadder to Bonneyparte's cannons. Them men-bodies as do get back home, well what's to come back for? Their fields swallowed up whole by the squire, all them ancient strips of family land. We've got beggars and paupers and battle-torn soldiers all over the place, ruined farmers, the lot. All scavenging round for work, not that there's any going round here. Ay, it's all changed. Don't go thinking Grasmere's just pretty views.'

How angry she sounded, but how loving.

'Home, did tha say?' Sally turned and asked. 'To Grasmere? To a field a few hundred yard from here?'

'I was born in a cottage that used to stand there. The Evening Star.'

At that moment Jack Nettleslack pushed open the door, smacked the rain off his hat and stamped his way across to his armchair, threw off the cushion which served as Nance's bed, lit a pipe and choked the room with the syrupy smell of honeydew tobacco molasses.

'Fadder might remember,' said Sally as she and Luke relocated out of the intimacy of the inglenook.

'What, lass?'

'Evening Star.'

Jack coughed so hard the pipe smoke interacted with the rushlight smoke and the statesman went the colour of the farm's exterior wall.

'Eh? Er... Oh ay, I do. Eveninstar wit lamp in the window all night long? Ay. Ole Michael and Isabel, wunt it? And that rascal of a son of theirs. Right sad tale that. Went tut dogs. Died at sea far away, so they say. Nabbut bovver. Broke his ole man's heart, ended his days. What were't bugger's name, now?'

There was silence while Sally threw peat on the fire and feverishly manoeuvred the bellows. Luke stared down at his broad-backed hands with their stubby fingers – his father's, his father's father's; made of Grasmere soil itself, honed for the manipulation of Herdwicks, employed in a hanged woman's strangling and its vengeful aftermath. In his grisly Greenhead hands he cradled his grief.

'Luke,' he said finally.

'Ay, that's ... it,' Jack tailed off, glancing across at Sally's troubled face. 'By yeck, tha's not Michael Greenhead's ... lad?'

Luke didn't reply. Sally's eyes appeared to gulp him down with pity.

'Why did yeh come back?' demanded Jack.

Luke clenched his teeth. 'Why did they knock the cottage down?' he snapped. Nance, stretched on her back on the floor, whined and shifted position with the general discomfort in the room.

'Pulled down a dozen years ago or more, twas,' said Jack. 'Dint think it'd still be there, did you?'

'I'd hoped … that —'

'Hoped what? Eh?'

'They might … Isabel anyway, might … forgive me,' he mumbled.

'Now what the damnbluddeeyell's to forgive, Luke?' Jack growled. 'We all mek mistakes. My Jackie never come back neither. Can't spend rest of my days vexed with him, now, can I, eh? Eh, Sally?' Sally shook her head.

'When did you last see him?' said Luke through set teeth.

'Our Jackie? Why twas—'

'Michael! When did you last see Michael?'

'Winter before he died. He were selling yowes and lambs and his flock was dwindlin. Ole Michael was full of hope that you'd come back at first. He seemed younger for a time, yet he was four score year or more, want he? I use to see him up in the fells looking out for his flock in all seasons, climbing among the rocks. But the years went by and he changed. Like he'd lost heart.'

Honeydew tobacco funnelled around the room.

'Sold all his yowes and lambs in the end. I saw him carrying his last one in his arms one day, full of tears, he was. I dunt need to tell thee, son of a shepherd, how much Michael needed them Herdwicks. How much we all do. They give us everything – sheep's head broth to aprons to candles, you name it. They give us our livelihoods. Awways have. I can't tell thee the number of times I've set off to Kendal with me packhorses laden with

Herdwick wool. Mind you, plenty's the time I've come back vexed with the price I got for it. "Too coarse, Jack, it's too coarse!" Too coarse my arse! Soft as a babby's buttocks, is that wool! Any road, in his last days Michael used to sit up by that sheepfold a lot, not building, just sittin'. Died up there an all.'

Luke had been looking into the fire, but now he turned and looked at Jack, and the statesman's eyes flinched.

'Isabel,' Luke said, his throat aching with the retention of tears. 'What about her?'

'Thy mudder left Grasmere a pauper far as I know, lad. Land was tekken and the Eveninstar pulled down. Isabel wunt never seen round these parts again. Passed on some years back, folk say. I'm right sorry.' Jack looked away from Luke and down into the fire. His eyes were glistening, as were Luke's. Sally placed a hand on Luke's shoulder. This compassionate gesture felt too much for Luke to bear, the way a tree might topple at the touch of a finger rather than the last brute swing of an axe.

He stood up. 'Where is his grave?'

Jack looked grimly round at him but didn't respond.

'Well thank you for your kindness,' Luke said to Sally, 'and for your honesty,' he added, glowering at Jack, and with that he left.

# 6

# Minnow Tansies

Dorothy Wordsworth surprised herself by the tightness of her grip on the handrail as she descended the oak stairs of Dove Cottage and peered through the tiny door halfway down that led out into the back garden. William was in his chair in the orchard, staring back at her. She didn't like the look in his eyes. It wasn't the faraway face which could stare through her while his brain sought the right word to end a particular line of verse; it was a much more uncomfortable, near-to look, straight into her, one which read her pain as though it was smeared naked in ink on her eyes. Well then, she said inwardly, if you want to know what I'm thinking about, William, it's this: you pleaded with me when we were on the Kirkstone Pass to think of the daffodils and there you would be – there we two would be. But

I now see that there were more than two of us that day, because you were quite clearly thinking of Mary as I stood transfixed by the daffodils. Dear Mary has been a friend to me since we were children, and I have loved her as a sister, but now we are three, and with Molly at Dove Cottage there will be four, and of course that's only the beginning. Gone, William, is the simplicity of our solitary life in Grasmere.

She thought with revulsion about one day replacing Molly as housekeeper at Dove Cottage and shuffling her mortal coil around the kitchen-parlour for the rest of her years, doing little of use but making a meal of it. William, the vampire poet, would meanwhile suck the lifeblood out of her, and once he had his little harem around him she'd become nothing but a bloodless, toothless crust of a woman waiting on him, just like Molly. The notion of it all had immediate ramifications for her appetite.

'I can't face broth or giblet pie today, Molly,' she said, making her way past the ignorant but endearing old dame and to the porch. 'How about minnow tansies? We've got the fish thanks to William's trip on the lake yesterday. All we need is tansy stalks and primroses.'

'Ay, well, Miss Dorothy, minnow tansies sounds a grand idea but I'm busy enough as it is without chargin' out to get flowers.'

'No, let me go. I've got a headache; fresh air and a walk is just what I need.'

'Why don't you go and spend some time wi't maister instead. He looks reet hangdog today.'

'No,' Dorothy replied firmly. 'I'll go right now to Butterlip How. I know I'll find them there. I'll see if I can get some cowslips as well.'

'I thought you didn't like picking flowers, Missy …' Molly called after her, but she'd already gone.

She was crossing the footbridge where Churnmilk Force became Easedale Beck when rain began to come on. She raised the hood of her cloak over her head and held it tight round her neck. At Butterlip How she bent down to pluck primroses, tansies and cowslips. 'What hope,' she muttered to herself as she ripped a stalk out of the ground, 'have I,' as another snapped out into her fist, 'of surviving alone,' – another handful – 'if I can't even uproot a silly flower without falling apart?' She looked at the bunched cowslip petals in her palm and pressed their yellow corollas to her nose. 'There, that wasn't so bad was it?' she lied to herself. She hadn't even tracked down the tansy stalks whose bitter juices Molly was to mix with the minnows, but it was enough, and she began trudging back home, feeling a little better for the walk, and the act of floral bloodshed.

As she made her way through the fields she thought about how William had referred to her in one of his poems as an enemy of nature, hacking down hazels with a tempestuous bloom in her cheeks. 'Well here's another thought, William dear,' she said into the clouds as if to his face. 'It wasn't only you, myself and Mary at Ullswater that day of the daffodils, there was someone else. Yes, quite a gang, weren't we? You might not have seen the other person – I didn't myself – but he was there, watching us. No! Watching me! And he is still there, watching me still. So when you say "think of the daffodils and there we will be", be sure that you mean all four of us, for we are no longer alone.' She smiled punitively, but from deep inside like a retch from the soul came the panic-stricken self-enquiry, 'What is happening to me?'

A silent deluge of mist blurred Luke's vision; the peppery hiss of rain on leaves drowned out the lyric of wren, robin and wagtail as he neared the blue-slate roof of St Oswald's. Rooks patrolled the churchyard as he passed through the lychgate and crouched between gravestones, squinting into wet epitaphs, fingering the grooves of headstones and tombs trying to decipher names. The sky had darkened, and though it was midday it felt like midnight. And no trace of Michael, or of the name Greenhead. Had they all died paupers and been buried to the hymn of the dunghill fowl? He sat down among a crop of flat graves, sheltered from the rain by black yew branches, and looked at the sunken ground, thinking about Michael sitting alone by the sheepfold. He needed something to touch, a grave, a memorial, somewhere to unleash his sorrow.

He stood up and began following his steps back through the village in the direction of the Forest side. Near Butterlip How he caught sight of a woman in bosom-friend and spenser paralysed in a field. An insolent long-horn stood facing her, cud-chewing and tail manoeuvres suspended. Eventually it swooned its neck down to the grass and the woman – who Luke now identified through the Calvinistic joylessness of her grey coat to be his pagan goddess, Dolly – began to edge forward. But the cow jumped, jerked its head and cast her a withering look. Dolly froze.

'It won't hurt you,' Luke hallooed. Deity and beast turned startled eyes in his direction. Only when he was near enough to slap her rump did the cow jog away, udders pendulating as it ran. 'They stare hard but mean no harm,' said Luke, feeling quietly heroic.

'Thank you!' gasped Dolly. 'Every horned cow puts me in terror. I can't trust them. They look so threatening.'

'But cows are cowards.'

'So am I,' she said with an embarrassed laugh. At least, thought Luke, I have that in common with her.

'I think they look sad,' he said, unconsciously projecting his own personal sorrow onto the animal, 'not threatening.'

'They do have a certain melancholy, I suppose.'

There was surely no more conversational mileage to be had on the cow, but they'd plumbed deeper than the usual farmyard banalities at least by exploring the innate bovine disposition. Luke was pleased to have found common – if unexpected – ground with her, and therefore felt encouraged to consider something similarly interesting, perhaps an ancient Greenhead wisdom on the subject of sheep. But although emboldened he was also unnerved by Dolly, with the result that the instant after he leant forward to speak to her he pulled back with a jerk, as though he were now on the back of said cow and attempting to ride it.

Dolly, helping him out of his discomfort, chattered away, declaring she was on an errand to Butterlip How for her housekeeper.

'Molly's making minnow tansies. William came back earlier from the lake with the minnows – although I would have preferred pike – and I offered to go and get tansy stalks, cowslips and primroses. The only problem is,' she added forlornly, now addressing the ground, 'I'm not good at picking flowers. It seems so cruel, so unnatural. I know it's silly.'

Luke gambled as to whether it would endear him or condemn him if he offered to uproot the blooms for her. He crouched. 'So you managed to survive the storm the other night?' he asked by way of diversion from his ransacking of the ground.

'Yes,' she winced as she watched. 'It kept William awake, but if it hadn't been the storm it would have been a poem. He doesn't sleep well.'

Luke pictured William striding across his bedroom all night in creative distress.

'I thought you were the poet,' he said.

'Oh no – well, nothing worth mentioning. I write the occasional line of verse, and sometimes I like to think myself maybe half a writer, but not like William. No, I write out his poems – and a journal for him.'

Luke was confused. William composed the poems but Dolly actually wrote them; Dolly wrote the journal, but she wrote it for William. Had he sustained some injury that had made writing impossible?

'Is he … incapacitated?' he asked, an unhealthy curiosity aroused.

She was stopped short by the word as though it had appeared on the ground in front of her and was not to be stepped in. 'Oh … I see what you mean,' she laughed, and he saw surprisingly few teeth in her mouth, a fact which only added to her gypsy mystique. 'No, not incapacitated in any way. I help William by copying out his poems and by taking down lines as he thinks of them.'

Luke couldn't help prying. 'And you write his journal for him as well?'

'Well, I write the journal for myself, I suppose, but William draws on some of my descriptions for his poems.'

Luke imagined William descending like a great jackdaw on her journal and flying off with all the nicest, shiniest words dangling from his noble beak. It was unfair to think so poorly of him – William might be the most agreeable person in the entire world – then again, no: whatever made Dolly miniaturise herself in front of William, it wasn't the miserable man's agreeableness. Why was she so in thrall to him? Was it the subduing power of poetic genius? But if William stole his best lines from Dolly's journal, clearly the appellation 'genius' was now open to doubt.

'I wish I could hear these descriptions of yours that inspire such great poetry,' he said.

They steered their way round vindictive kine all the way to a meek, pretty cottage dressed in white, with slate roof and diamond windows. At the back lay a cock's stride of a garden, and in front a field rolling down to the margin of Grasmere lake.

'I thought you'd never come back, Miss!' gasped an old dame in the porch with lips like a journeying caterpillar. Dolly handed her the murdered flowers.

'Mercy upon us, Molly! What made you think that? This is my home!'

'But you wus so long,' said Molly, reserving the disapproval in her eyes not for her mistress but for the tramp beside her. Dolly waved her away playfully and encouraged Luke into the kitchen. They watched Molly wash the Rydale minnows in salt, slice off their heads and tails, wrench out their guts, incinerate them in butter and egg yolks, fling the primrose and cowslip petals into a roaring pan and throttle the tansy stalks till they dribbled juice.

'There now,' said Molly.

'I'd invite you for tea,' Dolly said, 'but William is out at the back and—'

'And your husband will think I'm a beggar,' said Luke, spotting a dark figure snoozing in the orchard. 'I understand.'

'No,' she said in a way that sounded more like yes. 'May I ask, what do you... do?'

'I'm a ... a ... poet,' he lied, having been ambushed and not having written a line in his life, ever.

'A poet? How magnificent! Do you know, I suspected as much. Well, thank you anyway,' she said.

'For what?'

'Why, for rescuing me from all those cows. I'll try and build my courage. Farewell.' She slammed the door in what he liked to think was an affectionate way, and then re-opened it. 'By the way, I don't even know your name.'

'Luke. Greenhead.'

'I'm—'

'—Dolly, I know,' he interjected.

'Erm, Dorothy actually. Wordsworth. William is the only one who calls me Dolly. Goodbye.' She slammed the door again, and as he was walking away she re-opened it again. 'Here. Some paper just in case you lack some. It would be lovely to see one or two of your poems. By the way, William's not my husband. What on earth made you think that? He's my brother.'

Back in the village a sombre silvery light washed against the off-white walls of the Swan and slipped through its windows. Rain dribbling down glass wilting with age distorted Luke's view inside, and he saw bent and elongated faces staring down at dark tables. He stepped inside, unable to resist the inn's dubious comforts. Two men were clenching mugs long since drained of ale, while another, wearing Jack Nettleslack's rabbit-skin hat, was hobbling to the bar.

'How's Lucy?' said Jack to Goan, the dour-faced innkeeper.

more at his pint, screwed up his murky grey eyes and left. A breeze followed him out like a dog at heel. Jack turned to Luke.

'I know. Yeh thinking it sounds like useful work. Well tint just any work. It's months on end of cold, clashy, back-brekking days, dawn to dusk, with nowt to fill your belly.'

'Have you done walling?' asked Luke.

'Eh? Nae! But I know all about Vipond and his walling, I do. Nights on end in the fells nursing bleeding fingers. Men die on his jobs. Some from't work, some from't cold. Some at each other's hands.'

Luke left the Swan and made out the outline of Vipond stalking along against a sky ripening to sunset. When he caught up with him Vipond stopped and turned to face him by raising his arms in front of his chest defensively as if expecting to be set upon and stabbed.

'Who are you?' he snarled. 'What's your business with me?'

'I've a strong pair of hands.'

'You look like you need dragging back intut ditch you came from, offcomer. I don't want beggars.'

'I'm no offcomer and I need the work.'

'I an't seen you round here if you're local. What's your name?'

'Greenhead.'

Vipond's eyes tightened as he inspected him in all his dishevelment. 'You wouldn't last a day on Helvellyn. You'd be lying face down in Red Tarn.'

'I know the fells. I'll build your wall for you.'

Vipond looked him up and down with a view to ownership. 'It isn't my wall, Greenhead,' he sneered 'It's the maister's, him that owns everything else round here. Mek sure you're back here first light Tuesday.'

Dusk was in full swing as Luke pushed through the gate and stood over the ruined, sunken sheepfold. The evening sky was unnaturally light and a rainbow in the shape of a packhorse bridge arched over the fell-crests and buried its treasure on

Grasmere island. He stood at the edge of Greenhead Ghyll and saw, shimmering beneath the water, the cornerstone he'd tossed in a few nights before. To the momentary puzzlement of the few Herdwicks scattered about, he shouted, 'I'll find your graves, finish this sheepfold and make these fields ours again. That's my pledge to you.'

He set off back down in the direction of Nettleslack Farm. He'd distrusted Jack for the relish with which he'd told him of Michael and Isabel's death, and the blame the old man had pinned on him for it. But he needed somewhere to sleep, and when he arrived Sally at least seemed pleased to see him, and soon installed him in the grainstore, promising to pluck a hen for a mattress in the morning. He woke up during the night, amazed by the whiteness of the moon through the gaping hole in the roof. 'They're dead,' he said to himself, 'they're dead,' and he lay wondering where their bodies lay buried if not in the graveyard. He also wondered where their forgiveness lay buried. Drowsiness finally weighed on his eyelids and he fell asleep, his last, dispersed thoughts not dwelling on his parents but on Dorothy, the vision of her at Ullswater, and the image – within the privacy of his closed eyes – of her bathing now in the same argent light cast by the same moon above Dove Cottage, a light that mirrored the colour of her mystifying eyes.

# 7

# Vive la Révolution

'I'm the leanest fox in Lakeland, I am,' panted Yeoman Vipond as he submitted his naked upper torso to the first touch of another human being since his birth nearly forty years before. By chance, the other human being now touching him – the officially retired Doctor Lea of Grasmere, whom Vipond had chosen after hearing him to be a discreet and non-judgemental Quaker – was the same one who'd steered him through the birth canal in the first place.

'Have you been losing weight?' the doctor asked, tapping on his ribs.

'How a fella can lose weight by eating more cakes and puddings than he's ever done in his whole life is a mystery to me, doctor.'

'Hmm. Eating more, but losing weight.'

'Beats me, cos they go straight through me like water. But I can't resist them,' he said, letting out a chesty cough followed by a sneeze.

'Cravings, then?' said the doctor. 'And how long have you had that cough?'

'They come and go, can't seem to get rid of them.'

'You seem short of breath as well.'

'Ay. Mind you, it int easy climbing them fells day in day out.'

'I wouldn't advise such strenuous work in your present condition. What are you doing up there, might I ask?'

'Marking out a boundary, I've got a big job on, can't afford any "present condition", doctor. You won't say owt to no one, will you?'

'Trust me,' Doctor Lea said, shaking his head gravely. 'What about alcohol?'

'Nay, never been one for that. Leave it to the time-wasters in the inns.'

'Not a drop?'

'Oh ay, time to time.'

'Well I recommend you don't, not a drop. And how are you sleeping?'

'Fine, fine.' It was none of the doctor's business how he slept. He had said enough already. 'So what's the verdict, doctor? Will I live?' he asked with a wheezy and fake chuckle.

The doctor frowned. 'A healthy and nutritious diet is highly desirable, Mr Vipond,' he said, 'including an absolute minimum of half a dozen eggs a day – raw, mind – and six pints of milk.'

Vipond felt sick at the thought, but then again most food made him sick at the thought these days – apart, oddly, from cakes and puddings, which he'd never liked.

'And self-control in all things. Oh, and nuts, Mr Vipond, nuts.'

'Self-control!' Vipond growled to himself as he assembled the eggs, milk and nuts on his oaken table. 'What does that fat old quack know about self-control. I can spot a face full of gout a mile off.' He hated the idle rich even more than the idle poor. He, Yeoman Vipond, was the king of self-control. He'd been controlling himself all his life. Controlling his money, paying men half the wages they deserved because they were too desperate to refuse, storing up his wealth in a box in a dark room wreathed with cobwebs and patrolled by spiders. Controlling his land, taking a strip more every year from idle, complaining peasants who couldn't afford to keep it on because their rent was too high, or their wool too coarse to sell, or their grain not quick enough to market. There was always something with them, and always someone to prey on.

Controlling his appetites, not drinking, hardly eating, not spending on himself or anyone, not giving anything away, not whoring, not needing anyone. And controlling his servants, and hired hands, and reapers and threshers; taking his swingle to them, punishing their weakness and laziness, their lack of respect, being a hard master. Yes, Yeoman Vipond was the leanest fox.

Yet as he gagged his way through his meal he wished, not for the first time, there was a wife to look after him, and over whom he could play the domestic tyrant. And as he dressed for the hunt he considered how badly he was actually sleeping: fitfully, feverishly, wakefully. But he would not feel sorry for himself – that was for small men. The sickness would pass soon. It had to. 'Self-control!' he muttered again as he left the farmhouse.

'Childless!' cried Sir Edward Unthank Bart, injecting sudden pathos into his internal monologue, a habit he'd picked up after an affair with a minor actress who'd died of syphilis. 'Not a single legitimate heir!'

He sighed, scanning the vast acreage surrounding Unthank Hall and preparing to push once again through sylvan terrain amid the panting of dogs. 'All this. For what? For whom? What is left to me now but the rags of old age?

'No!' his inner voice roared in defiance of the gods – or at least those he imagined to be sitting in them. 'Hang old age! Unlike lesser men, I will not die unfulfilled.'

How on earth could a baronet of the recently united Kingdom of Great Britain and Ireland and a scion of the ancient d'Unthanque family – which had accompanied no less than William the Bastard out of Flanders seven centuries before – have been distracted from his destiny? He thought of the great hunters and conquerors gone before him, and relished the grand project that might make his heirless final years bearable. A string of mistresses, gargantuan gambling debts, a crumbling, six-hundred-year-old family seat, even the exorbitant tax on hair powder – all would be paid for, and his place in the Unthank pantheon ensured.

'And one day,' he avowed silently by way of a climactic end to his peroration. 'I will be a viscount ... perhaps even a duke.' His ambition, checked with a sigh of humility, fell short of the word 'king'.

He stood up tall on his white charger and aimed his gun at a jutting outcrop along the skyline of Rydal Fell. 'Do you see that rock, Vicar?' he bellowed into the fifty acres around his hunting lodge. 'Stone Arthur! A great king, Arthur. Defeated the Saxon invaders and changed the course of history. A revolutionary. Just like me.'

'You?' queried Parson Noble Snaile, a Beau Brummell ape in plain shoes, ribbed stockings, turned-back and casually half-buttoned coat, complementing his fake rusticity with an affectation of concern for the poor. At a distance he appeared almost to suffer flushes of genuine compassion, but Sir Edward suspected the fashionable Rector of Grasmere never dreamt of being anywhere other than at a distance from the poor.

'Quite so, Vicar,' he said as he rubbed his spatterdashes around the calf area. 'I am starting a revolution.'

'Hmm,' replied Parson Snaile. 'Where?'

'Here! Our village is stuck in the past with its barbaric, feudal ways. I intend to drag it into the future. Now, the blighter's in the woods here somewhere.'

'Surely the feudal ways are your ways?'

'They are the ways of my ancestors, yes, but I say smash the old system!'

'Ha-as it not ser-erved you we-ell?' said the parson, his diaphragm at the mercy of a horse in its stride. 'Lo-ok at yourse-elf compared to the sim-ple folk of Gra-asmere.'

'My point entirely,' Sir Edward replied, his voice well used to the demands of dispensing wisdom at an equine gallop. 'The common man has his little dwelling and his tiny strip of land, his one or two cows or sheep. And everything is free on the commons – pasture for his cow, peat for his chimney, turf for his roof, wood for his fire, stones for his walls. He has nothing to fight for, God damn him! Nothing to die for! Yah!' he shouted, and dashed up to his man, now only yards ahead.

'They'll 'ave him soon enough, sir,' his man called out, and they charged through the forest side.

'Does the com-mon man not have his in-de-pen-dence?' Parson Snaile cried out from the rear, his syllables pounding the saddle. 'His dig-nity?'

'I tell you,' roared the baronet, 'he is idle. It leads him to drink, to dissipation, to immorality. Where is the dignity in that?'

'And you think it is your duty to change him?' screamed Parson Snaile, by now far behind.

'Indeed I do, Vicar. Indeed I do. Our duty. You and I are the pillars of society. The Atlas that holds up the world. If the governing class doesn't govern there will be chaos. It is our duty. The revolution starts here. Vive la Révolution!'

Parson Snaile had, with a giant effort, caught up, and leaned out of his horse towards the revolutionary. 'These are dangerous times to use such a word, Sir Edward,' he gasped. 'What exactly are you proposing?'

The pillar of Grasmere stopped in his tracks. 'My revolution,' he announced from the coverts, 'is nothing to do with that despicable band of Jacobin regicides! I will defeat the French without setting foot outside Grasmere.'

'But we are at peace with France.'

'We might have made peace at Amiens two months ago but that does not mean we are now at peace, Vicar. It is called drawing breath. Make no mistake, we are still at war. Before long the knives will be out again.' He set off again. 'Soon it will be impossible to import grain again. Meanwhile the price of wheat and oatmeal continue to rise and our people lurch closer to starvation. And that isn't to speak of the terrible harvests. Whooping cough is a plague among the poor. These are desperate times, my dear sir, and they require desperate ideas.'

'How will you wage your revolution, sir, how?' Parson Snaile shouted, his horse neck and neck with Sir Edward's.

'With this.' hissed the baronet, handing a piece of paper between the horses. The parson read it aloud mid-air as his horse leapt over a thick, fallen tree. 'An Act of Parliamentary Enclosure for Helvellyn. Helvellyn?'

'Yes. My birthright. The jewel in the Unthank crown. I intend to conquer Helvellyn – and defeat the French into the bargain.'

'Are you mad?' yelped the parson. 'How can you triumph over the French by enclosing Helvellyn?'

'I can't hear you, Vicar, ride closer. Lakeland has more upland waste going to ruin than anywhere in England. Once I've enclosed much of the high ground I will get horses to drag my new iron ploughs through it and turn those rough common pastures into arable land, where cereals will be sown and grain harvested. No cattle, no sheep. That way this village, starved by Bonaparte, will come back to life and trounce him on our own soil.'

'Gottim!' shouted his man from ahead to the sound of hound hysterics.

'Ah! Good. Let me through.'

Beyond the deerhound-pack, slumped exhausted after the chase, head low and panting into Greenhead Ghyll, stood a wild Caledonian red stag. Sir Edward raised his rifle and took aim, and a shot rang out, making the hounds jump as one and look round at the source of the explosion, a barrel from which smoke was oozing.

'What the devil!' the baronet bellowed.

'Gottim!' repeated Vipond lowering his gun.

'You dog! He was mine!' Sir Edward roared, swinging his gun around and making everyone flinch apart from the stag, which had flinched its last into a pool of blood already diluting into Greenhead Ghyll.

'I thought you wanted me to shootim,' said Vipond calmly.

Unthank raised his gun, aimed it at Vipond and another shot rang out. He'd turned the gun away at the last moment and re-shot the stag, which turned out not to have flinched its last after all as a shudder of absorption passed through its corpse. Vipond turned away from his master, smiling. 'I'll tend tut hounds.'

'Oh, if only I could attend to him,' steamed Sir Edward inwardly as he turned his horse round. 'What would I give to blast that animal in the chest!' And he didn't mean the stag. What would he give to have the power to kill men at a time of his own choosing and get away with it. 'If I were a duke, or a king,' he dreamed, acknowledging the central frustration of his life, that he could never quite get enough power to satisfy his lust for it.

'Well? Can we do it?' he said, addressing Vipond with tight-jawed self-control. Vipond turned to his master and smiled.

'Course we can. Might break a few but that's a fair price.'

'Do them good I'd say,' said Sir Edward. 'There is nothing that appeals less to me than the laziness of the poor. You watch them wrestling on sports day and they fight like gods for their pride and for a belt to hang on their walls, but if you ask them to shift a few rocks for you they look at you like smacked children.'

'Well, I've found a half-decent gang this time,' said Vipond.

'So you can't foresee any trouble?'

'I won't stand for nowt now.'

'That's it. Don't give an inch.'

Sir Edward felt an involuntary surge of violent thoughts towards Vipond but all he could legally do was stare briefly at him with intense hatred. As he met Vipond's moist, unblinking eyes his over-responsive bladder began to give way and he broke into a run. He emitted into the trees, to his enormous frustration, a trickle weaker than the thinnest of mountain rills, which danced briefly on the tree roots in a gilt-edged stream. 'How can it be,' he muttered to himself as he went to remount his horse, 'that I am childless? And how dare that bastard look me so impertinently in the eye!'

'It sounds like a worthwhile project, Sir Edward,' said Parson Snaile emolliently, able to enjoy again the smooth feel of his own coat sleeves as his horse trotted back into the grounds of Unthank Hall. 'But it is all poor soil up there in the fells, surely.'

'Much of it is clay, yes,' sighed the baronet, taking deep breaths to recover himself, 'and, like the peasants, it is ungrateful and hard to cultivate, but I will do so. Lakeland is backward. I intend to reverse that.'

'But how will you get these peasants to give up their land?'

'My enclosure commissioner has mapped and divided out the western slopes, and we have a gang here about to build the boundary wall. I will get the indolent fools to work for me. I will show them the meaning of hard work.'

Sir Edward barked orders at his stable boy as they dismounted, and while they were entering the Hall Parson Snaile pressed his case.

'It will cause unrest if you take their land. You will need an army for your little revolution.'

'Unrest!' snapped the baronet as he guided the parson to the Great Dining Room. He'd had just about enough of this man of God playing devil's advocate. 'We already have unrest! Boundary disputes, farmer against farmer, shepherd against shepherd. Sheep-stealing is rife, dogging is rampant, stock is lost and killed in its hundreds. The unrest is between the peasants themselves. I rest well at night. With new allotments and boundaries every man will know where he stands.'

'And yet he will lose his strip of land and ancient rights to the common.'

'Those blasted rights were never his in the first place!' Sir Edward almost wept. 'They were a gift from the Lord of the Manor. Besides, he can use my fields if he pays me rent. I will pay him to work on my land, to build my walls. And when prosperity returns to Grasmere – when we win the war! – the peasant, the farmer, the shepherd, the farm-hand, they will all thank me for unchaining them from the feudal yoke.'

'An honourable battle,' said Parson Snaile half-heartedly.

'Honourable indeed,' Sir Edward mumbled as he slithered into slippers of red morocco, adding, 'and there's good money in it, of course, and good sport. I will plant larches, and some of the waste land will make excellent grouse moor.'

'Ah, tsk tsk, my good sir,' the parson risked. 'Your rapacious quest for land. What of the deadly sin of greed?'

'Greed?' Sir Edward erupted, searching around him and gauging on impulse whether this was an appropriate location for a duel with a member of the clergy. 'This is about public service, Vicar, not greed. We must sort these bucolics out once and for all.'

The king of Unthank Hall had had enough, and though fresh venison and claret was soon to be served in order to purchase the loyalty of the parson, he collapsed for a moment into his favourite Elizabethan armchair within the twelve-foot-thick limestone rubble walls of his family fortress, gazed up at a ceiling festooned with early Renaissance military motifs, and sighed that people should make his life such a damned, confounded battle.

# 8

# First Rood

In the nip of a half-broken dawn Luke crept out of Nettleslack Farm grainstore. He followed in the wake of two beggar children who scuffled along the path in front of him scattering the dew with their feet, no shoes or stockings, chasing a moth, swatted like flies by a mother who looked as though she'd given up being gentle with them years before. They were everywhere, these hard-faced widows of the wars. How many fathers, Luke wondered, had left Lakeland vowing to their loved ones a safe and soon return home, only to leave that promise lying broken beside their ploughed-up bodies on the battlefield, the realisation sinking like anchors into their wives' hearts.

'Let me alone, Mudder!' stamped the little lad, throwing to the ground a home-made hat wreathed with yellow wayside flowers.

'Getta move on, Jem!'

'I'm not going up. I'll stop here and beg, but I'll not go up there.'

When Luke reached the Swan alongside the beggar family he saw a small mound of humanity had gathered, rubble to be cleared from the vale and swept away into the fells. They joined the group, which stood clenched like the embryo of a mob, a grubby parade of smock-frocks, collarless shirts, ragged waistcoats, jackets and hats. Shortly afterwards a cart drew up and tipped out its contents like dung – gypsies, olive-skinned, high of cheekbone, brooding. Some mob, though: they were submissive as old cattle when, minutes later, Vipond arrived. He punched shoulders to indicate the ones he wanted for his Helvellyn gang and he might as well have spat at the rest for the amount of respect with which he turned them away.

'This way!' he snarled, handing out spades, sleds, hazel poles and bags of old sailcloth and tarpaulin. The new gang headed northwards out of the village on the Keswick road up Dunmail Raise. Luke had his ear cocked to the disgruntled dispersal of the rejected, and soon he heard footsteps behind.

'We can work as hard as three men, sir,' called the beggar woman.

'Mudder! Nae!' bawled Jem. The mother belted the lad across the ear. Jem didn't cry but looked up at Vipond with two fires of defiance.

Vipond turned to the mother as if calculating her worth.

'A day's work … for half a day's pay. Just one day, mind.'

The beggars joined the group at the back. The road stretched more than five miles northwards up Dunmail Raise and towards Wythburn Water. The gang splintered into pairs. There were two gypsies; the farm-hand Luke had met in the Swan was paired up with a bow-legged, leather-fingered man with straw hair, and Luke was coupled with the tall, thin Irishman who'd been the farm-hand's tablemate in the Swan.

'Swinton Gass of the 42nd Highlanders, chief!' the Irishman

declared with an interminable handshake. 'I've got four lungs – two for breathing, two for talking,' he joked, proceeding to recount without the slightest encouragement – in fact, without a single sign, bodily or verbally, from Luke to indicate he was even listening – his fondest memories of 'that great day', the 21st of March 1801, the Battle of Alexandria. 'Ah, sure,' said Gass in lengthy conclusion a good ten minutes later, 'we fought like lions on the glorious twenty-first!'

Luke murmured, when Gass had to draw breath, that he didn't remember Alexandria as being great, thereby giving away that he'd been there, and thereby finding himself being hugged more than half to death. 'I'm so glad to see ye, chief, so glad!' Gass cried as if they'd clambered out of the same womb as each other.

Luke stood looking back down towards Grasmere wondering whether maybe he'd got it wrong himself. What glorious day? Only blood and terror and childlike screams from dying men. The whole thing had been a living hell, from the dank fear of their arrival the night before, their campfires igniting the darkness and then the sky flickering to black. They'd huddled together like trembling rodents in the pits they'd dug on the sandhills, pouring sand on their blankets for warmth and trying without hope to sleep.

At around three in the morning, in the first gloom of dawn, he'd heard a noise; his ears pricked up and he squinted into the mist but could see nothing. Then, 'En avant! En avant! Vive la République!' came the roar out of nowhere. The French cavalry, and a battle-storm suddenly broke in the sky, to the thunder of drums and cannons and the lightning of gun-flashes.

Horses shot to the ground; unseated riders stabbed through with bayonets; dragoons dizzying about, some alive but most dead. Men pulled to pieces by grapeshot, roasted by artillery gun explosions, sliced through with sabres. When they all ran dry of ammunition they slung rocks at each other.

'Just children,' he said, 'turning to Gass. 'Scared children throwing stones at each other, killing each other. Slaughtered lambs, not lions.'

Gass was quiet.

'Anyhow,' said Luke with sudden pretend cheer, 'what was an Irishman doing in a Scottish regiment fighting for the English?'

'Hoho, you troy and stap me. The British army's full of us, chief, we luv a good foight, we do. They've been pulling us Catholics out of the bog for years now and enlisting us, telling us we don't need to swear legiance to no Proddie crown no more. They need us to fill their ranks, and we need their money to fill our mouths. Anyways, when it comes to foighting the Froggeaters we're all in it together, all British, all dyin' together like brothers.'

Halfway along the edge of Wythburn Water, whose surface displayed the imprint of Helvellyn's slopes, the two discharged brothers in arms turned eastwards and saw cloud shadows bleed up Helvellyn Screes. They followed a path up a track that wound through woods at the edge of the Swirls. Before long they'd reached the rest of the gang. Amid the pennywhistle of skylarks Jem was calling out as he tore through the heather with piles of small stones, spilling them, bending to pick them up again. 'Come on! What's tha waiting for?' his mother shouted, and Jem responded with something brazen, then tripped and vanished in the heather.

The two gypsies lugged boulders to the straw-haired man, who was on his hands and knees. 'If there's one magic word,' he said to them, 'it's fetch. Every yard of wall needs a ton of stone fetched. Never stop fetching and we'll be done with the walling before long. That's the plan, lads.' Luke and Gass, who'd just sat down at the end of the hike from Grasmere, set off again with a sigh of fatigue. Luke returned with an armful of stones and spilled them to the ground.

'Nae,' said the man he presumed to be a mason, 'them's no good, lad, too small. I need some big boulders first of all. It'll tek two of you, or use one of those sleds yonder.' Luke looked down at him, vexed.

'Who's in charge here? You or Vipond?'

'Me. He won't be up here with us all the time. Don't worry about him,' the man replied. 'He just likes to crack the whip; skulks around, hanging behind rocks. Misses nowt, mind. If you want to grumble, do it to me, and do it like this.' He clenched his teeth and widened his lips to show Luke. 'Ay, through your teeth. He reads lips. Keep out of his way an all, and work hard, you'll be fine. Hate him as much as I do, ay, but stay on the right side of him while you can.' He reached up and shook hands. 'Isaac Cragg, master waller. And this ere's young Master Weightman,' he said, pointing to the dim-eyed farm-hand. 'Now, let's build a boundry for these land-grabbing villains,' he said, the latter words through his teeth.

'Where do we start, chief?' asked Gass, having returned with bigger stones than Luke's and dumped them.

'With them long arms of yours,' said Cragg, 'pulling cobbles out of the ghyll yonder. We'll use them with slate to make a flat finish for each course.' He turned to Luke. 'You and Weightman help me on the first yard of wall. We need to dig out a six-inch sod. We've got seven yards to do for each rood, and a rood a day. With a bit of luck we'll stretch this wall right up over Browncove Crag, Lower Man and then Helvellyn one day, even if it takes two years instead of one. Once it's up, it'll stay up till kingdom come. Two hundred years from now they'll be wondering who the clever buggers was who put this wall up. They'll think twas the Romans.' Luke half-smiled. 'Right. Six-foot high, three-foot wide at bottom and tapered to eighteen inches at top.'

Cragg, Weightman and Luke raised their spades, and with his first chunk into the earth Luke thought of Michael. The earth they'd dug together, father and son, talking not with their voices but with their hearts; the winds they'd weathered for the flock, the leagues they'd walked, the crags they'd climbed, the years they'd toiled together, all of which had been the comfort of

Michael's old age and the joy of Luke's childhood. He pictured Michael shearing the flock in the shade of the clipping tree, keeping a fond eye on him. He remembered when he turned five Michael gave him a staff made from a sapling, which he wielded day and night for the next five years, to the long-standing forbearance of his mother. By ten he could pull a grimace in a fellside blizzard as well as any Greenhead through the ages. The old shepherd had been like a man reborn to have him by his side, and with every stab of the spade deeper into the ground Luke's sadness grew. The turning over of that soil, the desecration of flowers at a grave he should have left untouched.

The three men dug the foundations and, fingers black with dirt, Luke stepped over the mounds of stones to the edge of Helvellyn Ghyll. Gass was sitting looking silently into the water, having unplugged scores of cobbles. Luke knelt down next to him, felt the camaraderie of compassion, cupped his hands and swigged the cool liquid.

'Ye know,' said Gass after a wordless pause between them, 'I wasn't always such a big talker.' Luke wiped his mouth and looked round. 'I fought well but I got the life scared outta mae that day. Not stopped talkin about it since.'

'I'm the opposite,' said Luke, turning to him. 'I don't like to talk about any of it … but I didn't fight like you.'

Gass looked him in the eye. 'Howjeh mean?'

'I ran. Hid myself away. In the sand dunes. Came back when it was all over – when the fleet arrived on the shore to take us home next day. All I know of the battle is other men's stories – proper soldiers like you, the brave ones.'

Gass stared at him in silence.

'Come on, lads!' shouted Cragg. 'Stop gabbin'. We've got the trench, now time for the wall. No binding. It's about balance. We need some more boulders for footings now.'

Luke, Gass and the two gypsies dispersed again. They dragged large, uneven boulders hundreds of yards up and downhill to the trench using hand sledges. Weightman lugged some of the biggest stones silently on his own. Jem, his mother and sister carried a huge boulder between them and plonked it down almost on Cragg's foot. Cragg patted the boy on the shoulder and tousled Jem's hair. 'Tha's doing better than any of mine could, lad,' he said to him as Jem set off again with raw hands. 'Mine'd be sitting on their mammy's lap by now, jislin' and lickin' their soft paws like kittens.'

Luke stayed to help begin the wall, and as Weightman made to resume his quest for boulders Cragg seized his shoulder. 'Here, lad,' he said. 'Grab hold of this bugger with us, will tha, it'll do for the first footing.' The three men slotted the first footing stone into the sod.

'Right, we need two rows of these,' said Cragg. Luke and Weightman began heaving boulders.

'When I started out, donkey's years ago,' grunted Cragg as he jockeyed the rocks into position, 'this was craftsman's work, and down in the dale bottom an all, not up in the fells like this. You can't grow much on this land, any road, it's barmy. But I've got six bairns tugging at their mudder's pinny.'

Luke nodded in acknowledgement.

'There's nowt like the rugged fells round here, mind,' Cragg mused as they lifted and sank more footings into the muddy hole. 'Helvellyn, Great Gavel, Scawfell, Old Man of Coniston, Langdale pikes. Folk say they was all formed from volcano lava thousands and millions of years ago. The stone changes, you see,' he added, looking over at Weightman, as if expecting a reaction. 'Up north near Keswick, round Skiddaw, the rock's darker, smoother, more slatey. Over east in Eskdale it's like pink granite – hard as buggery to build with, tis. What we've got here isn't so bad, so we stand a chance.'

Luke looked across at Weightman, who shrugged boredly. Cragg pursed his lips, clearly vexed by his new apprentice.

Two parallel rows of footings began taking shape to form the new wall's foundation. The glacial and volcanic debris of Swirl Crags and Helvellyn Screes had provided the gang with enough

'Nice dream,' said Cragg. 'Had one of them myself once. Put me life into this walling, I have. Given up a lot to be up here in these fells year after year. When't wife were expecting our first bairn I were a farm-hand like you. Worked on a farmstead over in Easedale. When the money was better for building and walling and there was lots of work in the fields and dale bottoms – not like now – I learnt the craft.' He levelled off the course with slates and Gass's ghyll cobbles, and patted it. 'Turned myself into a stone mason, dint I. Learnt how to build houses, stuck together with lime mortar, and learnt how to build dry walls. And I learnt to stick the weather an all, and the weeks and weeks away from home. Then more bairns came along, and more, till I had to work nonstop to keep them blinkin mouths fed.'

The three wallers carried on in silence.

'Right, then,' said Cragg, 'time for the through-stones.' He scrabbled around among the heap being built by the rest of the gang, and found a large stone that he placed on top of the first course, bridging the wall's two faces divided by heartings. The throughs stuck out of each side of the wall like crooked teeth. 'Slope them all outwards,' he shouted, shifting with a snort the angle of a through. 'The rain'll drip out and down and it'll keep the hearting dry. That way the middle won't belly out in the frost and the wall won't rush.'

'Yeh stayed wukin up here all them years, right?' said Weightman.

Luke looked up and saw Cragg's relieved smile.

'I hated being away from't wife and bairns all that time,' said Cragg, with renewed vigour. 'But I got used to it. I had to. And the longer it went on, the easier it were. This work up here, the lads in gangs like this, got to be my family, you see.' Weightman nodded. 'Wife got used to doing without me. And the bairns. Began to forget about their fadder, they did – while I was up here earning money to feed and clothe the buggers.'

They placed the first set of throughs and began the wall's second course without a break, and Cragg now talked without pause. 'When I did get home,' he said, 'I felt like a stranger in me own house. So I stopped going home so much, telling the wife – and myself – I didn't have time. And these fells got to be my home – ay, just like they are for't Herdwicks. And all them lads who went to war and never came back, and left their wives and bairns widowed and orphaned, well I dint think for a minute I was doing that an all. The bairns are growing now. All that time's gone by for good.'

Lifting, positioning, packing heartings, placing throughs, another course, and another, with more heartings, and throughs, it didn't stop all day long, by which time the wall was narrowing to the height of a six-foot man.

'Right, now the cams,' shouted Cragg, and they began stacking small slates on edge along the top.

It was beyond sunset when Cragg heaved a weary breath and put a hand on the new wall. 'It's only a row, not even a rood, and there's hundreds of roods to make a wall, but for the first day … not bad at all.' The wallers' heads and shoulders slackened in unison with fatigue and relief.

Luke stood up and walked away from the gang. He gazed into the beautiful vales nestling beneath and wondered how he'd ended up as Unthank's hapless mule, slogging away for a handful of oats. He could just about see in silhouette far below a gentle elderly couple on an evening stroll, enjoying the leisurely season of their life, and he envied them. Only when he squinted to get a clearer view did he notice there was nothing elderly or leisurely about them. The taller of the two – who else but Wordsworth! – was barging along deep in conversation with … himself. And there, quite predictably, scurrying behind, was Dorothy, jabbing at a page with her pencil by the looks of it, no doubt catching all the poetic sweet-fruits straight out of her brother's mouth. Another hapless mule, Luke thought, surviving on a handful of oats. He turned away, unable to bear the sight of them, and focused on a gap in the wall lower down.

'We need to stop that hole there,' he called out to Cragg.

'Nay,' said Cragg, approaching the gap with a hinged board in his hands. 'It's a smoot is that. We dig a little pit tudder side and cover it wid board. Tek the pin out of the board, our little matey-boy gambolling about the place nips along it through't hole this side, board swings on its hinge and our pal falls int pit. Fancy a leg of rabbit on the fire? I do.'

'I wouldn't mind setting a trap like that for someone else,' said Luke.

'Ay, he's a right gammerstang,' one of the gypsies chipped in. They were talking about Vipond, even if Luke wasn't.

'Shifty-looking bastud,' agreed the gypsy's shifty-looking companion.

'Ay,' said Cragg. 'House has a chimney that sends more smoke in than out. Stinks of it, wheezes with it. Look at his eyes. They're cloudy with it, it's like they're weeping smoke. As I say, not to be trusted.'

'Sounds like a Froggeater,' laughed Gass.

'Nae,' said Cragg. 'Lakeland stock tut bones. Worst breed, mind.'

'Singing me praises again, Isaac?' said Vipond, having materialised supernaturally.

'Me?' replied Cragg looking him straight in the moist grey eye.

Vipond turned to the sitting wallers. 'Up!' he snapped. 'And stay up till the tents is done. No fire and no vittals till then.' The gang lifted themselves to their feet again and wearily erected their makeshift tents with the hazel poles and sailcloth. The fire eventually burnt beacon-like on the fell. Jem and his sister were dozing in their mother's lap by the fire when a figure appeared out of the dark, his eyes glistening in the flames.

'Here!' said Vipond, dropping a small coin in the mother's hand. 'Tomorrow I want you beggars gone. You can't tek the pace.'

Jem's mother stood up. 'That isn't even half a day's pay. We've not stopped! We'll be first up and last down tomorra an all.'

'I'll drag y'all downill first by your hair! In't no place for women-bodies and bairns up here. It's man's work. And you!' he shouted across at Gass. 'Whatf you been doing playing in the river all day? Dreaming? I want you gone in the morning an all. There's plenty of hard-working lads wants this job.'

Gass stood up. 'Ah cmon, chief, gimmae a chance. I'll work harder tomorrow.'

Luke stood up and decided to stand by his comrade in arms this time, unlike at Alexandria. 'If he goes, so do I.'

Vipond licked his lips, clearly enjoying being reviled, and was about to say something Luke suspected to be 'fine by me' when Cragg stood up.

'And I can't do without these two,' he said into Vipond's eyeballs. 'So looks like I'll be off an all int mornin'.'

Vipond's face was like broth on the boil. 'I'll be watching you,' he hissed to Luke, and withdrew. A black wind moaned through Swirl Crags and the gang retreated to their tents. Soon it would be dawn and the work would begin again on the slow march uphill, stone by stone, row by row, rood by rood, all for a handful of nothing.

# 9

# Cragfast

Lemon-flavoured sunlight blinded Sally's blue eyes already showing a hint of grey as she looked out from the porch of Nettleslack Farm across Grasmere. She could see over to Churnmilk Force, which spilt itself down the Easedale valley like breast-milk. She wondered, as she walked across the yard with three-legged coppy and pail under her arm and looked behind her uphill into Butter Crag, where the stranger was whom she'd nursed out of a fever only weeks before. She hadn't had a chance to talk to him that morning he'd left for the Swan at dawn.

She shrugged her shoulders and headed for the Nettleslack cow, which was roving towards her from the field. They met halfway and Sally led her to the byre saying 'Cummon then,

Judy lass'. She set the coppy and pail on the stone ground, sat down facing the cow's tail, ear tucked in to Judy's side and legs stretched far enough apart to make the fibres of her apron creak, and reached for her favourite two udders, the co-operative ones. Judy looked round at her as a matter of form and then set about chewing cud while Sally began strangling the sausage-like mammillas.

As she gripped, fingered and squeezed to make Judy's milk piss hard into the pail, Sally wondered why she'd wanted to talk to Luke that morning he'd left. Probably a mothering instinct, to check he had some food in his pocket, an oatcake or something. Or perhaps a sisterly instinct. She'd been close to Jackie before he left for sea and got himself drowned in a storm or killed by pirates or however he'd died. She missed her brother. There'd only been a few years between them and they'd understood each other, and how hard it was living with Jack, especially after Mudder. Jack wasn't easy by any stretch of Judy's udders, and Jackie had shared the burden, of Jack and of the farm.

Once she'd milked half the cow Sally stood up straight, back stiff and fingers rigid, and frowned at the thought of her body seizing up one day and then what would they do? Jack couldn't do it – Judy would kick him in the head rather than allow his clumsy hands on her teats. And it wasn't just her own body seizing up that she was worrying about. Judy was an old cow and would be dry before long. But she'd given a good pail of milk for the churn today at least, and that meant butter and cheese tomorrow, so Sally told herself again she wasn't one for fretting about the future and set off back to the house.

As she did so she couldn't help thinking about Luke again, and how he might be – though the idea was barmy – a reward, for all her sweat and tears and loneliness over the years. Now she was most definitely not the type to skip a beat for a man she'd just met, especially that washed-out rook-scarer, but all that brow-mopping had made her feel ... rescued, like in those tales her mother used to tell her by the fire as she tore her fingers through her thick, wet and knotted hair. He'd become her gallant knight, the prince to her Cinderella – or Rapunzel, or the Sleeping Beauty, or all three rolled into one – even if she'd been reduced numerous times over those few days to wiping parts less fairy-tale than his fevered brow. Since she'd seen Luke last all those silly romantic ingredients had been wrought into a big sloppy dough and tossed into the furnace of her heart, along with a peppering of pity for a man who'd been told by her bluddy thoughtless fadder – who regarded rubbing salt into people's self-inflicted wounds as a virtue, nay a Christian duty – that both his parents were dead, and that it was all Luke's fault.

Nae, she wouldn't wish the bluddy Nettleslacks on anyone. Mind you, with that filthy nest of a beard and that vegetable smell about him, who'd want Luke Greenhead under their feet all day, she told herself in a vain final attempt to become his mother, or sister. 'If I had my way,' she said as she entered the kitchen, now reinventing herself as a matron figure, 'I'd gettim straight into a biggot tub of water and scrubbim hard fut fust time in years,' but at that thought some unbidden sensation nagged at her. It was like ... no, she couldn't put her finger on it.

The walling had chained sunrise to sunset for ten days until at last Vipond gave the wallers their first break. The gang dispersed and Luke dropped downhill beyond the shades of the Swirls into a late afternoon of May Day sunshine. After the five-mile traipse back along Wythburn Water, down Dunmail Raise and past the Swan Inn, he appeared at Nettleslack Farm and made Sally jump like a deer at gunshot.

'I dint hear you coming!' she shrieked. 'Sneaking in like that. I thought you wut dog!'

It felt good to see her again.

'Fadder's up by Stone Arthur,' she said. 'Says he's gone after a yowe that's cragfast.'

The word 'cragfast' crunched in Luke's memory. Michael had taken him up onto Great Tongue on the fells above Grasmere when he was no more than twelve to rescue a cragfast Herdwick. It was when spring's sweetest grasses had infiltrated the most unreachable places on the fells and a callow yearling had ventured out onto a crag ledge. He and Michael had taken two ropes, one thick hemp about fifty foot long, the other shorter and thinner attached to a stick, and with a noose. Michael held the thick rope at the top and lowered Luke down the crag. Luke threw pebbles either side of the sheep to warn it not to step off the ledge, and then he hooked the noose over its head. But the rope holding him from above suddenly slipped several feet. He held on, frightened for his life, drew the sheep to him and bound its legs. Michael hauled him back up, groaning with the effort. When he got to the top Michael unbound the sheep and took Luke in his arms. 'I nearly dropped thee, son,' he wept, pressing him tight. 'I couldn't hold on, I'm sorry.' To remember hearing Michael say sorry to him felt strange, and to think of the risk his father had taken, for the sake of just one sheep, in nearly losing his only son.

It wasn't, come to think of it, the only time Michael had sacrificed him. He'd left Grasmere at his father's request, and thereby followed the path of temptation and iniquity. He had measured his every defect and failure in life against the boundless virtues of his father, but Michael was no saint, and had sent him more than once like a lamb to the slaughter. Sally snapped him out of his morose confusion with the clarity of golden haverbread.

After supping on it he offered to go and help Jack, feeling more kindly at that moment towards Sally's father than his own.

'Nae, he'll cope fine,' she said. Luke doubted a man of Jack's vintage would cope fine rescuing a cragfast sheep not long before dusk, especially considering how less-than-fine Michael had coped that time. Who would Jack be sacrificing on the end of that rope, he wondered. 'Time was,' Sally said, munching away, 'Fadder could lift a cow over the wall, but he's not so nimble on the pins now. Topples about like an ole hen. Gets the roomattics bad an all. Nance's the same. You'd never get them to admit it though. Proud as peacocks.' She frowned. 'I don't know how we manage.' Her auburn lashes quivered with the strain of pondering it.

'What about a hired hand?' asked Luke.

'We can't afford one! Sixpence a day a lad costs. Meantime I'm washing, cleaning, cooking, mending, being mudder and dotter to him. And that's just indoors. I haven't even got on tut planting, raking, weeding, picking stones, feeding the hens, milking the cow, churning the butter. We can't go on like this,' she said finally.

Jack appeared in the doorway. 'Hoo'doo, lad! Come to help out wit haymaking, has tha? Up at five, mind. Soon as the dew's off the grass we'll be at them fields wit sickles. Women-bodies can rake and turn the swathes after.'

'Nae, Fadder,' said Sally. 'Lettim off, he's been up in the fells for weeks.'

'Ee, if I were thy age …'

'Ay, but you aren't,' she chided. 'Now, Luke, you all right kippin in the store again?'

A home-made mattress in a grainstore compared to a stony fellside tent? Naturally. It seemed unusual, he considered once he got inside the store, that Jack should talk so keenly about the haymaking, when there was only one cow to feed in the byre next door and they couldn't afford a single hired hand. He hadn't seen any sheep either. As for tilling the land and growing crops, despite the talk of endless toil it was hard to imagine much going on. The grainstore looked as if it hadn't stored grain in years. Maybe they had stock and grain in some other place.

A cuckoo woke him up so early that the blackbirds were twiddling their feathers waiting for the worms. It was certainly early enough to help Jack with the haymaking, but there was no sign of him about the farm. Sally was in the down-house in no mood.

'Is Jack out in the fields already?' he asked her.

'Eh? Oh, ay. What in the divel's name are you wearing?' Luke looked down at the shabby gentleman's waistcoat, cravat, breeches, stockings and shoes.

'My only change of clothes.'

'Bluddyell! I better wash that smock-frock. Now get out from under me feet.'

'But—'

'Goo on!' she said, shoving him out of the door as if he'd been lying panting on the stone flags like Nance. After practically wrestling her into taking a shilling for his keep – and concluding that Nettleslack pride ran as deep in the rocks as Borrowdale lead – he retreated away from the farm into Grasmere.

Hardly had the sun poked its nose over the felltops on a beautiful May morning than he was free, enfranchised and at large. Before long he was following a path through woods strewn with pink confetti, a Maytide autumn of blossom-fall that painted pathways with lilacs, purples and coral pinks. The heart-shaped leaflets and pink-white petals of the wood-sorrel; the fleshy stench of hawthorns; the musk of distant deer; the downy touch of dandelions; the meek stoop of bluebells. A fallen ash trunk basked in the sun. He stood crumbling the biscuit-like bark in his fingers and squinting into the sun till his eyeballs throbbed. He felt drawn in, swallowed up, dissolved.

Further along the road, beyond the sparkle of celandines, he saw daffodils collapsed on the wayside. How quickly they'd died, he reflected, his mind turning to Dorothy at Ullswater. He wished he hadn't blurted out that he was a poet. Even though it had lit up Dorothy's face he was going to have to admit to her sooner or later that he'd lied – either that or become a poet as a matter of urgency. He didn't even know what to be a poet meant, apart from the obvious – wandering round looking glum and conjuring up largely incomprehensible combinations of words that occasionally rhymed, solely to impress educated people.

He was no poet and never would be, but she as it turned out was no poet's wife. She was his sister, therefore free, available, a fruit ripening on the tree and not so forbidden after all. He visualised Dolly – no, Dorothy was her name, not Dolly; only her precious brother could call her that! – he visualised her in the shape of a sharp green apple, and the thought made his taste-buds ache and his tongue venture out of his mouth in search of his lips. I must have that moist fruit, his tongue seemed to say.

The cuckoo, harbinger of spring's swoon into the arms of summer, piped its melancholy third. There the intruder was on a birch twig, jail-bars under its wings, eyeing nearby nests for a home! Luke looked down from the tree and spotted a man stretched out on the road ahead, with his ear to the ground. Either he was dead or he was enjoying listening to the subterranean rumblings of the earth, in which case he was a maniac. Only when Luke was overtaken by a coach did he realise the man had been listening out for the mail, and only when it stopped and handed the man a letter did Luke see, as he watched several wiry legs creep along the ground like a giant insect, that it was Wordsworth. Luke followed, but at such a safe distance that the mad poet disappeared ahead. By the time noon had struck, Dove Cottage stood only yards away. He hovered nearby, trying to decide what to do next, but eventually, fortuitously, who should be at her own home, as she habitually was, but Dorothy.

'What a heavenly day!' she declared when she saw him. In a surge of vanity Luke imagined it was because of him.

'Will you take a turn with me in the lane?' he stammered, cringing to sound so genteel.

Dorothy quarrelled with herself. 'I should really be collecting mosses, or cooking, or gardening, or building the fire, or darning ... but I've been sitting here on the wall making this shift for so long I can hardly see any longer.'

It took immense discipline of mind for him to avoid the image of her wearing nothing but her shift.

She accepted his offer. More than accepted, fair somersaulted off the wall and skipped up to him. 'Let's go to the lake,' she trilled, adding, 'William has just received a letter and is busy with it,' as if to say she wouldn't be seen dead with a mere mortal like Luke otherwise. They set off. Luke looked over his shoulder at Dove Cottage and saw, in the gloom behind a diamond-paned window, surrounding an aquiline nose, a scowl.

They stood looking out over Grasmere lake. Luke observed that steady pool, and the spiked crags beyond, with their milky cataracts amid the skirmishes of light and shade, and felt both the stamp and whinny of nature and its tranquillity. Dorothy was just as capricious. One minute she was hysterical with life, the next as still and unfathomable as the lake. She stirred, and placed the tip of her shoe in the water; he thought of the daffodils tiptoeing into Ullswater. He wanted so much to speak like a poet but he was as dry-lipped and dumbstruck as a cadaver.

'Dolly's View,' he suddenly burst out, to no one's surprise more than his. 'Let's call this spot Dolly's View.'

All at once the lake's looking-glass surface was smashed from beneath by a huge brown trout that must have weighed ten pounds, leaping into the air and crashing back into the water.

'If only William could catch one of those instead of blessed minnows all the time,' laughed Dorothy as they watched the ripples fan out over the lake like a peacock's tail. 'You are a mystery to me, Luke,' she went on to say in a warm, lyrical voice. 'You appear out of the clouds, and then you vanish into a storm. You suddenly reappear, subdue a cow on my behalf, then you evaporate again. Now here you are, silent as a ghost, but,' she added with a giggle, 'smart as a carrot.'

'A carrot on hard times,' he clarified, looking down at the dead man's suit to which he was tethered, which made her laugh out loud girlishly. They stood up and began walking away from the lake back towards Dove Cottage.

'You seem a little out of humour,' detected Dorothy as he walked lumpenly alongside her. 'Please excuse me for laughing. I know times are hard – William and I are as poor as church mice.'

Times had become harder now she'd mentioned that highwayman in the tracks of her thoughts.

'When I first came back,' he began, giving up his frigid attempts to impress and seduce her, 'I thought Grasmere, this lake, these fells, were the same as ... as before, but they're not. Everything's changed. It sounds strange but ... I can't see the life in it anymore – just the death.'

'Nature changes constantly, and dies, but doesn't it renew itself as well? Is it not timelessly unchanging?'

She'd cocked a compassionate ear but he wasn't in the mood for a lesson on the paradoxes of nature.

'I vowed,' he continued as if she hadn't spoken, 'to find their graves and recover our land, but I'm breaking my back building a wall for some greedy land-stealer called Unthank.'

Her eyes flashed away from him as though distracted. He'd hoped to prise *her* open, not wallow in his own confessional bile, and now it was too late, they were nearing Dove Cottage.

'To be at war with the future,' she said, 'when all you want is peace with the past.'

She was thinking about *him*, the literary giant who turned the rest of the world Lilliputian. 'He is very dear to you, isn't he?' he said through teeth gritted hard enough to send his gums purple.

'Who, William? Too dear,' she replied, her voice sinking. 'He's getting married,' she added in a voice as bleak as doom itself.

Luke had been cornered into commiseration and had to hide his pleasure at the news behind a sympathetic mask. But why should he commiserate? Shouldn't brother and sister be separated quite naturally by husband and wife? William couldn't expect to consume both Dorothy and his spouse. That would be gluttony.

'Is it not happy news?' he asked.

'Yes, yes!' she cried, sounding as if she meant the exact opposite. 'I encouraged the match myself, facilitated it even, and I want so much for him to be happy, but I worry…'

'About what?'

'What will happen of course. A poet like William should never marry. It will be the end of him. He will write nothing good after this, believe me. He is spent. Finished. He needs a muse, not a wife fattening with child by the day like a goose. And… and…'

'What?'

'Where will I go?' she faltered.

'Must you leave Dove Cottage?'

'No. Well, yes. I don't know. No. Oh, I do hope not. It would kill me! But we can't all live together. It would be too much. William's life is problematical enough, what with Annette and their daughter Caroline in France.' She sniffed with distress. 'Oh dear, I should never have let that slip. How frightfully disloyal of me. Please forget I mentioned it.'

Luke had struck meat at last. 'He has a daughter?'

'An improvident love affair ten years ago when he was in France after the Revolution.'

Luke recalled the monstrous improvidence of his own youth, but it didn't stop him judging William. 'And he just abandoned her?'

'Their relationship dissolved when William left France, and he never saw his daughter Caroline. He couldn't go back during the Terror anyway, and then he became so disillusioned with the Revolution that he couldn't face returning. But he wants to meet Caroline now and sort things out with her mother.'

'What, to be reconciled?'

'To make provision for Caroline, before he marries Mary. But where we'll get the money from heaven only knows.'

'Complicated,' remarked Luke, quite enjoying himself again.

'It is. If it weren't for a certain person all our lives would be easier.'

'A certain person?'

'Who owes my family thousands of pounds. My father was his solicitor, and died with his expenses unpaid. But I beg you, Luke, ignore my impulsive and indiscreet ramblings and forget what I've said. Please don't get tangled up in the Wordsworth web.'

Maybe too late already for that, thought Luke, and he couldn't promise Dorothy he'd forget what she'd told him either, but he didn't pursue it, having enough to pursue on a matter that, to his malevolent satisfaction, was presenting William in a less than heroic light.

'Surely your brother wouldn't turn you out of your own home, though. Would he?' he asked.

Dorothy turned to him in fury. 'What? Of course not! He'll beg me to stay, insist on it, refuse to let me go, even. And Mary is very dear to me,' she wilted, 'always has been.'

'Then don't leave Dove Cottage. But you can free yourself anyway.'

'Free myself?' she rasped. 'From what?'

'From William.'

'What are you talking about? William *is* freedom to me. I live for him, breathe for him. I should die if I lost him. Every word that issues from his lips I devour. Without him I would be nothing. Nothing! Just a little shell of a woman. Why would I want to free myself from him? I have given myself to him. If you see me sitting under the window with my back straight I will not be reading a book as some educated women might, but mending William's shirt. That is my vocation. He is a great poet. He calls me his muse. His inspiration!' She was panting. 'Oh! I am so ashamed to have shouted at you like that. I'm such a termagant at heart. I always was. An ungrateful little orphan. Please forgive me.'

Luke didn't need her apology. He'd seen a defiance in her, and this termagant side of her brought new hope. Nothing short of a violent mutiny against William would suffice, and this chaffinch had the potential to be as ruthless as an eagle-owl.

# 10

# Passions

Luke watched a flock of starlings breathe across the sky like woodsmoke, blown in and out of shape as they chased their own erratic flight patterns. Isaac Cragg peered up at them, too, his face scrunched with disgruntlement and the glare of the sky. May had been mild apart from the middle of the month, when hail and snow had cuffed the wallers so hard that they'd scampered down to the villages for shelter. But fair days had returned, and by the last week of June the wall's teeth, though not quite gnashing at Helvellyn's summit, had reached as high as Browncove Crag. Cragg surveyed the dizzying contours of rock into which they had to build the wall.

'Don't think it's me getting past it,' he said to Luke, paired with him that day. 'I haven't ever had such a hard walling job. I'm not as young as thee, mind – and not as young as me, neither, in them days. Nae. Summut's got to give. It's like building a wall up a bloody ladder.' He looked downhill at the drystone boundary sketching its pencil line between old waste and new intake, then looked uphill again, and shook his head. 'Fix them cams in tight, Luke. This wall's gonna be on its hind legs soon and they'll fall on us like axeheads if we don't.'

'How are ye now, chief?' asked Gass, who'd fetched an armful of stones.

'Summut don't feel right,' said Cragg.

'The days are fair, the sun's shining, we're making good progress, aren't we?'

'Nae, it isn't the weather. Summut don't feel good in here,' Cragg clarified, punching his belly. 'A gut feelin' I've got, starting to poison me.'

Gass and Luke looked at each other. Doom clouds had been gathering over Cragg's head for days. 'Hang on a sec,' said Cragg. 'Nae, it's in here,' he reconsidered, punching his chest. 'Ay, that's it. In me chest. In me yart.'

Gass turned to Weightman, who'd just arrived with rocks, and patted him on the shoulder. 'And what about you, young fella?' he asked cheerfully. 'How're ye doing, then?'

'Me?' said Weightman. 'Ay, I'm 'appy enough.'

'Why there ye go, chief,' Gass shouted down to Cragg, who was at the base of the wall on the other side, making a hogg-hole for sheep to squeeze through between pastures. 'Weightman's happy in his work. Heh heh, I tell you, ye'd make a fine soldier. Big-boned fella like ye would've made Sir Ralph proud.'

'Who?' asked Weightman, not turning round as he stuffed wedges into gaps in the wall-face.

'Sir Ralph, man! Abercromby! Greatest general on the field. We loved him. All of us. He was a father to us. Broke our hearts when he went. The fuckers!'

'What 'appened to him?' asked Cragg, pausing in his work to listen.

'Now there's a tale,' Gass said, leaning towards Weightman as if it was a secret. 'Sir Ralph was a bold, brave man. A hero. He was one of us, sure. He was there in the thick of it on that great day, right in the hottest furnace of the fighting. When he spoke to us, the whole regiment – and I'll never forget it – he said, "My brave highlanders, remember your forefathers." After that we were gladiators, and charged the French column down the sandhills with the ferocity of wolves. But more of them appeared through the smoke – whole regiments more, Weightman! We didn't hear the order to back off in the thunder of the guns. The Froggeaters charged us but we kept firing back and stood our ground like lions, hearing Sir Ralph's words in our heads. "Remember your forefaethers." Infantry, horsemen, they threw everything at us, on all sides, but we cuttem doon, man and horse. In the end they broke through our line and suddenly – there was Sir Ralph! Right behind me, Weightman, he was, squinting through the smoke. The Froggeaters had surrounded him and shot his horse from between his legs. Sir Ralph fell off, and a dragoon went for him with his sword. He damn near missed! Half an inch in it, no more. But the blade cut Sir Ralph's coat and scraped his side, drawing blood. Pure, blue blood. I shot the Froggeater and he fell to the ground. I felt proud, saving the old general. And he was good as new. At first. "Just a graze," he said. Ah, sure it was, sure. Just a graze. Days later poor Sir Ralph was dead.'

Weightman was holding two hearting stones in his hands, grinding them together. He looked spellbound.

'Oi!' barked Cragg. Weightman set to work and Gass disappeared in pursuit of stones. 'Gullible lad like that,' Cragg muttered to himself, 'standing around with all this work to do. Never mind fighting other men's battles,' he shouted across at Weightman. 'We've got our own one up here. Asleep in his tent is ole Helvellyn. Wek up sooner or later, mind, then we'll know about it.'

written a journal the pages would have been smudged with the sighs from his aching brow. And yet, as the sun went down, instead of skipping downhill like a milky yearling to be near her he felt like striking upwards into the mists of Helvellyn. He twigged that this impulse to circumvent destiny was nothing more mysterious than nerves – or, as military vocabulary might have it, cowardice.

Like a captured deserter he dragged his feet back down off Helvellyn towards the highway at Wythburn. As he glanced north in the direction of Keswick he was struck almost to the ground by a vision. A figure, a phantasm, was pacing pell-mell towards him downhill, wearing a scanty gown of Indian calico bleached in Whig yellow and carrying a white net bag. The spirit-form's hair – what could be seen of it budding out from the front of a tatty straw hat tied under the chin with a black ribbon – hung about the face in French-style fronds of coquettishly arranged dishevelment. But wait! The angel-incarnate moved in so distinctively graceless a manner, hopping and stumbling in the walking equivalent of a stammer, that soon all doubt in Luke's mind was suffocated. It was his pagan goddess.

'Dorothy!' he squawked.

'Luke,' she cooed back like the female across the dovecote.

'What are you doing here?' He couldn't believe the number of times he'd come across her in this vast, uninhabitable landscape. Fate wasn't so much discreetly intervening as bashing their heads together.

'I dashed up to Keswick this afternoon,' she said. 'I'm on my way home.'

'Keswick! It must be twenty miles there and back. On your own, in the dark?'

'I had to collect some medicine for William from the apothecary there. Besides, walking briskly is chief among my passions – I seem to spend half my time at the cobbler's! – and being abroad on such a beautiful evening excites me even more. Look at that astonishing sunset!'

Despite an earlier urge to climb Helvellyn to avoid her, the impulse now was to rescue her. 'I'll walk with you to Grasmere.'

'I don't need a chaperon – I'm a hardy traveller on foot ... but,' she added, appearing to blush, although it could have been the astonishing sunset in her cheeks, 'a little company would be pleasant.'

Luke had to sprint to keep up. 'Is William ailing?' he panted.

'Oh, only the usual injuries of hammering out blank verse.'

'But you're well yourself?'

'Not really. Toothaches and headaches, you know. I take castor oil and laudanum for them, of course, and a little wine, and rum, and brandy, naturally, and negus, and aquafortis – now and then. Oh, and occasionally I put my head under one of these spouts on the wayside,' she said pointing, 'which tends to work. But I don't like to go on about it.'

Luke's forehead corrugated in contemplation of her eccentricity. 'I remember a few family cures for nagging toothache. Have you tried massaging your gums with hen's brains, or having a horse breathe into your mouth twice a day?'

It was Dorothy's turn to wrinkle her brow. 'No ... I'll bear that in mind ... Tell me, how does your work fare on the wall over Helvellyn.'

'Very well,' he said, skirting round the truth, 'but I missed—'

'Look at the mountain ash!' she yelped as though he'd stood on her foot. 'Its grey-green feathery leaves will be the colour of blood by autumn. And that sycamore! Those drooping panicles will be wings by September. They're like fledglings getting ready to fly.'

All he was going to say was that he'd missed having a mattress to lie on at night.

A man with a calf's head in a basket walked past them and Luke felt the frothing of saliva in his mouth. How Dorothy had detected that he had no idea.

'Here, have one of these,' she said, fishing a leg of cold mutton from her net bag. 'I brought two; you look as if you haven't eaten in weeks.'

It took all his will power not to chomp her arm off at the elbow.

'I thought nature was your chief passion, not walking,' he munched, fixing on a topic not so much close to her heart as thoroughly embedded in it.

'Nature and walking are indivisible to me. Besides, if I were to reveal to you my true passions,' she said with a playful glance sideways, 'we'd need to talk about William Shakespeare.'

Not another William! Since he'd never heard of this Shakespeare – a fact which he suspected wouldn't have her swooning in his arms, unless with shock – he shifted on to the safer ground of banal and very English prattle about the weather.

'Have you noticed how you can't see the fells clearly in this dry, overcast weather between the hay and corn harvests?'

Luckily, Dorothy possessed within her gown a heart burning with passion for the weather. 'Oh, you do indeed have the eye of a poet, Luke! When can I see some of your work? It makes me feel half-poetic myself.'

'Do you write poems as well as William?' he asked, uneasy that his exposure – not as a bard, but as a fraud – was imminent.

Dorothy's eyes whipped round with delight. 'Would you like to hear some lines I wrote?' She didn't see him nod because she'd already closed her eyes – which made her gait even more snaking – and taken in a deep breath.

*My youthful wishes all fulfilled –*
*Wishes matured by thoughtful choice.*
*I stood an inmate of this vale,*
*How could I but rejoice?*

Having recited her half-poem blind she'd meandered straight into him, and got her stout leather shoes entangled with his big clogs in a way that might raise the eyebrows of her harried cobbler. 'No one in the whole world has ever been so inept at moulding words into a regular metre,' Dorothy said with a modesty that bordered on self-annihilation. 'And where did you learn to be a poet?'

The game was up.

'I'm not,' he replied with a poetic frugality for language.

She raised her eyebrows in surprise. 'Oh well,' she chuckled, 'I suppose you could always be a poet's muse like I am.'

Now that he appeared to have got away with not being a poet it was time for another confession. 'I'm not educated like you and William.'

'But surely you can rea—'

'Of course I can read, and write! My mother was taught by a local Quaker and she taught me. My father didn't care for schooling but she ... it was as if she had a better instinct for my destiny ... always said she wanted me to write letters to her if I ever left Grasmere. Michael never imagined I'd do anything apart from tend the flock, but he taught me about the winds and weathers, the seasons, the trees and flowers.'

'To be schooled in nature, through the senses, there's no finer education. And I can see how passionate it made you.'

Luke stared at the ground until his eyes stung, then he spoke, in a low, menacing growl. 'You talk of passions as if they were petty things, little pastimes to indulge yourself in. What if you become their slave? What if they make you do evil things?'

Dorothy looked shocked upright. 'What do you mean?'

Luke couldn't follow it through. 'Nothing. I meant nothing.'

They walked on in silence. A mist descended so thick and fast by the time dark had fallen fully that they could hardly see the yard in front of each footstep. The sky was a brooding grey-black mush and the stars had been wiped out by cloud. Somehow – and they both agreed that it was the first time it had ever happened to either of them – they got lost, on the road down to Grasmere, and ended up on an uneven, upward track.

'I can hear a waterfall,' said Luke, groping ahead like a blind man.

'It must be Raise Beck. We'll be up on Steel Fell if we're not careful.'

They turned and headed downhill, but the mist became so

dense that at one point they were obliged to go on all fours. As they did so, Luke couldn't resist peering round at the quadruped beside him in the yellow calico gown and remarking how strange and beautiful she was. In return of the compliment Dorothy donated an unambiguously affectionate smile. They soon found the track into Grasmere and, back on their hind legs once more, they passed right through to Town End. The mist had lifted and the moon was aglow when Dove Cottage finally teased itself into view.

A secretive whisper of 'good night' passed between them and Dorothy placed the closed Dove Cottage front door between herself and Luke. He turned to go.

# 11

# Rendezvous

---

He stayed, in the back garden, not sleeping like a respectable prowler in her arbour but dashing his head against orchard trees in his ardour. Once the owl had given over hooting and the cock was in its stride he clawed his way across the grass in the direction of Dorothy's heart. Dove Cottage was hiding beneath the camouflage of early summer leafage. Its whitewashed walls and peep-hole lattice windows glanced out, here and there, in the breeze, their whiteness subdued by guelder roses, scarlet beans and woodbine threading upwards in their invasion of the stonework. Any remaining space on the walls had fallen prey to ivy, mosses and damask, which hugged the stone so tight there was no room for their shadow.

He crept round the cottage towards the front door, and nosed inside a window. That other praetorian guard – not William this time but Molly – was pottering round the kitchen and glancing out at the sky when she saw him. She opened the door and bared her relic of a mouth.

'She int up!'

'When she is,' Luke grunted, 'I'd be obliged if you'd ask her to meet me at Goody Bridge at ten tomorrow morning. Tell her I'll be waiting.'

'The maister's—'

'Damn the master!' he snapped, biting off the end of her sentence. He was considering breaking through Molly's bodily fortification of the doorway and hanging the consequences when he looked up and noticed a dark figure within, grappling with a curtain, yet, despite raising his hopes, not opening it to welcome him. He withdrew, feeling snubbed but bloodthirstily resolute.

'What did he want, Molly?' asked Dorothy peering out of the window to see if Luke had gone, having been caught halfway into her petticoat when she'd heard his voice at such an ungodly hour of the morning.

'Yeh must stop seeing him, Miss,' said Molly.

'Must I?' said Dorothy pertly. 'Why?'

'He's a beggarman – he looks dangerous withem green eyes. What'll maister William say when he gits back from Keswick?'

'Molly! You make him sound like the devil! My brother writes poems about uneducated beggars and paupers and men dressed in smock-frocks and gaiters like Luke – that is half the point of his poetry. William turned his back on the French Revolution for his poetic revolution – for the likes of Luke.'

Molly hesitated. 'What French Revulsion, Miss?'

'Oh, Molly!'

Dorothy cast a quick glance out of her window again, this time not in search of Luke, but to check on her two pet swallows, whose nest had recently fallen off the ledge, then she took in a deep breath.

'Molly, as you know, I'm going to be whitewashing ceilings this morning after I've cleaned the grease off them, but first I'm going for a walk. Before I do any of that, however, I want you to tell me what Luke told you.'

'All I know is maister William wunt want the likes of that Luke in his home with him under this roof. Wiv got enough of them beggars ont doorstep as it is.'

'Molly, I've had enough of this. Tell me what he said or I will walk straight out now and chase after him to find out.'

'To meetim int morning, Miss.'

'Thank you. Where, and when?'

'Goody Bridge. Ten.'

'Good. Now I shall go for my walk.'

'Shunt I ...?' started Molly.

'No, don't be foolish, Molly. I'm going alone.'

As Luke wound his way up through Grasmere from Dove Cottage, feeling approximately midway between in love and insane, he saw a shepherd leading his flock of Herdwicks up into the fells to let them range on the fell grasses and slowly eat their way back down to the farm in time for winter. Wheat and barley that had been sown last winter were now fully in ear and ripening in the fields. His own ears ripened to the sound of arguing as he approached the stagnant outbuildings of Nettleslack Farm.

'Wheels!' cried Jack from the yard. 'We don't need wheels round here. Wiv done just fine without thum all my days and sentries before that.'

'Well now it's a new sentry, Fadder,' bellowed Sally, 'or dint tha know? Eighteen Oh Two,' she spelt out, 'not Seventeen.'

Jack turned to Luke, drawing him in straightaway. 'Are you using wheels up in the fells?'

'Er, no,' said Luke, 'but—'

'There you go. He said it, and he's a man of the world, aren't you, Luke?'

'Well, yes ... but ...' he said, placing his responses as carefully as a hen traversing a cowpat. He caught the tone of the look Sally was giving him as she stood in the doorway nibbling stale haverbread, but he was in it up to his waist now. 'It's too steep for wheels in the fells,' he said. 'Sleds are better for shifting stone. We're doing it mainly by hand anyway.'

'Ha! Now then! Hear that, lass?' cried Jack joyfully. 'By yand, not with big, ugly chunks of iron. These,' he shouted, waving his lengthy fingers at her. 'Trusty and cheap.'

Sally shook her head and rolled her eyes up to the fells. 'Fadder,' she said with mounting ire. 'Look at that old wooden plough outside. It's fallen apart, like the rest of the farm!'

'I've been using that bloody thing all my life, and so did your grandad before me. And his before him. And his bef—'

'Orrrright!' barked Sally, her interjection loud enough to trigger its own echo round the fells. 'But you'd need an ox-team of lads to push it!'

'Luke, talk sense intut girl,' sighed Jack with a shake of the head that made his old lips waggle. Luke was baffled. There appeared to be no work going on in the fields at all, wheels, wooden ploughs or otherwise. And he couldn't grant Jack's wish by championing the old breast-plough. It was little more than a long wooden spade, pushed along by the chest – preferably not Sally's. He looked down at Nance for wise counsel. Nance, a collie smart enough to do most everything apart from read and speak, indicated her neutrality with a nose-whine, ear-twitch and half-tilt of the head.

'We could've done with one of them light, iron ones,' said Sally. 'They're strong, and easy to use. All they need is a couple of Clydesdales.'

'Couple of bluddy Clydesdales? You, lass, are a blazing mystery to me,' Jack cried. 'Where d'you get all this stuff from? A couple of hours down in the village selling gingerbread and you come back thinking you're Turniptownzend, spouting all this miff-maff. Even if they are fast and light these iron ploughs, how d'you think we'll get one, lassie? Eh? Not to mention a couple of Clydesdales. Tcheeessssh!'

'Ay, I know that right enough,' Sally agreed. 'We've been left behind.'

'Nae, lass. What makes you tek on like that?'

'Open your eyes, Fadder,' she said, more in sadness than anger. 'Times have changed. We were using sickles all day long, flailing the corn by hand when we coulda bin using a thrashing machine. Ay, I've seen them, in Grasmere.'

'A thrashing machine! What the buggerinell's one of them? By yeck, what's it coming teh? Whole world's gone barmy. Machines. Pffooph!'

'A machine would've cost us less in the long run than letting this farm go to rackunruin,' mumbled Sally to the haverbread she was gnawing into a new shape. 'That's what's barmy.'

'Eh? Only reason a bluddy machine costs less is cos it spits out a handful of hired lads on the dung-cart, I'll warrant ye. Tint right, lass. Any road, this land isn't gunta go to rackanruin. Bin ours since Good Queen Bessie's time, has this farm!' he proclaimed proudly, standing upright in his yard with arms outstretched, 'and that's how it's staying. In them days Nettleslacks was ready to tek up arms against them Cabertossers creeping over the borders. That was the deal, and still is now.'

'We can't fight off the Cabertossers now, Fadder,' said Sally with a weary smile. 'We can't even feed the hens.'

Jack turned on her. 'Well if you'd got a nusband we mighta had a bit more work done round here.' Luke and Nance edged out of the line of fire.

'Oh, I'll just nip down tut market and hire one, shall I?' Sally screamed.

'Ay! Get thaself seen! Lass like you. Gettin on. Spent too much time sweatin at the dung cart, has tha.'

'Right then!' she said, flinging her boomerang-shaped

haverbread across the yard. 'I'll just get me best shawl and pop down to Grasmere.'

'Ay, you do that, you daft girl!' roared Jack after her, at which point crimson rage flooded the statesman's face and the fingernails of his right hand launched an assault on the chilblains of his left palm. Sally was as good as her word, not grabbing her best shawl but her only one, and stamping away out of the farmyard with a basket under her arm.

'Tell thee what, lad,' sighed Jack to Luke as they went inside, 'pass me that sugared onion on the table for me chilblains... Oooh, that's better ... Ee, I wunt fancy being the fella she ends up with, not in that mood. Bluddeeyell! She'll eat him up for breakfast. Presarve us O'!' Nance stormed out of the house with her tail between her legs. 'By yeck!' said Jack, shaking his head as he watched the tail disappear. 'Thar she goes again. Man can't say a blinkin word round here.' Luke thought of going after Sally to mollify her, but the image of being trampled to death by a wild longhorn came to mind, and he thought again.

Dorothy had lost count of the number of times she'd walked through Rydale and along her favourite path to White Moss, but rarely if ever had she done it without William. She never had got out after jarring with Molly first thing in the morning. Beggars had called, the mail had arrived, then there were the deliveries of paints to be ground for the walls and dung for the garden, and whitewashing the ceilings and manifold other diurnal tasks, and she hadn't had a chance to venture out until evening had come round.

As she sat on the wall at the foot of White Moss an owl hooted in such a human way that she started with fright, convinced it was William calling out to her. Only when the hooter sounded again, in a much more tremulous way, could she reassure herself it was indeed an owl. She stood up and began making her way to the top of the Moss, spotting glow-worms and noting to herself that it was just as well all Grasmere and Rydale's children would be in bed by now, otherwise they'd be dancing around with glee to see the glow-worms here, and no one would be abed before the devil's hour.

When she reached the top she decided, in a moment of wildness, to do something she'd never done before – not here anyway, and not anywhere without William – and lie down on the hard ground in the posture of a corpse in a coffin, with arms crossed over chest.

'Mortality,' she muttered into the young summer air from her mock grave. 'No one shall even know of me two hundred years from now.'

She uncrossed her arms and placed them by her sides palms downwards. She stared through the trees up into the sky as if in pantheistic worship, reflecting on the important distinction within her that this didn't feel like the splendid manifestation of God, but of the deity of nature itself. She saw a strange lightness along with the obscurity of evening, a peculiar moonless glow. She flexed the fingers of her right hand and the shortest finger brushed against something hard – a twig, maybe – and she imagined it to be a human finger-bone, and that she'd reached through the side of an adjacent coffin and touched the hand of her soul's companion, her love for the eternity of death. And in one of those tumults of mental confusion accompanying intense experience, the finger belonged to Luke.

How could he possibly have implanted such a passion in her, and how could she be so deeply affected by a man with such poor judgement as to love a plain, spluttering little orphan as herself? But how he sought her out; stared at her; prised her open; terrified and excited her; flattered her as though *she* were the poet, not William. Her brother often said she possessed the gift of seeing into the life of things. Well, now it felt as if Luke had the gift of seeing into the life of *her*. Never, but never, had any man – who wasn't William – ever made her feel so ... so ... vital!

She closed her eyes in terror, lifted her arms and crossed

them over her breast again, not this time in imitation of a body in the grave, but out of modesty. She immediately felt safe, and allowed the timeless murmur of nature – the hushed breezes of evening through trees and grasses – to breathe through her whole being. She shivered with delight at the sensation, and without being in any way conscious of what she was doing she cupped, beneath her hands, which were still drawn across her chest, her own bosom.

Sally's feet punished the ground all the way down to the village. Her face was as rigid as a cooled horseshoe as she stood in the middle of the green and displayed her wares for everyone to see. Maybe Jack was right, she thought as she winched her lips into a smile. Maybe it was time to find a husband, if for no more romantic reason than that she could do with an extra pair of hands. She wondered how many women got married just for an extra pair of hands. It was unlikely to bring her happiness, but nor was the workhouse, or poor relief, or beggary. There was, of course, one person whose hands – or hand, anyway – might interest her, but like all men he was incapable of reading her absurdly indecipherable and contradictory signals. And besides, he was probably trying to decode some other woman's absurdly indecipherable and contradictory signals by now.

A character sauntered up and showed an interest in what she was hawking. He inspected, nibbled a little, spluttered, then coughed up some money. Ten minutes later he sauntered up again, smiling, and handed her more money. He appeared to be immune to it, he seemed even to enjoy it, perhaps to be one of the rare few to be healed by it. Sally smiled back.

'Hwhat brings thee hout of doors to sell thy fine whares, mam?' the man asked, his voice sounding either as if his tongue was on fire or as if he were attempting to be genteel, or both.

'Why, to earn myself a few pennies, sir,' answered Sally with a forced chuckle.

'Ah!' said the man, chewing over her response, along with

a corner of her gingerbread. 'Costs a pretty penny to feed the bairns, eh?'

'Bairns, sir?'

'Bonny face like that and not feathered your hown brood? No whon made a honest woman of you?'

'Too honest, me, sometimes, I think sir.'

'I can believe it. How many then?'

'Come again?'

'How many a pretty penny d'you need?'

'Oh,' she said, realising he meant money. 'Enough to keep a roof over our heads.'

'Our heads?' he repeated, with a delving look. Sally cottoned on.

'Me and me alfella. Just the two of us.'

'And where is yhour habitation, my bonny maid?'

'Come again, sir?'

'House, lass. Where do you live?'

'Oh, forest side.'

'Aha!' he said, licking a gingerbread crumb off his top lip. 'Well why don't I take you?'

'Tek me, sir?' she questioned, deciding that he'd been behaving as spicily as the gingerbread.

'Home, lass, home.'

'Oh. Most kind, sir! Most gentermanlike.'

The man smiled, seeming to like that word.

# 12

# Thursday Week

Luke stood at Goody Bridge in waistcoat, silk cravat, breeches, stockings, leather shoes and nerves of aspen, not looking out on the wonders of an Easedale landscape spun into the white yarn of Churnmilk Force, or doing what one of those vultures of the picturesque might do and turning his back on the whole thing to modify its glories in the black mirror of a Claude glass. Instead, he stared morosely at the tops of his hands, horrified that the skin on them was already beginning to look like slack pork and his clock hadn't even struck forty. He was as sure as a fresh-cut sundial that it was vaguely roundabout ten. When he began to feel Dorothy was more than a second late he started convincing himself it was madness, wretched lunacy, to think someone like her might incubate feelings for someone like him.

Then she appeared down the lane. The long, slow minute of her arrival was an age of nervous embarrassment. He couldn't look at her – it would be too admiring – but he couldn't look away – it would be ill-mannered to pretend he hadn't seen her, and might raise questions in her about his eyesight. He couldn't bear the silence between them either, even though she hadn't strictly reached him yet. He made a panicked calculation that she was within earshot no less than seventy-five yards into his personal space, and gabbled like a turkey fleeing a farmer.

'I thought we might take a walk up to Churnmilk Force below Easedale Tarn. I used to play there as a boy and haven't been back since. It's my favourite waterfall. After heavy rain it leaps off the fells in thrilling, spilling cascades. I love tranquil ghylls, too, that curl over mossy stones, hurrying down hillsides and sneaking into the vales, but a violent cataract makes me feel so alive!'

'I do beg your pardon?' Dorothy said as she finally came within earshot. 'I didn't catch a single word. What were you saying?'

'Nothing,' he said with a prosaic thud, dismayed not to have won her over with his first ever semi-poetic extemporising. They set off up into Easedale and Dorothy, whose normal behaviour it was to gabble nervously herself, twittered away about the swallows in her garden, over whom there had been a crisis.

'They came about ten days ago,' she chirruped. 'I thought they were going to build a nest outside the sitting-room window but they decided to build under my bedroom window instead. It was so lovely to watch them flitting round and round and then bustling up so close to the window pane with their soft white bellies and forked tails that I could see their breathing. I could hear them outside the window every morning, even when the shutters were closed, building their nest, and I could see them sitting in it every day. It made me feel so close to them, knowing the two of them sat just outside my window morning and evening looking down on the garden, even if they flew off late on and slept somewhere else. It was as though we were all one family, sharing our beautiful cottage. But the other morning when I rose and went outside to look at the nest it was gone! It had fallen down. Can you imagine? The ruins lay in a large heap on the window ledge. I was distraught – the poor dears had to begin the whole nest again!'

Well at least now he knew how the damned swallows were, and a fantasy leapt within his breast of dashing the detestable birds against the window casement if he ever got his ageing hands on them. But all the while he'd watched her in wonder, and felt the strong temptation to do away with all this chiff-chaff by cutting out his heart and handing it to her.

By the edge of Easedale Beck, Churnmilk Force's dribbling offspring, they sat down to rest among grass measled with oxeye daisies. The gold-green leaves of the ash leaned in to listen, and foxgloves stretched their necks. A young robin hopped onto Luke's leg to Dorothy's delight and perched there for a moment. Luke didn't dare move for fear of scaring it away, but had to breathe eventually and it flew off. It was probably just as well, as it wasn't long since his murderous fancy about the Dove Cottage swallows. He felt a little calmer, as though the very act of resisting throttling a robin had settled him.

Dorothy, too, had become tranquil after all that nervous blubbering, as William would put it, about the swallows. Luke's eyes – always soothed by the sight of waterfalls – retreated across the spear-grassed ground onto Dorothy's visage.

'Nature never did betray the heart that loved her,' she said dreamily.

'What?'

'It's from one of William's poems.'

'Oh.'

He couldn't stop himself. He'd had enough. 'Dolly! ... I do beg your pardon ... Dorothy! There are other things in life, you know, apart from the trees, the birds and the flowers. And I don't mean your brother, either, or his poems. Does nothing, no one, else matter to you? You say I'm a mystery but what about you? Do you actually exist out of beloved William's shadow?'

Dorothy stood up. 'How impertinent!' she snapped, slapping her thigh as though it were his face. 'I am devoted to my brother, and his poetry.'

'William will soon have a wife!' he ranted from the ground. 'One day, sooner than you think, he'll have children. Can't you see that you're caged in by him? You can't spend your whole life scurrying along like a little grey duckling in William's wake.'

Dorothy, rigid with anger, could have passed for an ill-disposed statue hewn from Eskdale granite. Her reply was accompanied by a darkening of the sky as she stood over him. 'How dare you! Our parents died when we were children. We were separated, for many years. Then my beloved brother and I were reunited, and so we remain. I make no apology for the fact that we are now inseparable. Utterly inseparable! And besides, who are you to tell me I'm caged in? You're trapped yourself, Luke, by your guilt over something you did after you left Grasmere, though what that is I'm sure I'll never know.'

Chastened as though by means of a birching switch, Luke went quiet.

Dorothy wasn't finished with him yet. 'Why did you leave Grasmere in the first place? Why did you turn your back on nothing short of everything dear to you?'

He lay down, his eyes closed – although he could tell that she was still towering, goddess-like, over him – and spoke in a glum monotone.

'He came to me one evening when I was eighteen and told me I had to go away. "This land," he said, "and the Evening Star yonder – your birth-right – will pass into strangers' hands if you don't." I asked him why, and he said he'd made a promise, to keep the Greenhead fields as surety for another man's debts, and he now had to sell them. "But if we lose them all," he said, "thy mother and I will never lie quiet in this earth."'

'So you went? As any dutiful son would. Where is the shame in that?'

led myself, by the hand, into hell.' He contorted his face until it resembled that of a demonic effigy. 'And now look at me. No youth, no beauty, no innocence, nothing.'

Dorothy put a disconcerted hand to her mouth.

'I little thought…' he began again.

'What?'

'My pleasure-seeking would breed such … despair.'

'Was the memory of Grasmere and home of no comfort to you? A reminder – like the sight and scent of the daffodils that so moved us – of another world, another life you once led … and still could?'

'Comfort? It was a curse! When I lay in some hovel in London and the memories of my childhood and Grasmere flooded back, I felt my hideousness more sharply. To think of what I'd squandered. No, the thought of it all only made things worse. It fed the thing that killed me in the end.'

'Mercy on us!' winced Dorothy. 'What do you mean?'

'I tried to take my own life.'

He hesitated, and his eyes filled with tears.

'But I … took someone else's instead.'

'You … killed … ?'

'Alice told me,' he yammered as Dorothy's eyeballs stared at him as large as goose eggs, 'that he might not even be dead anyway – the child I mean, not Kears – all she'd done was give him away … she couldn't afford to feed herself let alone a newborn … and she knew she'd never get any work with him under her arm … and would be back on the streets for the rest of her life.'

'What are you talking about, Luke? Who is Alice?'

'A street-walker. We only spent one night together but she was different – she seemed to care about me, like me even, and it made me realise that my greatest desire was no longer for pleasure itself but for an escape from loneliness, endless loneliness. So Alice and I would look out for each other; we became friends; in a way she came to feel like a sister. Then she disappeared ... It wasn't that unusual. People came and went in that world. But I had a bad feeling. I used to walk along Oxford Street in the evenings by lamplight looking for her. I gave up in the end. I found out later she was in jail.'

Luke was by now striding up and down along the edge of Churnmilk Force. The only thing between him and the torrent was Dorothy, standing morbidly enthralled with her back to the waterfall.

'I managed to get a pass into Newgate Jail,' he continued, now breathlessly, 'to see her, thanks to the chaplain. She told me she'd been accused of murder – of her newborn son – by a gentleman, a powerful nobleman. She said he would stop at nothing to be rid of her, not because of the scandal of his having got a whore with child, but because he found out she'd abandoned the baby. But she said she wasn't even sure he was the child's father.'

'Did she have any idea who the father might be?'

Luke didn't reply. Dorothy's horrified face reminded him of a mediaeval stone gargoyle he'd seen on a church somewhere.

'I left for the war soon after – I was press-ganged into it but went willingly; I had to get away from London – and I expected to die in battle ... wanted to. But I didn't, and after Alexandria I ended up drifting back in on the Thames again like some ghoul, some floating corpse. That was less than a year ago.'

Dorothy frowned, and spoke timidly. 'What happened to Alice?'

'She was hanged – I helped her die with my own bare hands,' he said, holding them up.

Dorothy shook her head to signal she couldn't bear any more, but he ignored her.

'Straight after the hanging I went in search of this woman Kears, who'd taken the infant from Alice and promised to find him a good home. I found her and demanded to know where the child was. Her husband, a brute who looked well-used to violence, accused me of threatening behaviour, and said quite casually that the poor mite had starved to death.'

Luke stopped and faced her, grabbing her shoulders and pushing her back towards the edge of the Force.

'I went into such a rage, you see?' he howled, shaking her. 'I knocked him to the ground. He came back at me, but he was no match, not for my anger. It was as if it had built up over all those years. We fought with our bare hands and I left him lying there painted in his own blood. I didn't wait around to find out if he was dead but that harridan wailed out that she'd see me hang for it.'

He let go of her trembling shoulders and slid from her with the enervation of grim defeat. Dorothy recoiled from him as though she'd just been violated.

'I left London that same day,' he said at last. She made no reply. He watched the long, white locks of water sprout from the head of Churnmilk Force's stone face, then he sank to the ground like a scuttled wreck and buried his head in his hands.

'Luke,' Dorothy said at length, so sweetly and softly it felt like a kiss. 'I'm so sorry to hear you've been through so much, and to see you so torn apart.'

He looked up at her.

'Have you heard,' she said, 'the Greek myth about Narcissus, after whom the daffodil is named?'

He shook his head.

'Narcissus was a beautiful but proud youth who fell in love with his own reflection in a pool. When he reached into the water to touch it, his image vanished, and he feared it was gone forever. The surface calmed and his reflection returned, but he was so scared it might disappear again that he lay by the pool gazing into it, transfixed, until he died. A flower is said to have grown where his body once lay.'

'A daffodil?'

She paused.

'Luke ...'

She hesitated.

'I ... I was wondering if you might like to join us for tea ...

Matthew Connolly

at Dove Cottage?'

He gulped with disbelief that such a genteel proposal should come on the heels of such sordid revelations. He shed secret tears of rekindled hope.

'When?'

'Perhaps one day the week after next. Thursday week?'

To seize her Thursday week rather than now, and at Dove Cottage rather than here, and – worst of all – not her but *us*, in other words, with the brooding bard in attendance? He wanted to tell her no, he didn't have the patience and he didn't agree the conditions. But his heart wasn't in it, mainly because his heart was in her, up to its neck. And besides he had to admit, if sulkily, that this was progress, maybe an inch forward, of sorts. After all, she did at least now know the truth about his despicable history, and she was still amenable to supping tea with him. His nerves in tatters, he could only manage three mortal words in response.

'Thursday week it is.'

# 13

## Merry Neet

---

The annual Easedale Clip was one of those events for which Sally Nettleslack could at last get a break from her chores on the farm and work her fingers to the bone elsewhere. Soon after sunrise she threw on her only shawl, hopeful that somewhere among the men straddling uptight sheep there might be a shearer nursing a desire for a spinster. It wouldn't be the first time her hair had turned the odd head among the hired hands.

Nance paced around the fire-house, ears twitching and tail swishing like a sickle, her saliva rendering the area around the porch potentially unsafe under foot.

'Nah then, lass,' declared Jack from a stool, 'are we right?' Sally looked round about to reply, but Jack was addressing Nance, and the latter jumped into his lap making the former nearly fall off the stool. 'Ho ho, looks like tha art, then.'

Luke was up and about outside, having sought once more his gentleman's outfit in his bundle. It was Thursday, and he'd been wandering round the farmyard agitated, kicking hens, gnawing his nails and squinting into the sky to decipher the time by the loose arrangement of clouds, none the wiser for it. Once the Nettleslacks had disappeared downhill he decided to tag along after all, and trotted off in sheepish pursuit, catching up down by Butterlip How on the way to Goody Bridge.

'Nae, not again!' cried Sally as she inspected, amid a poorly stifled smirk, the shabby waistcoat, breeches and stockings Luke was wearing above filthy leather shoes.

'What?' said Luke, cantering alongside her stiffly.

'Whatyeh doing in that daft gettup?' she said, linking arms with him. 'Yeh look like a blinkin squire. You'll be't laffinstock of the farmyard. It's a clip, not a weddin!'

'I've been invited to tea.'

'By yeck!' laughed Jack from behind. 'You look like brother n' sister yootoo.' Luke turned round. Jack's eyes were sparkling, but with a look of grief not amusement.

'So, brother,' teased Sally, 'that's why you've got itches in them britches, eh? Where's tea?'

Luke liked thinking of her as a sister. 'Town End,' he said.

'Why you coming up Easedale way?'

'Killing time.'

'Who is she, then?'

'The poet Wordsworth's sister.'

'Wudswuth!' she scoffed. 'Gotta be poets wi' a daft name like that.' Her bearing turned proud and her bosom inflated. 'Well, you aren't the only one who's got tangled up.'

'Who ... you?' he asked.

'Ay, why not? I'm no Wudswuth but I'm not just a workhorse neither, tha knows. Right fine genterman he is an all.'

It couldn't be William, could it, thought Luke in horror. Silence fell as they passed by Goody Bridge into Easedale. The interlocking of his and Sally's arms began to feel unnatural. For some reason he didn't like, at all, the idea of Sally being tangled up with any man, least of all Wordsworth. She seemed resentful of him and Dorothy, too. Their kindred interlocking of arms was already loosening – the novelty of siblinghood was already wearing off.

'What mischief did yeh get up to all them years away, then?' she asked out of the blue.

He checked behind to see how far back Jack and Nance were, and then grabbed her wrist. 'That's all in the past, d'you hear?' he snarled. 'All in the past!'

'Ay,' she said, flinching and pulling her hand away. But a hand seized both their shoulders from behind. It was Jack, and the clack of iron on whetstone announced that the Clip was at hand. Sally wriggled free of father and erstwhile brother as soon as they got in the farmyard and didn't look round at Luke once. His mood stabilised as ever at the sight of sheep, but he was disturbed not only by Sally's question but by his reaction to it. And anyway, what the devil was he doing here in the first place instead of running at a fast clip to Town End?

No Lakelander ever hired a man to clip his sheep because none could bear to part with a penny for the job, so they all worked for each other for free. The Herdwicks, those wire-woollen vagabonds with Roman noses and eyes as ancient as the rocks they inhabited, approached the day with little relish. They'd already been chased down in bleating battalions from the felltops by panting collies the day before, and the mixed flocks, flaunting an assortment of nicked lugs and smit marks, huddled in vast numbers in tiny pens, sneezing their displeasure. Some scrambled on top of each other, not to escape the pen or to rehearse mating but because there was no room on the ground. Others bent low and mooed like husky cows at the scraping sound of wool-thirsty men honing metal only yards away.

Underneath the clipping trees – including a five-hundred-year-old sycamore that cast a shade so broad as to make a man shiver with cold in the heat of the day – stood the clipping-stools, solid and shapeless as the rumps of the women-bodies. The shearers began trudging through in single file and silence, apart from the odd snigger, possibly at the sight of Luke's suit. The swordfight of click-click-tap-tap started up as the shearers tried out their weapons above their heads then reached for their hones, with which they did a final, ostentatious, scrape. Then one by one they nodded at the exploding pen of sheep and shouted 'Ruddy!'

Two farm-hands who were awaiting the command – the first a lad with fair hair as thick and wiry as Herdwick wool, the second a man of about thirty with rampant baldness – unlocked the gate each time the call came and grabbed the nearest sheep, lifting it high into the air and flipping it on its back. The pen was shut and the farm-hands flung the sheep upside down into the waiting clipper's arms. Luke had forgotten the comforting sight of a heavily fleeced, upturned ewe soaring through the air at him. Minutes later – and easily identifiable as the only man in the whole yard not in smock-frock, gaiters and felt hat – he was on a stool and clipping, glowering at the Herdwick-haired lad, who'd deliberately bowled the sheep at him instead of passing it.

The bald man, whose feet were as long and wide as rabbit-smoot boards, seemed distracted in his activities by the presence of Sally Nettleslack gathering fleeces, rolling them, tying them up and piling them high in bundles, about to lift the first bundle and carry it into one of the barns.

'Naaaey!' he shouted, the way a piqued horse might, 'you shunt be lifting all them, nah. Ere let me.'

'Most kind,' sighed Sally, dabbing her brow with the back of her hand and whooshing her hair about for no obvious reason. The smoot-footed hand yanked the bundle from her, grinned, heaved the bag over his shoulder and lugged it to the barn. This he repeated seven, eight, nine times, grinning and swaggering with the confidence of a man ever closer to calling the marriage banns with each bundle. The output was awesome, even if the swaggering legs began to stagger beneath the bales.

'Ready!' Luke called out, with one eye on what he was doing, and a spare eye on the bald man hanging around Sally. He tucked the sheep's head under his left arm and began opening the body out. He clipped right down the belly and along the neck. The fair farm-hand grabbed the beast's flailing legs and tied them. Luke turned the sheep on its right side and gave it a thorough going over, his right hand shearing and his left hand turning the wool. Once he'd reached the middle of the back he flipped the sheep and started again. It had been a long time, and it felt right. A good, hard clip might also steady his nerves for the road to Dove Cottage, upon which he fully intended to launch himself after lunch.

Quiet fell. The penned sheep had calmed, the ones between the clippers' knees had stopped kicking, and the collies, all barked out, lay curled round themselves in the midday sun, only the more intelligent ones – Nance foremost among them – reclining under the vast boughs of the sycamore for brain-protecting shade. A whistle blew, and tools and sheep were dropped to the ground. The men washed their hands and climbed up the stone steps to the hayloft and sat round a large table. The women-bodies had readied boiled beef and pease pudding, and everyone ate lunch in the speechless mode of an austere monastic order.

The work went on long into the afternoon. Jacketless Herdwicks, thin and white as swans' necks, amassed in their new skimpy waistcoats in a fold at the far end of the farmyard, wandering round anxious that their lambs might not recognise them. Finally, the last sheep was shorn as the sun died at the back of the sky. Lamps flared up throughout the farm, someone shouted 'supper's ruddy' and the shearers re-trod their gloomy pilgrimage up the stone steps to the loft. The women-bodies had lit lanterns and candles and prepared bread, jam and tea.

In a sudden and magical transformation the shearers became

cheerful, chatting away about the cut of the sheep, the weight of the wool, what the fleeces might fetch at market. Single and double chins wagged among the mean-spirited but stout-hearted women-bodies. About the colours of clothes and smell of babies; the colour of babies and smell of clothes. About cold shoulders and hot snubs, and stony remarks that sent ripples across lakes. And into their chatter of crops and stock and all the rest of it they weaved grief, illness and death, comforting each other with brutal embraces. 'D'ye hear about Goan's girl? Went a few weeks past, she did. Only six year old, poor babe. Like a skinned leveret at the end.'

After the supping was done, the tip-tap of clogs up the loft steps brought a fiddler, a concertina player and – hearty music to the shearers' ears – a handful of hard-baked lasses from Grasmere. Beer was unbarrelled with abandon and soon the menfolk were spinning the women-bodies – and from time to time even their own wives – around the sweat-tanged barn in the dusty candle-shadow of the Easedale Clip Merry Neet.

'Dance with me!' shouted Sally into her father's ear. 'Billy Tindle keeps wheeling me round, squashing me with those biggevy feet and whispering things. Quick!'

Father and daughter stamped a square-eight that made the earth shake.

'Tha knows, don't tha?' Sally shouted into her father's ear.

'Knows what, lassie?'

'Yeh can't carry on mekkin ale at home. We can't afford to buy barley. So enjoy thaself now, have a merry neet, but don't expect to be drinkin' from now on.'

'By yeck what tha yammering about, lass?' he bawled into the noise. 'We grow our own barley.'

'Fadder,' she shouted, 'gone's the days when Nance gets drunk on fermentin' grain in the farmyard after't rain. Gone!'

'Presarve us O!' cried Jack. 'Well we can awways buy anudder field, lass.'

'Buy? With what Fadder? Hen's eggs?'

'Wi' nowt, lass. Ee, you bairns knae nowt about t'world. We buy a field, tell't vender we'll pay for it when't varra first crop's tekken of 't. Then we sow't field with acorns – the first crop'll be oak timber, lass, and not for donkey's years. Haha. That's howter do it.' The statesman then sighed, shook his head and shouted to the fiddler that as the self-appointed head shepherd of the Clip he wanted to sing a song.

'A sang, a sang!' everyone shouted. Jack stood upright and proud, his eyes glazed over to effect the blurred mystique of the performer, and he sang.

'Let sheep run a fortneet and than comes on clippin',
And bleatin', and fleecin' of woo;
They submit, without whimper, to tying and strippin',
And feel leetsome they hardly know how.

Now clippin' of done, comes weshin' of hands
And kestin' off scoggers and brats;
A fleece is hung up on a powl in t' lang-lands,
To be run for without shun or hats.

Next out wid a punch bowl, and yal i' girt plenty,
Wi' horns and glasses to drink frae;
And piggins, and mugs, bit nought varra dainty,
And nought 'at a clipper need shrink frae.'

Jack was lifted up on a clipping stool and carried round the room downing a pint of ale while everyone sang at top speed.

'Here's a good health to the man of this house,
The man of this house, the man of this house;
Here's a good health to the man of this house,
For he is a right honest man.'

They all cheered and raised a glass to the statesman. Luke, ale in hand, laughed to watch it all, and to see Sally looking so roseate with the crack, even if it was the blush of ale. He felt what he imagined to be brotherly love for her despite their altercation earlier – maybe even because of it – and he caught a glimpse in his mind of William's protectiveness of Dorothy. What loving brother wouldn't protect his sister, especially from the likes of him. He almost had a sympathy for the malcontent. As he watched Jack wheeling Sally round the floor, Luke wished he was doing the same with Dorothy, instead of getting drunk and failing to screw the courage to go and sip tea with her. His ale-oiled vision was starting to twist around the room at the same speed as the Grasmere lasses. He tottered over to Sally, who was standing watching the merrymaking. 'Sally!' he shouted into the din. She didn't look round. He moved to within bawling distance of her ear. 'What should I do?' he yelled into it.

'With what?' she shouted back, not looking round.

'About Dorothy.'

'Whatever tha yart tells thee,' she said, at last turning to him, with icebergs in her eyes. What his heart told him was to go and take Dorothy in his arms, but he couldn't say that to Sally, or do it to Dorothy. The bald man who'd been predating Sally earlier suddenly took her in his arms and launched her into the middle of the room for a hayloft-trembling quadrille. Luke watched Sally smile, even if falsely, every time he whispered in her ear. After a while Luke slouched down the loft steps and outside, his head loose on his chest as if his neck had snapped. A late-arriving merryneeter barged past and nearly knocked him over. He thought, as he looked round, he'd seen the man before, but it was dark, and he was dizzy.

He heard Sally shout something like, 'Come on, Lance, before Billy Tindle has me leaping over't besom!' He sprawled back up into the loft to see who Sally was dancing with, but he couldn't work it out because the man was wheeling her round and round, whispering things into her ear that made her genuinely smile. As for that other predator with lost hair, he was inhabiting a dark corner, sulking into his ale-pot and looking on with covetous eyes.

He left for good this time. It was late and he was tired, and drunk enough to fight with anyone who suggested he was drunk. With the comic resolve of an inebriate he vowed to go and see Dorothy without a moment's hesitation first thing in the morning. He staggered back along the road to Nettleslack Farm, meandering like Wordsworth, but minus poetic inspiration, and finally succumbed to the snug cradle of a ditch, in which he soon slept like a newborn, dribbling.

# 14

## Termagant

Dorothy drew William's writing-table to her, sharpened a quill with a penknife, dipped it and with her left hand flattened the page of her leather-bound journal. She gasped – by mistake she'd pricked the quill on the top of one of her fingers and made it bleed. She looked so closely at the bead of blood on her finger that she imagined she saw her own reflection in it. She sucked the skin, leaving her lips slightly salted with ink and blood. She looked out of the window, then down at the little table – her brother's prize possession, one he polished so often it shone like the sun itself – and picked up the pen.

*Thursday, 9th July, 1802*
*A sunny and showery morni—*
'No!' she shouted, slapping down the pen, upsetting the ink

and scattering the swallows on her window ledge. William would have to look elsewhere for inspiration for his giant philosophical poem about nature, or for its everlasting prelude about its author. Today she couldn't face gathering the twigs for that nest. Today she would not be so prosaic as to record the weather, or mention the tedium of starching the linen and hanging it out, or write that she'd walked a dozen miles to Keswick and back, or that she'd read incomprehensible fragments of German metaphysics to William while he lay in bed with insomnia ... or note that she'd attended him with honey and lard when the piles had popped out ... or that she'd set fire, at his request, to copies of his poems he wasn't happy with. And so on, and so on. No.

For once she would write her journal to give herself pleasure by it. Her hand shook. A tiny insect she'd accidentally-on-purpose doused in ink ran for its life across the page, and she followed it with her quill, the scrawl imitating the insect's desperate and haphazard trail. After much scratching and blotching, striking through and blotting out, on the page and in her mind, she paused.

There was so little time. William had been up for hours. He'd gone out for a last walk but would be back soon and ready. Why had Luke not turned up for tea the day before? Blast him, he was so unreliable, so reckless! For all she knew he'd thrown himself fully clothed into Grasmere lake – of course at great risk of death – for no other reason than that it made him feel alive. He was like a child, in pursuit of a kind of insolent liberty. It wasn't freedom, or wildness, or whatever he might call it, it was lunacy.

They would both send her to the madhouse! It was hard enough looking after William, who was injuring himself more than usual on his poems. She could feel herself burning with ... with ... oh, she didn't know what ... mad rage? The quill hovered over the journal, swooped down on the page and tore across it.

When she stopped writing, stood up and shoved open the window casement to look out at the island in the middle of

Grasmere lake, she felt the itch of tears on her neck. She decided she was no good at all with men. She picked up the pen and wrote, her mouth clenched. After this latest outburst of ink she stood up again, panting, eyes dancing with tears, and headed for the door. Through muffled sobs and trumpetings into her handkerchief she scurried downstairs, outside in her white bedgown and homemade felt slippers, carrying a white net bag, and down towards the lake.

It was a sunny and showery morning in the ditch as Luke shook the insects out of his hair and made the final yards of the journey to Nettleslack Farm. The only limb that felt even more tender than his head was his heart. Intoxication had fizzled away, along with the dribble, and although he was a day late for tea with the Wordsworths and stank of sheep, stale sweat and ale, he felt – inexplicably – absolutely great. Greater than great even. Euphoric; alive at last to the greatest passion of his life.

At the farm, standing on the table looking warm and edible was fresh haverbread, but no sign of its incendiary-haired baker. He pilfered a piece and loped outside, snagging against ragworts and their poisonous yellow flowers, scattering the butter-yellow butterflies that had been sipping their nectar.

He brushed the rain off his waistcoat and thought of Dorothy as he picked his way across the farmyard. Suddenly his legs became bogged down in despondency and he stopped. He knew he shouldn't have trusted that euphoria. The relief at having confessed everything had long been replaced by the fear that he'd ruined everything, but now the whole outrageously impossible implausibility of a loving union with her had hit home, as he'd sensed it would the nearer he got to the consummation of tea with her. He leant against a tree, staring outwards over the Nettleslack land, barren of wheat stooks and barley spikes that would soon need harvesting. He sighed, wondering if anyone of any education passing by at that moment might think him an interesting-looking fellow, perhaps a poet, gazing on nature and composing an ode on the subject of dejection. Was this how he wanted Dorothy to see him? He decided it was just as well he was late – he might, after all, get to see her on her own if the grisly sibling wasn't around to spoil things. He spotted Sally looking even more debased, on her hands and knees, rear end up, face full of red effort, but at least she was exhuming potatoes and turnips instead of chewing on melancholy.

'Here, let me help you,' he called out.

'Nae,' she said brusquely. 'You get along. You'll need a brisk walk after all that ale.' Luke was unable to work out whether she never wanted to speak to him again or, worse, couldn't care less one way or another. He worried about what he might have said or done at the Merry Neet, or beforehand. He'd been very tired – not drunk – tired, and emotional.

'And what about you?' he force-laughed. 'Cavorting with that bald-head.'

'I spent the whole night cavortin' away from him, I'll 'ave you know.'

'Come on, he'd have danced you straight down the aisle last night if you'd let him.'

'I'll do a jig on Billy-Bluddy-Tindle's grave before he gets me down the aisle. Any road, where you off? Tekkin tea?'

'I'm a day late. I hope she won't mind.'

Sally laughed, scornfully, and shuffled away on all-fours.

From Nettleslack Farm down to the highway took him past where the Evening Star used to be – not directly, but he hoped to draw on some ancient Greenhead pluck for a trip to Dove Cottage that was beginning to feel like the march to the scaffold. As he approached the patrimonial fields he spotted the last person he was expecting to see trespassing on Greenhead territory. Not an invading Scotchman but ... could it be him of all people, standing right among the larch saplings shouting at somebody or other – no, fulminating against larch plantations themselves? He crept closer to listen.

'In spring,' the poet shouted, 'you will have turned green long before the native trees, and not a green harmonious with anything around it, but one so strange and bright that it will make this spot totally disagreeable.' He turned and looked round to see if anyone was watching, but Luke had camouflaged himself behind a tree, fortunately a native sessile oak that didn't draw Wordsworth's wrathful eye.

'In summer,' the mad bard continued, pointing an accusing finger at the seedlings, 'when all other trees are in their pride, you will be dull and lifeless. In autumn you will be of a spiritless, monotonous yellow; and in winter, when every other deciduous tree of the forest will seem only to sleep, you will appear absolutely dead. A curse on the man who planted you!' With that, Wordsworth took off his round, worsted travelling cap and threw it at one of the larches, then turned and made to climb over the gate. Halfway over he paused, screwed up his eyes with displeasure and climbed back into the field. He went and retrieved his cap from the ground and set off again to the gate. As he was climbing over it the second time he noticed Luke, who'd stepped out from behind his tree to get a better look. As Wordsworth crossed his path Luke scowled politely and his opponent answered with an extremely black look. Not a word, poetic or prosaic, passed between them.

Dorothy couldn't bear to pick a flower out of the ground, William rampaged about the place all but committing arboricide – they were as mad as March hares, these nature poets. Luke decided, as he began making his way to Town End at long last, that it was wise to steer well clear of the whole Wordsworth crowd. Unfortunately he was at the mercy of a stronger, more carnivorous, urge – to have Dorothy for dinner once she'd had him for tea. And so he followed in William's footsteps, all but bearing his fangs.

Dorothy ripped out roses, lilies and poppies from the cottage walls, scattering their sweet fragrances through the air as she

the lake was up to her waist, and her garments were so heavy with their drink that she couldn't move, she hurled the white net bag full of flowers across the water and watched it rise and fall on the surface, tugged by a breeze towards the little island. A minute or two later she let out a desperate cry.

# 15

## Departure

It had been quite a pilgrimage, ensnared several times by cowardice, drowned briefly in despair, once taking the wrong path, and twice waylaid by insistent beggars – perhaps mistaking him, in his near-threadbare gentleman's outfit, for a gentleman, despite the presence on his feet of filthy clogs following the demise of his leather shoes after the Merry Neet. But he reached Dove Cottage. As it turned out he was in dogged mood, having been thwarted long enough, and even if the gloomy bard was home – maybe even at that very moment in a state of inspired composition – then damn him he would interrupt anyway, a day late for tea or not, and if absolutely necessary risk ruining one of Wordsworth's most immortal lines. He banged on the door. He could hear ponderous, shuffling feet. The door opened and there, looking as if she'd fossilized further since he last saw her, was Molly.

'She int in!'

'I'd hoped to speak with her.'

'Well she int home.'

'Is she out walking?'

'Nae.'

'Well I will find her. Where is she?'

'Gone.' The word dripped onto his head along with fresh raindrops.

'Gone?'

'Hour or so ago. Wit maister.'

'Where, damn you?'

'France.'

When he came to his senses and regained his vision Molly invited him in, perhaps because she thought he was going to faint and that as usual she'd be the one having to clear up the mess. He hadn't actually fainted, but he'd gone dizzy enough to see a million dark, swirling colours and all the stars of the Milky Way in his eyes, all with Dorothy's face in them.

Molly ushered him into the stone-flagged kitchen-parlour and sat him down by a defunct fire over which swung cheerless utensils. The cottage's low, beamed ceiling hung above walls panelled with dark, stained wood. Molly shuffled around, fussing and grunting over a cup of water. He stared out through the diamond windows into the garden. Dorothy must have known days earlier, even weeks, maybe months, and she hadn't told him. Clawing vengefulness began to stir in his breast.

While Molly wrung out a soaked bedgown and pottered round the parlour looking for something unspecified, he slipped through into the garden and up to the orchard. It was the first time he'd been there in daylight. The view over the lake took in the island that floated upon it, and Silver Howe and Helm Crag loomed beyond. The half-wild garden was overrun with weeds and reeked of dung, but it was crammed full of flowers and vegetables.

He noticed they'd pilfered gowans and wild orchids from beside the lake to adorn their cosy nest, and wild thyme from the fells. Dorothy had obviously been trying to tame nature for her pathetic little plot. There was a newly built shed, and the arbour from where no doubt Wordsworth would decree poetry while his muse and slave slavered over the words as they issued from his mutton-mouth. Luke grabbed at the arbour and tugged it till the branches cracked. It sprang back into place and leaves fluttered to the ground. He struck the shed, too softly to damage it but hard enough to damage his hand.

'Oyyy!' croaked Molly. 'This is privut propty!'

Luke trod disrespectfully back down through the Wordsworths' nauseating nook of mountain ground. He heard voices outside at the front, then a loud rap on the door.

'Nae, nae. Not again!' Molly cried. 'Blinkin beggars! Wait in 'ere,' she said, pointing to the kitchen-parlour. 'And stay put.'

He immediately began snooping around the adjoining room, a dingy, wood-panelled and stone-floored bedroom. On a double washstand he saw a cut-throat razor and quite naturally imagined driving it into Wordsworth's neck, but he saw no evidence of Dorothy. He crept upstairs and into a light front bedroom which smelt of fire-smoke. The bedroom floor tapped with raindrops leaking through the roof. There was a bed, and beside it a chair and small table. On the table alongside a book on botany was an assortment of plays by that Shakespeare man. Molly was still battling with the beggars, so he sat on the bed's home-made mattress and picked out a ragged copy of a play called *As You Like It*, remembering Dorothy gibbering with enthusiasm about it. He looked through it for a second or two and understood nothing, then put it back on top of the other plays. By mistake he knocked them over, and as he bent down to gather them up he saw a brown, leather-bound book on the floor by the bed. He picked it up, but as he went to open it he heard footsteps on the stairs. They didn't sound like Molly's. They sounded quicker, more urgent, firmer. He stuffed the book inside his waistcoat and stood up. A large shadow benighted the bedroom doorway.

'What the divel!'

It was Molly after all, and she wasn't one for ceremony, and was merciless with minnows, but the way she brandished the edge of William's ice-skate at him was uncalled for. 'If you only knew what poor Miss Dorothy had bin through this mornin' before she went away you might've shown a bit more respect.'

He didn't ask or want to know what she'd been through, but Molly told him anyway. 'She damnear died in the lake yonder. Maister found her on the little island in the middle. Like a drowned bird, she was.'

'What was she doing in the lake?'

'I'm sure I don't know. Some miff-maff about wantin' to feel free. Any road, she's gone now. Yeh hear? Gone! For Lord knows owlong. So best sling tha hook.'

Luke slunk away from Dove Cottage clutching his waistcoat and the granite conscience of a criminal. Then came a shout.

'Wet a minute, Ah've just found it. I don't want to give you this, specially now, but I promised her I would if I saw you, which I hoped I wunt.' She handed him an object wrapped in brown paper. 'It's from her. She said tellim this is as good place as any to start an edjacation.' Molly withdrew, shaking her head in contempt, and Luke set off down to the lake with his gift, and the brown book.

When he got to the water's edge he sat down. He checked around him to see if Molly was watching him, and took out the book. It was Dorothy's private journal. With malicious glee he opened it and began flicking through from the beginning.

*Saturday 17 April. A mild, warm rain. We sat in the garden all the morning. William dug a little. I transplanted a honeysuckle …*

He flicked.

*6th May Thursday 1802. A sweet morning we have put the finishing stroke to our bower and here we are sitting in the orchard … upon a seat under the wall which I found my brother building up when I came to him with his apple …*

He flicked again.

*Wednesday 30 June. William slept ill, his head terribly bad…*

And again.

*Friday July 2nd. A very rainy morning there was a gleam of fair weather and we thought of walking into Easedale…*

He threw it to the ground. It might as well have been written by Molly. He would hurl it in a ditch, or even better into the lake, or burn it, and deny its owner the full, shocking, inconsequentiality of her life as servant and second housekeeper to her brother. He looked down at it in disgust and saw that it had landed open on a page dated Thursday 15th April, the exact day he'd been passing along Ullswater. He picked up the journal and read.

*When we were in the woods … we saw a few daffodils close to the water side, we fancied that the lake had floated the seeds ashore & that the little colony had so sprung up. But as we went along there were more & yet more, & at last, under the boughs of the trees a long belt of daffodils along the lakeshore, about the breadth of a country turnpike road. I never saw daffodils so beautiful they grew among the mossy stones about & about them, some resting their heads on the stones as on a pillow for weariness & the rest tossed & reeled & danced & seemed as if they laughed with the wind that blew upon them over the lake; they looked so gay, ever glancing, ever changing. The wind blew directly over the lake to them. There was here & there a little knot & a few stragglers a few yards higher up, but they were so few as not to disturb the simplicity & unity & life of that one busy highway.*

At last! Not just chaff from the chaffinch. He'd found a poet nesting in her prose. He skimmed through the journal again, this time excitedly. On the inside back page was written *Friday, 9th July* – that very day's date – and beneath it words not long since blotted dry. It was scrawled at speed and almost illegible, and a tiny insect of some sort had got caught up in the ink. There were other blotches, watery ones, maybe of rain, or tears.

He squinted, and slowly deciphered.

*A sunny and showery morni—*

*The weather be damned! I tire of the yoke. What of my own passions, hopes, dreams? He consumes me! And I tire of waiting. He must have changed his mind about me – come at last to his senses. We were always going to be torn apart from each other, divided by such a chasm. Was he simply a beggar on the doorstep after all? What a fool I was to think men who do not wear fine clothes can feel deeply. And yet I have used him. I wanted William to feel he was losing me, and abandon the French trip. That way the wedding might be called off. If William does not tie up his affairs with Caroline and the girl, how can he marry Mary? And our life here will not be lost forever. And all his greatest poetry will not be behind him. William is for all time, but he will only live on this earth once, and though he thinks Mary might bring the sweetness of peace to his life, the consummation marriage brings will kill the longing which makes his poetry immortal. The sweetness of peace will not get the Recluse, his masterwork, written. He will waste the rest of his life on everything else but that. He will tinker at the edges of true greatness but die having failed to achieve it. Everything and everyone must be sacrificed for William – including Mary, including myself … and Luke!*

He was lost for words, but rescue was at hand, for when he picked up the gift and tore off its brown paper wrapping, all the words Dorothy had judged he'd need were right there in front of him …

*LYRICAL BALLADS,*
*WITH PASTORAL*
*AND OTHER POEMS,*
*BY W. WORDSWORTH. 1802.*

# Part Two

Part Two

# 16

# Rage

'And you say your commissioner personally staked out all the
boundaries in his perambulatory survey?' inquired Parson
Snaile, puffing his way up Helvellyn, wiping his nose with his
sleeve and secreting steamy droplets down his temples.

Sir Edward Unthank Bart, several roods ahead and stroking
his new wall, looked round and caught the parson with his
hands down the back of his trousers scratching his rear ingress
– yes trousers, not pantaloons and breeches, he noted, making a
snap judgement of loose morals based on the sartorial evidence
before him – not only trousers but open-necked shirt and
vaguely long hair. Two other men were climbing uphill behind
them, watching.

'Yes, personally, Vicar,' the baronet replied. 'Are you sure you're up for this climb? You look rather tired.'

'Tired? By no means, Sir Edward,' he replied. 'You are looking at a man in his prime. I could wrestle you to the ground on this very spot to prove it.'

'That won't be necessary, Vicar,' he said, adding after a pause, 'and I didn't see you as the wrestling type, I must confess.'

'You sound surprised Sir Edward. Need I remind you that it was a man of the cloth such as myself who invented buttocking?'

The baronet would have spluttered into his drink if he'd had one at his lips. 'Buttocking, Vicar?' He racked his brains to remember how this fool had become Rector of Grasmere.

'You know, pulling one's opponent forward and onto the ground with a wrenching action. One can use one's shoulders, or slip right underneath and throw him over one's back, which is called a full buttock. A cross-buttock is when—'

'Yes intriguing, Vicar, thank you,' Sir Edward interrupted.

The baronet groped the wall again and nodded to himself with contentment that a good, professional job was being done. His investment was paying off so far, his revolution well under way. 'Remind me, Vicar,' he asked, curious now about his provenance, 'how you came to be a man of God, if I may ask, that is.'

'Of course. I was dropped by my father into the soft lap of the Church, simple as that.'

Sir Edward stopped and leant against the wall. 'You mean you had no sense of personal calling, Vicar?'

'None whatsoever.'

'Hmm. And, if I may be so bold, did you not actually believe in God?'

'Why, no sir, I did not. Or, to be more exact, I'd never really thought about it. Never had the time. I was always too busy with my painting and other vocations. But being a gentleman, I considered it churlish not to devote myself to God despite this – at least on Sundays. Which is why, in bed each night, a vessel of wine in hand of course, I read out loud to myself the early drafts of my Sunday sermon. And on the seventh day I emerge from the rectory with all the might of Christian righteousness and breathe divine fire over Grasmere's sinners, then leave them in the gorgeous silence of awe.'

'I see,' grimaced the baronet. 'And the other six days?'

'On the other six days it is work, work, work. Painting, extending the rectory, expanding my knowledge of flora ...'

'What, the sexton's daughter?'

'No, Sir Edward. Flowers!'

'Ah.'

'Gardening, Sir Edward, is my great love. But being a Christian and therefore equipped with a living and breathing conscience, I am fully aware of the temptation to excessive indulgence, even if horticulture is to the greater glory of God. Indeed, if I may say this in confidence to you,' he said, scuttling up to the baronet, 'I have recently fallen into the habit of visualising myself in purgatory, bound hand-and-foot, face down on the ground in flames, for having concentrated far too much on gardening. Which is ironic considering my garden is based on Milton's Paradise.'

The parson sat down on the hard earth and let his spine bend forward. The two other men at the back stopped as well. 'One thing I do believe,' Parson Snaile sputtered, 'is that a man should either climb a fell or talk – not both at the same time. My illustrious parishioner Wordsworth – you know him, I'm sure – insists that only when the legs are in motion can the mind truly think, and the heart fully feel. Well it is my firm belief that the ideal posture for spiritual and intellectual flow is to be reclining in a warm chair by the fire, with spine and shoulders at ease, in a kind of ... as it were, contemplative slouch, for want of a more delicate expression.'

Sir Edward presumed, as he looked at the round-shouldered ape beneath him, that he was at that moment in a contemplative slouch, or at least its outdoor equivalent.

'We must press on, Vicar.'

Noble Snaile combed his fingers through his remaining strands of hair and released a 'ppffoooph!' that sounded like a rallying call to his weary muscles for one last heave, either that or a decoy for the discharge of wind which resonated simultaneously. 'My other great love,' he panted, 'is landscape painting. And for that, Sir Edward, a man must have good air.'

'Good air?'

'Yes, good air.'

The baronet looked round at him almost cross-eyed with puzzlement.

'No matter,' said Parson Snaile, groaning and hauling himself back on his feet. 'I am a man pulled in many different directions through life simultenously. I confess that with my numerous vocations I don't know where I am half the time. How much further is it to the front of the wall now, do you know?'

'Oh, a fair way yet,' sang the baronet, taking active pleasure in the parson's gradual waning.

Further uphill Parson Snaile stopped again, panting against the wall, and waved his hand over an infinity of open fell land. 'So let me get this straight,' he gasped. 'I'd get a portion of the allotments?'

'Correct, Vicar.'

'But I must give up my right to the tithes, is that correct, too?'

'Er, well, it is, but you don't need to pay for your boundary wall. It costs me well over four shillings for every rood, but if that's what it takes to do my Christian duty, then so be it.'

'Most generous and noble of you, sir, I'm sure,' the parson said with a glissando falling through his voice that implied he wasn't sure at all. 'But how will I survive without tithes?' he cried, the anguish reverberating through the rocks. 'What about my little luxuries?'

'Luxuries, Vicar? England is pinched to the bone. What luxuries?'

'Those modest extravagances, sir, which go with the dignity of my ministry. A little cotton is all I ask, and worsted, and cambric, and silk for my stockings, of course. Am I to be denied handkerchiefs, table linen, morning gowns?'

'Tithes,' protested Sir Edward, 'are a poisoned chalice. Think of all the bad blood they create. You can never tell what men mutter about you behind their closed doors. They might be saying you take too much from them, and they might ask themselves how you spend the pennies they scrape together for you. They might wonder at the glories of your garden, the luxuriance of your stockings, the crimson delights within your wine decanter. They might one day ask why, why am I paying Parson Snaile all these tithes when I can hardly feed my children? That, Vicar, is the curse of being a tithe-collector first, and a pastor second.'

Parson Snaile stood erect and shouted out with energetic self-pity. 'You will have me barter away my sacred ministry for the humble life of a peasant farmer?'

Sir Edward Unthank's chest swelled, and he replied in a declamatory way, as if he'd rehearsed his lines on a small stage nearby, and they were a message for all humanity. 'A statesman-farmer, my dear Vicar, but surely even more the shepherd of your flock? And imagine all that land. Your own Garden of Eden. Think of the glory of standing alongside your lost sheep, tending the soil and the hearth during the week and praising God on Sundays. But you are so much more than your flock, Vicar. You are one of the symbols of England's greatness. Throne and altar – the two arms with which Atlas holds up the world. And we must fight together to defeat those pagans and plotters who would have religion itself dethroned. Believe me, Vicar, you will be a better parson for it if you join forces with me – and a richer one.'

'Well at this juncture, Sir Edward,' the parson said solemnly, 'I feel I must ask about the poor of my parish. Will some provision be made for—?'

'Damnation!' exclaimed Sir Edward, looking ahead of him. 'Only up to there.' He turned round to the two men in their wake and waved them forward. Then he turned to Parson Snaile, his jaw tight and his eyeballs swollen with quashed rage. 'Forgive me, Vicar. You were saying?'

'Oh, never mind,' said the parson, looking a little intimidated, but clearly unable anyway to feign enough enthusiasm for his moral point to repeat it.

'I'm just an ignorant peasant, I am,' said Cragg as he and Weightman tried to shake the bruising out of their hands before lifting and dropping a huge footing stone into a circular trench. It was a trench not for the wall but for a stone shelter now that it was too high up, too windy and too cold for tents. 'But I've spent long enough on these fells to know what's what.'

'What's what then?' asked Weightman.

'Eh? I keep it all inside, see, in here,' continued Cragg, rapping his chest.

'What?' asked Weightman, tracing with his eyes the line of the wall as it skirted Helvellyn Lower Man, now only eighty feet or so below the summit.

'Shoulda seen it coming,' Cragg said, ignoring the interjections. 'When they started tekkin all't lowland fields, knocking all them small-oldins down that've been there for donkey's years. Field after field. Every last blade. You can't graze, you can't grow corn, you can't fold sheep. Once a man has to sell his cow, his pig, his geese or his sheep, he's got nothing left but his wage. And when his wage is nothing, that's that. Ay, I shoulda seen them coming.'

'Who?'

'The powers that bluddy-be!' hollered Cragg as the other wallers, dumping stones for the building of the shelter, listened in. 'They're pinching all the common land. Your land. Lord of the Manor, Magistrate, Church, Parleyment.' He spat on the ground. 'It isn't Bonneyparte we should be fretting about. Wiv got a right battle on our hands wit powers that bluddy-be. Vipond's working us to death. We'll have no strength left when't time comes.'

'For what, chief?' asked Gass, his soldier's ears pricking up.

'To fight back!' shouted Cragg, checking around him for signs of Vipond. 'We're in this together. That's how we get out of it.'

'Like an army!' cried Gass.

'Army?' sneered Luke, who was working on the shelter and thinking bitterly about how it resembled a certain sheepfold he'd never got to finish building. 'A worn-out, starved, penniless army.'

'Ha ha!' laughed Gass. 'Didn't do us no harm at Alexandria.'

Cragg turned to Luke. 'We meet not have much to fight with, but plenty to fight for. And wiv got one thing they can't tek from us.'

'Stones?' guessed Weightman, clearly trying hard to prove his head wasn't made of pork.

'Rage, you dafsod, rage! Feel it in your heart. I can.'

'Rage, chief!' shouted Gass, raising a fist into the sky. 'Rage!'

The other wallers looked round at each other with befuddlement, not rage.

'We should've stopped 'em fixing them enclosure notices on the church door,' said Cragg. 'They wunt have dared step through a mob of us there with hatchets. Ay, we could've had a right ole clamour.'

'Let's smash the wall down,' shouted Weightman, his rage peaking too soon. 'That'll learnum.'

'Nae you dafdivel,' snapped Cragg. 'That'll get the lot of us transported. If only wid got a petition, genst the Helvellyn bill, and took it to Parleyment, to the Ousacommons.'

'Petition?' scoffed Luke. 'Who here can write his name?'

No hands or fists were raised. 'A lot of exes, then. Don't you see? Parliament is full of the landlords who are stealing the land anyway. The House of Commons is the last place to protect our commons and houses. Face it, they're stealing our land and we're helping them.'

He threw down the rock he was holding and looked at Cragg with disgust.

'All right!' snapped Cragg, looking round clearly anxious that heads were nodding. 'You keep your ideas to yusself. If you ain't got the balls for a fight, leave it to them who has.'

'Least you lot get compunsation. What do we get?' said one of the gypsies.

Weightman, presumably now empowered with the rage he didn't even know he had, rounded on him. 'You thievin' squatters build your hovels at neet and if yuv gotta fire going by sunrise you think the land's always bin yours. Well it int!'

'Nae!' reprimanded Cragg. 'Stand together, lads.'

Vipond's cloudy grey eyes were camouflaged by the rock behind which they concealed themselves as he lip-read the wallers. His instincts, like those of the wretched, agitating wallers he spied upon, were to fight and smash the system to bits. Yet he longed to crush the downtrodden peasants beneath his feet as well. Beat the slaves, beat the masters too. He hated them all. But one. She'd begun as no more than a scheme, then a fantasy when he was alone coughing and spitting a treacle-like fluid into the night, wishing she were there to care for him, to be company. He'd never needed anyone, but she was different. He felt hot, then cold, and then felt a sharp stitch in his chest that made him wonder whether this was what soft-hearted chumps meant by love. A hand seized him from behind.

'What the hell do you think you are doing? Hiding?'

Vipond turned round to face Sir Edward Unthank and Parson Snaile.

'I—'

'You were planning? Or guarding? Or maybe gaining perspective? Do you have the first idea how far behind schedule my wall is? It should be long over the top. There will be no money in it for you, and no more work if it's not done by the end of the year. And if that means staying up here all day and all night, then so be it.'

Sir Edward gestured to one of the roughnecks who'd been

# 17

# Rushbearing

Noble Snaile had noted well by the time of Rushbearing that the flowers were beginning to have had their day, and that the mellow sighs of the scythe were leaving gossamer stubbles and clearing a path for autumn. Heather roared purple on the fellsides but down in the vale, from harebells to honeysuckles to roses, flowers were wilting. Yet he didn't need his Claude glass in order to detect a lack of poignancy, a pallor that was the prelude to the rich pathos of autumn, where flower and leaf corpses would strew the lakes and carry one's senses inexorably into excess. He simply had to find the time to get up in the fells and do some painting.

Lakelanders, the parson had spent long enough in Grasmere to learn, prided themselves on their wholesale resentment of offcomers all year round, but especially in August. In this month rich southerners who were too parsimonious to go on a proper Grand Tour of Italy and France flocked up to the new finishing school of the fashionable, Grasmere, to watch the locals perform the ancient Lakeland ritual of accepting tourists' money without gratitude or warmth. Villagers collected in small groups and chaffered their disapproval, shaking heads and tutting about the weather, lack of work, war, price of food, floods of beggars, airs of tourists. Any sightseer uplifted by the scenery was soon downcast by the locals.

One thing Grasmerians could rely on as they congealed together on the Rushbearing and Sports Day was the unreliability of the weather. All that a glorious burst of sunshine through the church windows could guarantee – apart from the way it set fire to Parson Snaile's vestments and endowed him, to his great pleasure, with an all-over halo of divinity – was that rain was sure to follow. It always had its hands round the neck of Rushbearing Day and accompanying festivities, threatening the amateur landscape painter's worst nightmare: an overcast vault and drab scenery.

But at least the arrival of tourists held the prospect of a swollen congregation, the thought of which sent Parson Snaile's pulse into excess as he made the final touches to his sermon and checked the colour scheme of his vestments in the glass. His performance was only minutes away and the church was less than half full. Very disappointing considering that his flock were soon to see before them not the warm, approachable friend to all he was when out and about doing good in the parish – or in the alehouse on the odd evening – but a volcano of a Christian shepherd.

The wallers were on a day off Helvellyn, and as Luke shambled into Grasmere in soiled smock-frock and hat he spotted a gaggle of young maids dancing downhill from Helm Crag, bearing armfuls of rushes. There was a time, he thought sadly, when everything else would be abandoned – injured lamb, axe, mouthful of mutton, everything – to behold a bonny lass, more radiant than the arc of a rainbow, sweeter than a nightingale.

But he hadn't come to ogle the bonny lasses, however delicious they looked, particularly in his new and somewhat troubled romantic circumstances. He'd come in fact to make good on his long-neglected promise to find his parents' graves. He drifted towards St Oswald's, where the rush-maids had rushed to bear their harvest. He brushed his hand over a handsome marble monument with the name Sir Edmund d'Unthanque inscribed on it, and sat in a narrow oaken bench, his eyes drawn to sunlight gushing through the windows onto an altar candle. He remembered Michael talking of faith being a light amid the dark, and he thought about the faith his father had once had in him, and about that Wordsworth woman in whom he'd put his faith, and who'd humiliated him. The church darkened, the candle trembled and went out, and folk began shuffling in. Rain drummed its fingers on the windows. A decrepit veteran of some species levered itself into Luke's pew and laid out its bones so close that Luke could identify the stench from different zones of its body. The last thing he wanted was for the – was it a man? – to lean closer, but he did.

'Rain, eh,' he whispered with a wink, 'turns this church into Noah's ark. Only way't preacher can get creechers like us in two by two.'

A procession began, of girls carrying rushes garnished with flowers. The fairest girl was predictably crowned the Rushbearing queen, and stood at the front of the pageant flourishing an elaborate garland that made the uglier girls' nosegays look flimsy. The queen placed her garland on the pulpit while her plainer subjects scattered rushes on the pews and on the soft, swept earth. The dizzying over-fragrance of rushes burrowed into Luke's nose and made the old man almost on his lap sneeze, unleashing a cough that bucked on for minutes. The preacher – Luke recognised him as Unthank's odd-looking companion on

Helvellyn – mounted the altar, gleaming with summer sweat, tongue dark as claret.

Bells rang, candles were snuffed out, and, with extensive reference to scripture, the preacher usurped the liturgy with his litany. He declared the author of all falsehood to be ravishing the souls before him as he spoke, polluting Grasmere with the multifarious sins of adultery, fornication, lewdness, uttering of oaths, quaffing of ale till bestially insensible, clandestine wedlock, non-payment of tithes, and knowingly forking corn on the Sabbath. The defender of the faith pronounced finally, and at length, that for such sins absolution was unlikely, excommunication probable, and eternal damnation by no means to be ruled out. Once the sermon was over and the sermoniser's spittle had dried, indelibly, on several front rows of heads, Luke's pew-fellow turned to him.

'Queer feller, isn't he, eh?'

'Hypocrite,' muttered Luke. 'Drunkard. Land-pilferer.'

'Heh heh, I like tha spirit, son. No one likes a nippercrit, eh? Pal of mine use to talk like thee.' He burst out with another cough, sending a ball of gobbet onto the earthen floor, the spittle fizzing among the new rushes, and he tried to speak while continuing to cough and spit. 'Dint like (reugh, reeugh, reuuugh eeeeghhh tptoooph) – a nippercrit neither, ole Mi (reugh, reeugh, reuuugh reeugh, reuuugh eeeeghhh) chael. Godfergivemeh,' he croaked. 'I dint mean no disrespect.'

'Did you say Michael?'

'Ay, might've just gobbed on me ole pal.'

'Under here?' Luke said, pointing to the moistened rushes on the floor.

'Dint tha know? They lay them rushes to soak up the niff o'them that's underneath. Only thing is, damn rushes get right inside me bad chest.'

'Greenhead, was that your friend's name?'

'Ay, that's it. Statesman Greenhead. Wunt much of a church-goer, had run-ins wid parson, but a Mannagod all't same ...

Mebby,' he added, his face overheated with another cough, 'he was ex (reugh, reeugh, reuuugh eeeeghhh tptoooph) ecuted.'

'What? Executed for not going to church?'

'Nae, lad. Parson wunt that harsh – least I don't think so. Nae I said excomooneycated. Parson used to do that sometimes with them as dint go to church.'

The woody knock of Luke's enraged knuckles on the pew roused heads that had been bowed, some in prayer, some in the ostentatious pretence thereof, some now emerging with whiplash from opportunistic naps. The rain-clouds had passed over without further comment, and there followed an exodus of biblical zeal, during which Luke lost sight and scent of his pew-fellow.

He watched as ten tense statesmen looked up and down Silver Howe and waited for the signal. They were off, clambering up the twelve-hundred-foot fell, leaping over walls and skimming through bracken. Amazingly soon afterwards they were leaping and stumbling downhill again, on legs that looked as if they were made of sloe jelly, careering as recklessly downhill as Luke had in his impassioned London years. The winner gasped, the rest panted on all fours like spent collies in smock-frocks.

Luke sauntered over to the village green to see what the crowd was gawping at. Wrestler John Lioll was the name on most lips, a flaxen-haired farm-hand built like Helm Crag. His father, rumour had it, hadn't been gentle with him, and his father's father hadn't been gentle with his father. Lioll was, so Luke overheard, frustrated that he had no wife and children to thump.

His opponent was wild Ed Hogg of Wigton, no taller than a donkey but apparently sensitive enough about it to be a danger to any man. His face was a wall of stupidity stuck on an oak-trunk neck, with small black holes for eyes. Some onlookers said Lioll and Hogg had an 'axtergrind' and others said they had a 'boneterpick', but all agreed they would fight by the rules, because there was no glory in Grasmere wrestling without dignity and respect.

They went at each other like fiends, grunting neck to neck, grasping and grappling shins and buttocks, one propelling the other through the air and flipping him on his back with a slap on the grass – all to roars of 'good lad!', 'nae!', 'ay!', 'that's it!', 'hold him!' and the occasional 'grab his arse!'

Hogg had, before the final bout, declared himself twice the man of Lioll, even though a third his size, but it was Hogg's pink flesh that purpled and buckled first, and Lioll won bout and the belt.

'Drink?' asked Luke, the only man reckless enough to talk to Lioll after the crowd had dispersed. 'Wunt say nae,' scowled Lioll as he swaggered through the door of the Red Lion. Four times over the next hour Luke said 'Drink?' and heard the refrain 'Wunt say nae.'

But he wasn't listening to Lioll, he was harking back to his youth in London, during which time he'd had his earliest dalliances with drunkenness and its bosom companions, violence and lechery. He'd had a dead-end job filling barrels for a merchant who'd invented an ale that kept its flavour on long sea journeys, and would drag the pale-ale casks onto barges that sped along the Thames – that great emblem of the Empire into which he felt like tossing himself again – to ships destined for the officers of the East India Company. This was an elite club of Englishmen half the world away in India, whose tireless work colonising, civilising, exploiting – not to mention barking at their Indian servants – made their privileged throats terribly parched. Pure English ale, all the way from jolly old Blighty and not tasting brackish, was exactly what the poor lambs needed. Luke had worked like a dog, developed an insatiable taste for alcohol and sampled all manner of evils as a conseqeunce.

'Diz you know,' he slurred some hours later as he clocked why he'd come to Grasmere in the first place, 'that they bury bodies under the shursh? Diz you know that?'

'Nae,' said Lioll, inspecting his giant hands. 'What's that to me?'

'My farzer is buried under the shursh floor. Whass about you?'

'Me?' Lioll said, looking up from his hands. 'Nae, I'm here, not undert church floor.'

Luke jerked his head back and furrowed his brow. 'No,' he clarified, 'not you, your farzer.'

'Mind this,' said Lioll, slapping a finger on Luke's right nostril.

'Izzy sill alive?' Luke persisted at his own risk.

'Uh?' Lioll grunted.

'Izzy dez? I never spoke to Mygul affer I lef Grazmere. Wish I haz. I luffed the ole man, and he luffed me.'

'Hah!' laughed Lioll, swigging his dregs scornfully. 'My ole man belted me like a pup, till I … ne'er mind.'

'Whass?'

'Eh?'

'Till you whass? What ziz you zoo?'

Lioll looked round the room. No one was listening. He turned back to Luke confidentially. 'Belted him good and proper dint ah! Once an' frawl.'

'What with?'

'These,' he said with a grin, brandishing his hands like spades.

'Dizzy stop affer that?'

'Get me another and I'll tell thee,' he said, sucking the dregs from his pot. Luke emptied his own and ordered two more. Lioll looked round again and leant in. 'Did fer't fucker,' he whispered. 'Ay, bare 'ands. Said twas an accident of course, like, but nae, twas no mistek. If I hadn't done him in he'd've done me.'

Luke thought dizzily about Alexandria, how he'd seen men shot in the face, their skulls broken with rocks. He felt sick. He stood up, but a spade-like hand clamped onto his arm.

'Where you going?'

'Home.'

'Nae. Not now I've telled thee my big secret. Tha's not going nowhere.'

Luke looked into Lioll's eyes. He'd seen enough drunken brawling to know those eyes meant it. A long pause elapsed, then with the wildness of a man who had nothing to lose but his life, Luke thrust his pot in Lioll's face so hard that two waterfalls of blood cascaded from the giant's nostrils. Lioll picked Luke up and threw him across the bar into the open arms of two men at a table. They pushed him away and he slid to the floor with the same fluidity as their drinks. Lioll battered him about the head and stamped on him as he might in a clog dance. Only seconds later, half-hearted rescuers had flooded the inn to try and stop Lioll going the distance. Out of their hesitant midst burst Wild Ed Hogg of Wigton, whose axtergrind and boneterpick with Lioll were a thing to behold.

Sally stood outside St Oswald's threatening the Rushbearing children with her last stock of gingerbread, while the fiddler played the Rushbearing March and led the procession through the village to the Red Lion, with their poles, crosses, hoops and sticks all decorated with rushes and flowers. The fiddler shouldered open the inn door and stopped mid-crotchet at the sight of Hogg wrestling Lioll in a way that was highly flexible with the rules. Hogg held Lioll's head in his hands and was fondling it with his clenched fist. Lioll was trying to squeeze Hogg's leg into submission. Thrilled children peered through the doorway while their parents dragged them back out. Sally bustled through, saw the wrestlers in fierce embrace, and saw another bruised, bloody, swollen face, one she knew well.

'Stop this now!' she screamed. Lioll and Hogg, clearly having awaited a vexed matriarch, separated and brushed themselves off. Sally crouched over Luke, dabbed his face with her apron and offered him gingerbread. The fiddler played a jig into the lull and gradually tickled the atmosphere into something more jovial.

Merry was made late into the evening. For her heroics, Sally was danced up and down, and round and round, by innumerable drunken bachelors. She noticed Luke, a gelatinous broth of blood, mud and alcohol, eventually ooze out of the inn, pick up one of the children's Rushbearing sticks and set off in what he probably thought was a straight line towards the church.

The main door of St Oswald's invited her. Inside, someone was walking through the church in what Sally imagined he, too, thought was a straight line, muttering how indecent it was to be merrymaking so near the Sabbath, and how he would go directly to the Red Lion and tell them all to go to bed at once. She spotted Luke clearing, with his pilfered Rushbearing stick, rushes from a patch of floor. He held his nose and his breath, presumably to avoid their toxic sweetness, stabbed the stick in the ground and began scraping. With his fingers he widened the trench and soon Sally was holding her nose and her breath, not at the smell of new rushes, but the stench of ripe corpses. She made her way gingerly towards him. He froze. Then he carried on digging, more urgently. Her voice rang out.

'What are you doing?'

He didn't look up, but waited, soil in his hands, tears in his eyes. She placed a hand on his shoulder with compassionate pressure.

'Here, grave-robber, tek a sip of this,' she said, nursing him in a nearby byre.

'What is it?' he slurred.

'Whey-whig.'

'Whass waywig?'

'Mint buttermilk in whey. You forgotten all the ole ways round here? Tastes sharp but a good cure for drunkenness.'

'I'm not dzrunk!'

'Shh,' soothed Sally, puffing up an armful of fresh hay for a pillow.

'He wasn't down there,' he said, placing his head on the hay.

'What you talking about?'

'He's spose to be buried under the church.'

'Your fadder? Nae, he int down there. Now shush while we get some sleep.'

'How d'you know?'

'Cos it's rich fowks who get buried under't floor, not poor ones.'

It rained, straight through a hole in the roof onto his forehead, as if Sally had placed him there on purpose to sober him up. A comfort came over him as he lay, almost bestially insensible, listening to the drizzling outside and feeling its regular drops on his drunken brow. Beside him lay Sally, adorned with the silken silveriness of the moon. He gently tugged her fingers, which, to his surprise, came to him. He turned his face to hers. She looked so beautiful close up.

'Sleep!' she chided, but tenderly.

The morning after, Luke felt a presence next to him, not of Sally, but of his old friend abjection. With a nauseous shudder, which made his eyes stand out like plums and his lips sphincterise, he recalled his colourful attempt – red with blood, blue with bruises, black with mud – to seduce Sally. Nothing remained of her apart from a vague, sensuous impression on the earth, like the musky flat patch in a field where a deer has rested overnight. Only the most grossly vain side of him entertained the idea that Sally had been flattered by the advances of his fingers. He stepped outside the byre and, to force the stiffness out of his legs, stamped on the ground the way a small child might mimic a soldier. He set off to Helvellyn with a heart full of hatred of himself, and everyone else for that matter.

# 18

# Red Tarn

The summer harvest came and went. Hired hands swished their sickles as soon as the corn was dry, cutting, tying and stooking an acre a day, leaving a foot-long stubble in their wake. Up in the fells the bracken harvest arrived and departed, a red and warm phase when farmers gathered up the flames of dead ferns, and slung them into carts attached to disenchanted-looking horses whose days ended with a slap on the backside that sent them clopping back down to the farmsteads.

Up near the summit of Helvellyn, these enflamed weeks, this short early autumn idyll of prophetic blushings in bracken, mountain ash and wild cherry, soon withered into a grey-whiteness. For the wallers, the stone shelter that had given them at least some kind of refuge two months earlier had become prison walls wailed at by icy gales trespassing inside the cracks and gaps. In they came in secret, invisible streams, violating the folds of clothes, worming round necks and toes.

It was just after dawn as Cragg booted his wallers awake. 'Gittup you idle buggers! I'm not building this wall on me tod.'

Luke lay listening to him muttering oaths, thinking how much like Vipond he sounded. 'What'f I been doing up here all these years? One more rood till't top. That's enough for me. Up you bastards!' he shouted, kicking everyone again. Luke responded to Cragg's kick by jumping to his feet and squaring up to him. He could smell the master waller's food-starved stale breath in the cold air. Cragg's eyes looked like flint against the sky.

A ghoulish wheeze of laughter broke the silence.

'Heh heh heh! Fighting are we, lads?' said Vipond.

'Keep outta this!' snarled Cragg. 'Git back behind them rocks again, why don't you? Only place safe for thee round here.'

Vipond's face changed. 'Like to see a bit more of the wife, Isaac? Going about it the right way, you are. Mind you, plenty of other fellas seen a bit more of her over the years, so I hear, so join the queue.'

Cragg and Luke turned to Vipond with suspended ferocity.

'And what about the offcomer?' Vipond sneered. 'Why he's a Greenhead, he isn't no offcomer,' he laughed. 'I remember thy mudder, the barmy old scarecrow. Heh heh heh! Used to walk round with a funny hat on. Dint know what she wus doing. Heh heh heh!'

The wind moaned over Helvellyn as Luke punched Vipond. Blood drooled out of his mouth as Cragg pulled Luke off.

'Good luck Greenhead,' Vipond said through punctured lips. 'You'll need it.'

'Come with me,' said Cragg, putting his arm on Vipond's shoulder. Luke watched the two men disappear up into Helvellyn's mists, and then followed them.

Cragg and Vipond scrambled onto Helvellyn's flat, shale-covered summit amid a wind bent on blowing them over. The mason picked up a shard of slate and waved his arm across the wall-pencilled landscape visible through a sudden fracture in the mist. 'How many of these walls have we knocked together over the years, eh?' he bellowed to Vipond, who carried on mopping his tomato lips with the back of his hand. Vipond coughed and more blood came out on the back of his hand, rivulets of it within the mucus. Cragg turned and looked eastwards down the escarpment to Red Tarn. 'Scores,' he answered himself, 'and for what? Carvin't place up, wiping out whole communities, ancient families, the real folk of this land. Our folk.'

'Ours?' shouted Vipond. 'Not mine.' The wind blew even more irascibly from the north, straight over the escarpment.

'Course yours,' said Cragg. 'Who d'you think you are?'

'I were born for better things.'

'You?' laughed Cragg. 'You was born wi nowt, jus like me. Nae, wuss than nowt. Nae family, nae home, chucked in the wukhouse as a babe-in-arms. Yeh forgotten all that?'

'Wait and see. One day you idle buggers'll build my walls over the fells. I'm a genterman.'

'Genterman?' bawled Cragg, his voice barely audible above the wind. 'You've brutalised every decent, hard-working man who's ever set foot on these fells. Mind tha back, man. One day the common folk will want all this land back. We'll see how much of a genterman they think tha art then.'

'Listen tut champion of the common man! Who's bin building all them walls up here all these years? I'm not the one suppin wid divel.'

'I did it to feed the wife and bairns,' Cragg roared. 'Not to turn myself into a genterman.'

'You wunt've stayed up here if you dint want to. Scared of the missus, was you?'

'Don't you sinuate nowt!' shouted Cragg, grabbing Vipond's arm. The wind suddenly changed direction, blasting straight into them from the north and thrusting them nearer the edge overlooking the escarpment and tarn below.

'Get yer hands off me!' yelled Vipond. 'I know all about thee. Watched thee many a time. Seen it with me own eyes. Bit too cosy up here wit lads to go back home, wunt tha, eh?'

'Nae!' roared Cragg ... or was it Vipond? Luke had been edging closer from a distance, but through mist, and he couldn't make out which of the two it was, especially after a sudden violent gust had knocked him to the ground. He waited for a lull and a gap in the mist before going any further. When he set off again, pressing blindly through the freezing vapours, he heard footsteps, distant at first, but then stumbling quickly towards him. Out of the mist appeared a blanched face with charcoal-smear eyebrows and cloudy round eyes. A graveyard of blood-stained teeth stood behind blue lips.

'You shunt have done that,' grinned Vipond, who then strode away, coughing and spitting out something that looked like birdlime. Luke made his way to the edge overlooking the escarpment. He peered over, and tried to make out a shape. It was round, bobbing on the surface of Red Tarn like a head, connected to something longer and body-shaped, bubbling up fat with water.

# 19

# Michaelmas Daisy

He stood shivering by Dolly's View on the edge of Grasmere lake, looking out at the little island and its stone hut. Icy stars swarmed above, and the moon spilt its wraithlike milk over the water. He could almost smell the nocturnal breezes hissing through the tall, moss-clad firs beneath which the tiny building hid. Over to his right he saw an abandoned, upturned skiff bearing the upside-down name Georgie. He looked down at his feet, onto which the lake was tiptoeing ashore, and felt an object sloshing against them. He plucked it out of the water and shook dry a bunch of flowers caught up in a white net bag. Some wild roses among them were tied with what looked like a lady's bonnet. He threw the flowers back into the lake and stuffed the bag in his bundle, which he tied to his arm round the shoulder. He turned the skiff upright and heaved it out into the black lake, clambering in and nearly toppling over. With his hands he paddled, first one side, then the other, through the achingly cold water.

With each stroke further from the shore Helm Crag appeared to bear down on him bigger and blacker until it towered over him, as if the giant, kneeling monk it resembled was now standing menacingly erect. He leapt with terror at the sudden sound of dogs – yelping and barking far off on the fells. Had his hunted, haunted mind imagined it? He lunged even deeper through the water, but not in a rhythm designed to buoy up his oarless craft. The upset skiff rocked this way and that, like a horse sensing its rider's fear and losing its own nerve. Soon all control was lost, and the skiff bucked him into the lake and glided away out of reach. Underwater reeds set about investigating his legs, and he thrashed around in a tantrum of panic, causing enough commotion to prick up the ears of the hounds on Helm Crag, if there were any.

But he was trapped, and up to his mouth in icy lake-water, and he began to sense, with rising horror, that he was about to drown. This was what it must have felt like for those boys in Brotherswater, and for Dorothy that day back in July, and this was the end he'd chosen for himself when he'd jumped into the Thames. He felt the blood in his veins begin to slow like a river made sluggish by ice. But not again, not now, not here if he could help it, and with a mighty cry he kicked his legs free of the reeds and lunged forward in a desperate effort to swim. He splashed his way across to the half-sunken skiff, dragged himself in and lay coiled up and shuddering as the night breezes propelled the stricken vessel through the water.

When he stirred from the shadows of his closed lids it was with a start, on hearing the ridiculous quack of ducks. After the gluey, delicate business of opening his eyes he dragged himself up and awake and saw that he'd come ashore at the island and it was morning. He climbed out of the skiff and pulled it aground behind him. He headed straight for the hut and pushed his way into its ruined interior. Here he gathered as many dry, dead leaves as his withered strength allowed and lay beneath a blanket of them. In this state he stayed, motionless, through the light and shade of numberless hours. Maybe even days, he didn't know.

Hunger and thirst finally nagged him to get up and go down to the edge of the lake. He crouched, splashed water into his mouth and guzzled. It tasted of soil and made him retch. Over the next hour he explored the tiny island and discovered, washed up on the shore further round, the oars to the skiff. Before long he was sitting in it out in the lake, assuming the intent look of a predator and holding the white net bag in tense readiness. He knew there were pike and trout in there somewhere, as well as minnows, and after a lengthy expedition, with no big success, he spotted the tubular neck of a milk-white swan as the bird glided through the water like a bride along the nave.

If the inhabitants of Grasmere had turned their heads to the island that evening they might have spotted a string of smoke spiralling out of two hands rubbing against each other with the vigour of an ice explorer. The smell from that fir-and-alder-twig bonfire they might have recognised as charred swan.

He fished, slept, and perched on the knoll at the island's summit to watch the weeks come and go. He saw it all, autumn in its wedding garment one day, its shroud the next. The trees performing their slow ministry of divestment, the thistledown in flight, the Michaelmas daisy in flower, the ghylls and becks boiling like kettles with autumnal sunshine. Varnished leaves collected and roasted in the golden pyre of October soil. On some days soft late-autumn colours melted into each other like fruit – the orange of fern and mountain ash, the lime and lemon of oak, the cherry of sycamore. On other days Helm Crag and Silver How snuffled behind grey ribs of mist, the ferns that feathered them looking sallow and wintry.

Gaze though he did, he could hardly bear to look on any of it. He wanted to go to ground, to bury himself. At night his dreams were of terror, of flight, and self-annihilation. One late October day, when bitter winds had snapped the last autumn crocuses and he stood looking out on the leaf-strewn lake, he felt a great outpouring of sorrow suddenly break over him. He howled out so loud that it turned the heads of Herdwicks in far fields. The sky darkened, a breeze swelled, and rain began gunning the lake surface and springing off the dead leaves. He stood beneath the deluge like a lost child, heavy-chested with sobs. When the clouds budged and grumbled along and the rain stopped, the lake turned glassy.

He looked down into its dim mirror and recognised, amid the reflection of an azure sky, himself. Or was it his father? He remembered Dorothy talking of the youth Narcissus, who'd died gazing at himself in the water. The closer he looked, the more he saw neither himself nor Michael, but the broken face of a boy. He felt a sudden flash upon his inward eye of the daffodils at Ullswater. It was like the film of flame on a low-burnt fire, as if something had been rekindled. It made him think of the lantern-glow in the window of the Evening Star.

Seized with a sudden passion, he ran back up to the hut and rooted around in his bundle for those dead daffodils from Ullswater. He stripped the weed away from the two remaining bulbs and scampered to the lake's edge that faced across to Dove Cottage. He flung the rags of the dead flowers in the water and crouched down clutching the bulb-shaped hearts. With his fingers he scraped a large hole in the muddy soil by the water's edge and buried the nut-like bulbs close together, sprinkling soil back over them as though covering two tiny coffins. 'Back in the earth and free,' he muttered, 'down to your roots.'

Outside the hut that evening, as a late harvest moon swung low in the sky with its big red-orange face only just out of reach, he stood with Dorothy's journal in his hands, reading it by

the first human being Luke had decided to approach in many weeks, but it felt right as he climbed into the skiff and rowed across the lake.

When he drew near, the owl-impressionist – a scruffy young beggar lad – stopped hooting and hung in silence, perhaps expecting the genuine owl to embarrass itself further by issuing a call of recognition, even attraction. Luke paused, too, and let the boat drift. In this moment of suspension he felt Helm Crag's solemn image carry far into his mind and imprint itself with all its weight. He shook himself and came back to his senses. The lad, he now saw, was Jem, the poor little ragamuffin from Helvellyn. Luke looked at him with the fondness he imagined a father would only normally set aside for a child of his own. Jem didn't reciprocate, but he always was a bold little beggar on Helvellyn.

'That's a good owl,' Luke croaked as he dragged the skiff ashore. He hadn't spoken in weeks. His throat was like tar. Jem stopped hooting and looked up at him.

'I can do a cuckoo an' all,' he said.

'Are you out here on your own? Where's your mother?'

'Dead.'

'Dead? How?'

'Drowned herself in a pond, she did. Dint want me numore. Dint want erself neither.'

Luke tried to hide his horror with a smile.

'Where are you staying?'

'Up by Goody Bridge. Maister took me in but misses isn't back.'

'Where did she go?'

'Off lookin fert maister on Helvellyn. Yesterday.'

'And she didn't come back last night?'

'Nae.'

'How many are there?'

'Six lasses.'

'Six!'

'An' me.'

'What's the family called?'

'Cragg.'

Luke winced at the thought of them all alone there. Jem pursed his lips, in preparation for the next brace of owl hoots, or cuckoo calls.

'Stop!' Luke shouted. Jem's first discernible note tailed off like the dying drone of interrupted bagpipes. 'I want you to do something,' Luke said. 'You do it and I'll fix you and the six Cragg girls some meat supper.' His promise was extravagant, and he could tell Jem knew it. The lad said nothing, but the hooting didn't fire up again. 'On the forest side of Grasmere,' Luke continued, 'is a place called Nettleslack Farm. Ask for it if you can't find it but don't tell a soul why. When you get there look for Sally Nettleslack. Tell her to come back with you straightaway to Goody Bridge, and tell her about Mrs Cragg going missing, but don't mention me. It's not safe. I'll see you both there in a few hours, with supper piping hot.' Jem ran off hooting into the village.

Luke wedged the skiff in a convenient little boathouse at the foot of a large residence on the western shore. He set off to Easedale with a purposeful stride, not really knowing the purpose but clear that he now had to hunt, kill, cook and feed a sizeable animal to a houseful of ravenous half-orphans. His exile alone was over.

# 20

# Wedding Mourning

Dorothy lay in bed trying hard not to think about the past three years alone together with William in Dove Cottage. She tried not to think about the present, the last night of that unique and golden time, because she knew she'd get no sleep at all if she did. And she couldn't bear to consider the future, so she lay suspending her thoughts, in a state of stillness, staring at the ceiling, the effort of which had the eventual effect of sending her to sleep not too many owl-hoots into deepest night.

She woke up in the morning surprised to be feeling so fresh and well, but aware, as she blinked her eyes from sleep and rolled tiny blobs of dried tears between thumb and finger, that she hadn't had time to think about what day it was. Then she remembered and went back into her previous torpid state staring at the ceiling. No physical feelings, no thoughts, no emotions.

After some minutes she began vigorously working at the wedding ring. The 18-carat gold band William had bought in Calais a few months earlier – of which she'd been the custodian – had become stuck in the soft furrow it had made in the skin of her wedding finger and it didn't want to shift, which was fine because she didn't want to shift it, even though she knew that sooner or later she'd have to. She'd been wearing it all night and the top end of the finger was red and strangled, the bottom end carcass-white. She forced the ring to turn and it felt as if it would rip the skin, a pain she felt happy to bear, in fact keen to suffer. It was turning, but she most definitely wasn't ready to take it off. The day was already beginning to feel like a funeral but her one night being married wasn't quite over, even if the secret wearing of a ring meant for another woman was far from the full bridal trousseau she'd dreamt of as a girl. William would have to prise it off her, however.

She lay still and played dead again, wondering whether she might fool the wedding party into thinking that the vicious cold she'd had in London on the way back from France – a result, she imagined, of sea-sickness and travelling in an excessively long-bodied coach with no fewer than twelve passengers in it – was the reason she was in bed and unable to go to the church. She had in fact suffered countless colds and other petty maladies throughout the summer, ever since falling out of the skiff on Grasmere. But what had really knocked her sick had been her dread of the wedding, and that severe concentration of feelings in connection with it that had been building up since William had announced news of it to her back in April. 'Grasmere,' she murmured mournfully. She hadn't seen her beloved Dove Cottage garden for nearly two months. There were so many things and places she missed that she could hardly bear to name in her mind – her walks through Grasmere and Rydale, her swallows, her journal, her poems, so many things and … people. No wonder she was wasting away.

Just before eight he came to her and she jumped up out of the bed to greet him, tearing the ring off her finger and giving it to him with the most passionate embrace and deepest blessing. He took the ring and placed it back on her finger, blessing her fervently in return, and saying 'never, never, never'. They stood together, head touching head, face to face, in silence. She removed the ring again and gave it to him for the last time, and watched him part from her. He didn't turn back, and she heard his footsteps down the stairs and outside. She ran to the window and saw him walking down the avenue towards the church.

William had seen the mess she was in at the beginning of July and had told her she'd turned into some kind of wild Bacchante running into the lake in a frenzy. He'd absolutely forbidden her to mention one name as they left Grasmere for Dover, and she'd been so delirious with the fever the fall from the boat had brought on that she hadn't objected. Besides, as they'd made their way down through England and across to France, he'd linked arms with her more often than ever before, making her feel cherished again. The fear of losing her had perhaps refocused his heart.

Then there'd been the stay in Calais with Annette, and the child, Caroline, who'd issued from that radical coupling ten years before. William had felt a desperate need to see them both, and yet he'd been quite cold when they'd met them at Calais. He'd shown little patience with Annette and paid Caroline scant attention. As for herself, she'd been so emotional during the weeks at Calais, so sensitive, flinching and weeping at everything.

One evening, rather than delight in a walk along the beach – which always made her remember crying the first time she'd seen the sea as a child – she'd been heartbroken to watch little Caroline running along giggling and collecting shells as the sun set. She'd wanted to take Caroline in her arms and bring her back to Grasmere. William said no, Caroline would get all the love she needed right there, beside those roiling waves under that heavenly sky. He'd closed his mind and heart to Caroline. Mary was to be the mother of his children. But Dorothy couldn't detach herself so easily, and her pity for poor, innocent Caroline had brought many tears. She'd hoped Caroline would remember that beautiful evening and cherish the memory, even if it turned out to be her only memory of her father.

Yet despite all the tears and pain, she and William had achieved an intimacy that had felt as unbreakable by the time they'd returned to England as it had been when they'd first moved into Dove Cottage four years before. An unbreakable intimacy. He was getting *married*! She was horror-struck at the duplicity, the secrecy, the adultery of it. Poor Mary. How could they do it? How could *she* do it?

'Gracious!' she cried through the closed window. 'I must stop this now. This is the morning it must be broken.'

Around nine she was still there, watching and waiting, but she became distracted and fell into a reverie, during which the autumnal scene outside became dominated by the figure of a man walking from a distance towards the house, but she couldn't identify him. He had William's gait and build, but it wasn't William. And he was looking right up at her, smiling and reaching his arms out to her. But ... was he a ghost? She reached her hand out to him and it smashed through the glass, cutting her on the wrist. She stretched her bleeding arm out to him but felt nothing receive it. The spectre was gone.

'Dorothy!' somebody cried out. 'What are you doing? You'll fall. Dorothy!'

It was too late. The life together alone, the intimacy, the privacy, the poetry. For a moment everything was suspended – a silent, respectful interval between one life and another. Then she threw herself onto the bed and lay again in stillness, not hearing, not seeing, not feeling anything.

She could hear footsteps. She jumped onto her feet and found herself running down the stairs and outside, faster than ever into his arms, weeping on his breast. She was so beside herself that he had to carry her across the threshold.

# Part Three

Part Three

# 21

# Discovery

Sally liked to think she was the type to fold up her feelings, put them out of the way and get on with her toil, not quit the churn and pound her way down into the village reprimanding herself. They should never have gone to the Ambleside tup show. No longer would they salve their Roman-nosed flock by smearing a gallon of tar and sixteen pounds of rotten butter all over them to kill off the keds and ticks and other Herdwick infesters. No more would they release the rams into the meadow and watch the ritual of fifty-foot run-ups, leaps, clashes of skulls and unconscionable headaches, all before they were loosed on the ewes. The Nettleslacks had answered the tinkling call of the market bell with nothing, and had haunted the show like phantoms, Nance dribbling throughout and bearing the increasingly ironic grin of a collie stiffened by palsy. They'd returned with nothing apart from dejection. Jack had complained on the way back of a splitting headache, perhaps in sympathy with the rams, but probably, Sally had suspected, because she'd barked at him for pestering her to go with him to a bull-baiting.

As she paced into Grasmere she listed on her fingers those who might know the whereabouts of the name on her lips – farmers, shepherds, hired hands, men in inns searching for hope inside tankards, butcher with seven sons (three of whom had married the gossipiest girls in the vale and were beginning to regret it); blacksmith and joiner, grocer and tailor, shoemaker, miller, victuallers, schoolmaster and wheelwright, draper and maltster, lord of the manor, poet and sister. The list spanned more than three dozen fingers, and Sally spent the short, long-shadowed day ticking off as many of her digits several times as she could manage.

By evening – or the creeping façade that darkness superimposed on late-autumn afternoons, turning four o'clock into dead of night and reshaping straight-spined Grasmerians into hunchbacks round fires, lighting candles in nooks – her spirits and legs had faltered. She'd all but given up hope when, near the head of the lake on the western side, she saw, in a garden of a house, in a chair, in his shirt-sleeves, a man. With hoary locks sprouting from a three-cornered hat whose front brim brought to mind the side view of a mince pie, his face was gazing up at the canoe-shaped moon as though he were bronzing – or silvering – himself in it.

'Beg pardon, sir, I'm looking—'

'What the? Who's there?' the man spluttered, he and his chair collapsing and his shin receiving a scalding of tea. 'Ow! Ow! Oo! Oo!' The malleable and generously fleshed face he wore set off in three directions of revived pleasure, however, when he saw Sally. 'Good morning,' he said. 'Oh do forgive me, good evening. Or should I say good night? But we've only just met. Hahaha! Ow! Ow!' He bent over his leg and proceeded to stroke his shin.

'I'm looking for a man, sir,' she said, fixing him straight between the eyes and hoping she wouldn't be misinterpreted.

'Hahaha! Now there's a thing. I'm faithful to my flower-bed at night, and my marital bed in the day. Hahaha!'

Before she could back away she found herself planted on the recuperated chair, sampling gingerbread, being offered a cup of tea, and moon-bathing. 'D'you sit here every night?' she asked, wearing down the edges of the gingerbread with rodent tenacity.

'Every night ... well, most... well, from time to time ... I suppose... these days,' he concluded with a sigh that issued a cloud of melancholy breath into the November air. 'There isn't so much going on at this time of year. It's more to keep them company.'

'Who?'

'Why, my dear, you must think me a lunatic sitting here under the moon. I do my gardening at night, you see – even though it is only mid-evening as we speak. It all happens among the shadows. See this,' he said, pointing to a yellow, rose-like flower, 'the evening primrose. It waits until the sun is down before it opens, and feeds on the moonlight. It is shaped like a crucifix in its centre. It brings God to me as I sit here at night. That quiet, still presence in the dark that a Quaker seeks, a silence pure enough that one can almost hear the grass grow.'

Sally shivered and wrapped her only shawl tighter round her shoulders. 'Here,' said the gentleman standing up, 'let me get you one of my wife's old shawls. Nothing like good, thick sheep's wool in this weather.' Before she'd had a chance to say thank you kindly but she really must be going, the mad but lovable old man had scuttled off indoors in search of a shawl. He returned a minute later looking dispirited.

'Please take this,' he said, handing her a woollen shawl. 'She was wearing it the day she died. It is a treasurable memento, and it still bears her unique scent, but it really would be madness for me to keep it to myself, especially now that I can hear the old dame insisting I give it to you – if you'll have it, that is.'

Sally put it on, sad to think she was taking a thing so prized but unable to refuse. 'Thankyou kindly, sir, but I—'

'Of course we must stick to the wool, now more than ever,' he said with sudden gravity.

'Stick tut wool, sir?'

'The cotton revolution must not be allowed to succeed. Our great country transports forty thousand African negroes a year to the cotton plantations of America. We must all boycott cotton and stick to wool. The slave trade is in its death throes, abolition is near at hand, I'm sure of it. But now more than ever we must resist cotton. Here, do have your cup of tea.'

Sally duly took and sipped the tea, and duly spat it back into the cup.

'Oh dear, I forgot to say. Evening primrose tea. Soothes me into a drowsy peacefulness that is perfect for a night's – or should I say day's – sleep. Better even than camomile or cottonmilk. But it is an acquired taste. I also eat the roots and leaves, they go well with a glass of wine. Now do you think me mad? I expect not, hahaha!'

Sally kept her counsel.

'Ah, maybe you do,' he continued, rambling away again. 'Oh well. The divine pleasures of lunacy. Give me snug hearth-rugs, closed shutters, curtains billowing over carpets while the wind and rain rage throughout the vale. Where will you find me? No, not indoors but out here. Hahaha! It used to drive my poor wife cuckoo. So you see, we were a pair of lunatics. Hahaha! But what,' he finally asked, a concerned frown blotting out his grin, 'brings you abroad at this time? A man, you say?'

Sally delivered a detailed description. She'd delivered it so often that day that it had become a portrait painted with cruel but accurate brushstrokes that she felt captured the subject perfectly.

'Hmm,' said the gentleman, caressing his left ear lobe with thumb and forefinger. 'I can't say I spend much time watching people come and go in Grasmere, but one place I do observe is the lake – you can see from up here how good a view I have.' Sally looked round and took in the lake, gleaming in the moonlight. 'And when one observes things in detail, like with my flowers, well, one gets to see things. Do you see that little stone hut on the island? Animals used to be kept in it, but now gentlefolk go there on picnic excursions occasionally in the summer. Otherwise it's deserted. Or at least, it was.'

Sally screwed up her eyes the way she imagined Lord Nelson might survey the horizon for the French navy. 'I see no hut,' she said.

'Well it is rather hidden, which I imagine is why he likes it. I've seen him making fires. Wild and curious fellow. Bit of a recluse, I'd say. Poet, perhaps – one tends to get them a lot round here, like the red squirrels. Or maybe he's a Quaker like me.

'Quaker? What's one of them?'

'There are many of us about, my dear. We believe God does not speak to us through those splendidly dressed churchmen we prop up with our tithes, but directly to us, ordinary individuals simply dressed. It's a radical view but Lakeland is full of madcap non-conformists – it's probably the wind through those wild fells. Now your friend down there sits many an evening looking up into the stars, at worship I shouldn't wonder, in his own al-fresco meeting-house. I quite envy the fellow. Does that sound like him, my dear?'

It was enough confirmation for Sally to know that a madcap non-conformist of a wild and curious nature was on the island. 'Ay, that'll be him.'

'What is he doing there?'

'Don't know, sir. He should be up on Helvellyn building a wall. Haven't seen him in ages. But there were a murder, month or so back. Fella got tipped off the top.'

'You think your man might be on the run? In hiding?'

'Some folk round here says he did it. But Nae. Not him. He wunt do that. You won't tell no one you've seen him, mind, will you, sir?'

'Trust me,' he replied gravely. 'I won't breathe a word. But take care.'

'Ay.' She turned to leave, offering to bring him some of her own gingerbread at a more convenient moment by way of thanks.

The gentleman's features erupted with delight. 'Oh you must, my dear,' he roared, taking her hand. 'The name is Lea. Doctor Lea. We shall compare recipes – secretly of course. We could even open our own little gingerbread shop right next to the village school. Ha ha ha! Now,' he added with a moon-eclipsing frown, 'I'd let you use my little boat, but alas, well, it's been stolen ... or gone missing at any rate ... like my beloved son,' he said, exhaling another cloud of melancholy. 'I normally leave it down at the boathouse below here on the edge of the lake, but for some reason I left it on the far side when I used it last. Never mind. It was full of leaks anyway. I used to go fishing in it when I was younger. Liked to think I was a bit of a hunter myself, heh heh. The only hunting I do now is for my spectacles.' He'd cheered up, but clouded over again before Sally could get a word in. 'I named the boat after my son, you know. Georgie. He went away to sea and I believe the ship sank with the loss of many lives. Ah well. Perhaps some kind soul further round the lake might lend you a bark. Good luck, my dear, and do come back. And remember, wear wool. Oh my, I almost forgot. Here, take this. Quaker's Black Drop. You might need it.' He handed her a small glass bottle filled with a ruby-coloured liquid.

She made her way down to the lake's edge and found Doctor Lea's boat exactly where he'd said it wouldn't be. She pushed the boat out in the pitch dark, propelled herself across the lake and scraped ashore. As she crept up the bank of the island and tiptoed through the bushes and trees, she suddenly panicked at the thought that the man in the hut was not Luke but some salivating cut-throat – or worse, a dangerously over-sensitive poet.

The ashen moonlight revealed no recumbent body inside the hut. As Sally ferreted around she came across a bundle containing a white net bag and two ragged books, both of which looked as though they'd been immersed in water and dried out. One was entitled *Lyrical Ballads* and the other was a notebook or private journal of some sort. In normal circumstances Sally liked to think she wasn't the type, but she skimmed through the journal anyway, and with intense interest. The writing was scrawled and blotchy, and the ink had run, but she managed to read quite clearly a recent entry ending with the words, *Everything and everyone must be sacrificed for William – including Mary, including myself ... and Luke!*

Her heart chugged with anger, jealousy and hurt. Who did that Wudswuth woman-body think she was?

He'd been here but he'd gone, and he could be anywhere now. She had to give up the search and get back to her ailing father. She dumped the two books in the white net bag, ran back down to the skiff and pushed it out into the icy black water. So icy was the air, too, that she wondered whether it might even snow. She rowed back to the east shore of the lake. The skiff scraped ashore and she jumped out and ran through the dark woods and fields in the direction of home.

The snow was coming down heavier. Cold pinched at her but when she saw the silhouette of the snow-capped steeple of St Oswald's she knew there was only half a mile to go. The moon had lost its way behind snow-clouds but the ground was illuminated by the whiteness settling on it.

Only a quarter of a mile now, but a bitter one up towards the forest side. Eventually the lights of the Swan came into view. She peered through the window. Hardly a soul about. She stepped in and told Goan Jack was sick and that she needed rum. She stood by the fire and worried her heart into a froth that he'd gone forever, that she was too late. For both of them.

'There you are!' declared a familiar voice behind her. She turned, relieved, thinking it was him at last.

It was Lance.

With the slaughtered beast drooping and dripping over his shoulders he crossed paths with a carriage on his way to Goody Bridge, but the fine-looking lady inside, with a red, full-lipped mouth and wearing a gargantuan ostrich plume in her hair, didn't look at him so much as straight through him. Luke hoped he'd given her the impression, with a nod and a contrived nonchalance, that the corpse on his back was his own and that he did this kind of thing pretty much every day. He reached Goody Bridge and Cragg's cottage. Six grim girls stared through a window at him, the youngest beginning to weep at the sight of the bearded, bloodied ogre with woollen shoulders at the door.

He brought Cragg's cottage back to life by winding up the clock, scalding the milk, milking the cow, raiding the peat-stack, picking the potatoes, and roasting the lamb. The Cragg children, fed and no longer fed up, became playful. The hours passed, evening swallowed up the afternoon and it started snowing. Luke was unsettled at the thought of having sent Jem out into a gathering blizzard. Finally, the front door creaked open and snowflakes swirled through the cottage. A diminutive white monster crunched across the floor to the peat fire crusty with frost. Luke, who was crouching by the fire taunting the flaming ashes with a stick, cried out with relief.

'Jem! Are you all right? Did you see her? Did you ask her to come?' Jem needed a minute to defrost his voice and let the fire burn the life back into his palms. He answered all Luke's questions with a glum shake of the head. Luke stood up and looked out of the door at a sky that was grey-washed with snowfall. 'Then you'll have to look after the girls while I go and get her.'

Jem broke through his iced-up throat. 'There was a dog whinin' and whimperin' its head off. Right din, twas.'

'Did you not see Jack, the statesman?'

'Him as sleeps all day?'

'Sleeps?'

'Ay. Dog took me to him. Couldn't wek him.'

'What about Sally? Was she not there?'

Jem shook his head and looked around. 'Where's that supper?' Luke handed it to him and he went about it with the greedy enthusiasm of Christmas morning. 'Oh, ay,' he said after a few minutes, cheeks ballooning with lamb and potatoes, 'there was someone else went past me. On his way tut farm I reckon, but I was on me way back by then.'

'Did you see what he looked like?'

'Nae, snow'd come on by then.'

Luke busied himself dressing for a blizzard and fearing the worst, that Vipond was on his scent and would be lying in wait at Nettleslack Farm. The Cragg girls huddled round Jem as though he'd been appointed substitute father, and Jem insisted to Luke that he could cope while he was gone. Luke shut the door behind him and tried to order his priorities. Was it better to go to Nettleslack Farm first, since Jack was clearly unwell? Or should he set off towards Helvellyn in search of Cragg's wife Elizabeth? Or should he head for Grasmere village, where Sally might have gone to find a doctor for Jack? He set off into the snow.

The huntsman of a hound trail would have had cause to stop and scratch his head at the brilliant way his quarry had confused him by leaving snow-prints leading in countless directions away from Goody Bridge. One set went north as if in the direction of Dunmail Raise, Wythburn and Helvellyn, but the prints looked as though they'd doubled back on themselves; another set headed south towards Grasmere village, but they also appeared to have reversed; while a third set headed east in the direction of the forest side. This set looked freshest and cut the deepest imprint in the snow, suggesting feet having stamped in frustration.

Nettleslack Farm emerged ahead dimly, surviving the four o'clock blackout on one taper. Luke opened the door and crept through the firehouse to Jack's chamber. His eyes fell upon a poignant, almost sacred, tableau which featured Sally, complete with undomesticated hair, gazing down on Jack, who was gazing back up at her pathetically, while Nance looked on with the pious serenity of a nativity-scene cow. Dear Sally, he thought. She'd become like a sister to him, and he must love her like a brother – not guarding her jealously the way William did with Dorothy but cherishing her. He then noticed, in the shadow of the corner of the room, a hand, swishing a long stick, and two fiery eyes.

Jinnyspinner swished his stick out of the room as if scouring the floor for leeches. Luke looked across at Jack, shocked at the sight of him. He'd undergone some form of rejuvenation, to the young blade Luke imagined he'd been innumerable decades before. He hardly recognised him. Jack looked across at Luke, who felt he'd aged dramatically when he first saw himself in the reflection of the lake. Jack appeared not to recognise him straightaway. The moment of adjustment to the change – Jack looking younger, Luke looking older – left a pause in the air, as if between symphonic movements. Nance's tail wagged at a tempo likely to mark the new movement *allegro con brio*.

'Ahreet!' croaked Jack from the bed.

'Well you look all right, Jack,' said Luke. The old man was grinning.

'Oh ay. Right as Burradale rain. I've bin slorping poddish and I've had some of that magical stuff of our Sally's.'

'Gingerbread?' asked Luke turning to Sally. He felt a cool breeze from her eyes.

'Bit starker than my gingerbread, is that,' Sally said, observing Jack's absurd smirk.

'Ay! I've never felt so damn marvlus.'

'Had a pint or two?' Luke tried again.

'Nae. When I'm neudled I dance, and kiss the blummin village, then I blub away for't wife who went before her time, and sing sad tunes about our Jackie lost at sea. And them as don't blub with me gets a thump in the chops, I tell thee.'

'So what's ailing you?' Luke asked, trying hard not to accuse Jack directly of malingering. The reply was delivered via a burst of laugh-spittle.

'Are you bloody daft, lad? Can't you see? I've got the ague. I'm on me last legs.'

'Who's to doubt him?' said Sally to Luke. 'He's been abed with a headache ever since the tup show. Never been like this before, have you Fadder?'

'Never, lass, never. I feel so clearedded, and so tranquil-like in here,' he said, striking his soul. 'It's like I'm walking with God, never mind with me dog.' Nance tilted her head, a gesture which captured the general feeling of mystification. 'So I don't want no blubbin from thee when I'm gan.'

Sally rolled her eyes and her sleeves and brushed past Luke into the downhouse. Jack went grave, his voice withdrawing to a whisper.

'Sit here, Luke, right up by't bed. Ay, that's it. I've bin wanting to talk to thee. I sent Sally out searching everywhere for thee. We're in trouble, and trouble opens folks' hearts.'

'What kind of trouble?' Luke asked, fully aware of three kinds of trouble he was already in – pursuing an absconding mother in a blizzard, telling a family of six their father was dead, fleeing a gang of villains out to hang him for murder, although the last one was sheer paranoia ... hopefully.

'I haven't got long. I'll be dead in two shakes of a lamb's tail so I'll tell it short and blunt,' said Jack, which Luke imagined was a first for a yarn-prone Grasmere patriarch.

'You'll go on forever,' said Luke.

'I don't want to! I must be three-score and ten.'

Luke sighed. 'Michael must have been about that age.'

'Eh? Oh, ay, God rest his bones.' He paused. 'That's one of the things I wanted to speak about. But first, listen up good, lad. The swindler has got his eye on our Sally, and once I'm gone he'll have his mucky hands on this farm.' Luke had thought Sally's friend was a fine gentleman, not a swindler. He put the remark down to irrational paternal jealousy. 'I can't say a thing to her, mind,' Jack carried on. 'Daren't. She'll just say it's her life and I might get me own way now after nagging her all year to get married.'

'Married? You don't think…?'

'I do. That's why we're in trouble. This farm and this land belongs to Nettleslacks. Has done for hundreds of years. Just like your crowd, the Greenheads. Our ancestors drove the sticky-fingered Scotch back up north in return for this land. But common folk like us don't really own land, we rent it from rich folk like Unthank. So when I pop me clogs it's Unthank's land if anybody's – unless you-know-who gets his hands on it.'

'Who?'

'The swindler!' Jack shouted.

'But who is the swindler?' Luke shouted back.

'Bluddy Vipond, whoodyeh think?'

'Vipond!' Luke yelped, sick at the thought.

'Ay! That's what I'm tryin' to tell thee. But I can't stoppim, cos I'm dyin.'

'You're not dying!' Luke roared. Sally reappeared. Silence fell. Sally looked at them both suspiciously, then disappeared again.

'He's a snake,' Jack continued. 'Says you killed that Cragg feller an all. Did you?'

'No,' replied Luke calmly, his paranoia having turned into fact. 'He did it.'

'Aha, that's what I reckoned. Good. Wiv got summut on him now. We have to get to Unthank. He detests Vipond, every bugger knows that.'

'But he's Unthank's estate manager.'

'Ay, and that's a mystery, cos they hate each other's guts. If Unthank knew the snake had knocked his master waller off the cliff he'd have it in ferim, he would. So we get to Unthank – which isn't easy cos he spends all his time in London – or we get to Vipond. Well you do, any road.'

'Get to him?' asked Luke, unable to avoid the fantasy of a gravestone bearing the inscription *Here Lies Lance Vipond, 17— to November 1802. He Gotteth His Comeuppance.*

'Presarve us O! Talk to him,' said Jack. 'Menace him. Don't

let the bugger chase you tut gallows, chase him back. And mek sure our Sally knows what a snake he is.'

'I'll do it,' said Luke. 'I've got a few things to sort out with him already. Like what happened to my mother.' Jack went quiet, stiff and pale, not dissimilar to a corpse. Perhaps it wasn't attention-seeking malingering after all, Luke thought. Jack came back to life, and spoke in a voice sombre enough to suit the reading of his own eulogy.

'It's a funny thing, lad. Thy mudder's jus' what I wanted to talk to thee about. And I wunt be at all surprised if these is me last words.'

Luke drew closer, not believing they would be Jack's last words but hanging on them anyway, just in case.

'Remember I told thee I never knew what happened to Isabel? Well, that wunt the full story, lad, or you might say, twas a bit of a lie. I dint think you could tek it. But you've got a tough Greenhead heart, I can see that now, just like Michael. He never give up. Never!' Luke made a quick mental calculation of the numerous times he'd given up on things in his life. 'And that's why I'm telling you now,' Jack continued, 'so you never give up.'

The statesman drew a breath. 'Isabel were a strong 'un, Lord knows, but once Michael'd popped his clogs it was too much for her. She stuck it out for a good few years, mind, but then her head went daft.'

Luke winced.

'I know it hurts to hear that, lad. Folk felt right sorry for her, but she was barmy. Her heart was broke and her head gone soft. Some local lads picked on her. Younguns, like. Laal swines got a good sock in the chops when I caught up with them, mind. Heheh, made them squawk like capons, I did.'

Luke felt strangely soothed by the image of Jack thumping the little swines.

'But there were one swine bigger than any other.' These were the words Luke really began to hang on, and the way Jack was getting into his narrative stride, sitting up straight and fixing his eyes on him, it didn't look as if they were going to be his last. 'Poor Isabel got afraid to live alone, see, and the swine told her he'd look after her if she went to live as his housekeeper. Treated her meaner than those younguns ever could. Made her work in the garden scaring off rooks. Didn't feed her scarce nowt, so folk say. She ran away in the end, just wandered off one day, but not before the swine'd sold the Evening Star. The cottage was knocked down and land ploughed over and that were it. Bad tidings, lad, I know, but remember thy folks loved thee till the end.'

'Who was it?' snarled Luke. 'Vipond?'

'Nae, nottim. Now,' the supposedly dying statesman said hoisting himself up onto his elbows, 'I don't want thee rampaging round Grasmere getting thy own back. Promise me, in Michael and Isabel's name, you'll go after what's right, not what's revenge. It's an evil thing, anger. Eats away at a man. I ranted at the bloody world when we lost our Jackie. But I had to let him go. Let go of all that rage. And ole Michael were sad right enough when you never come back, but not angry. He loved thee, they both did.' Luke stood up biting his lip with grief and anger, staring at the ceiling and wondering how on earth he could follow the old man's advice and not go after the swine, whoever it was.

'Here's another thing,' said Jack, lifting an arm to Luke. 'It's bin like having me own son again to see thy face around the farm these past six months.' Luke turned and held his hand. 'But I won't lie quiet when my time comes – and neither will the whole blinkin Greenhead tribe, God restum – if you walk outtta here with them big shepherd's fists scrunched up and ready.' Jack squeezed Luke's big shepherd's fist. 'There's bin enough of that in the family already, d'you hear me? Enough!' Jack no longer looked rejuvenated, and he shrank back down into his bed.

Luke let go of the withered hand and walked over to the window. He felt an overwhelming urge to hunt down both the snake and the swine and point them roughly in the direction he'd sent Kears that day in London – viz., to hell. But he also wondered what exactly there'd been enough of in the family already. Revenge? Fighting? Killing? And which family did Jack mean? Greenhead or Nettleslack? He turned round with several questions on his lips. Infuriatingly, Jack had uttered his last words after all – for the time being, at any rate – and fallen into such a profound sleep that not even a rope for the rescuing of a cragfast ewe would drag him out of it.

# 23

## Found and Lost

It was beginning to look as if Jack might one day join the great Grasmere poet William Wordsworth in immortality, not on poetic merit but because, despite all assurances of the ague, it appeared he wasn't going to die, even now at three-score-and-ten and more or whatever he was. As he rose from irretrievable sleep and slid back down again, Luke and Sally swung the emotional pendulum between heartbreak and vexation. The only change in Jack during this bedside era was the gradual disappearance of his odd, intoxicated grin.

When at one point he was awake, and Sally wasn't around, and the unmistakable signs of life issued from the patient in the form of blustery flatulence, Luke decided to push patiently for answers. 'Jack,' he whispered. No answer. 'JACK!'

'Uh? Eh?' The statesman snapped back to life, opened his eyes wide and looked at him with dread.

'Jack,' repeated Luke. 'Enough what in the family?'

'Uh?'

'You said enough of that in the family already. What?'

Jack's eyes glistened and a faint smile wafted through his barley-stubble beard. Clearly it wasn't too late for an over-embroidered yarn, deathbed or not. He sat up. 'Ole Michael and me,' he began, 'we'd both been losing yowes one after tuther for weeks on end. This was going back donkey's years now. Every time we looked another was gone, and't sound of copper bells was getting scarcer across the vale. We took it in turns to watch the flocks at night, but dint see owt. It was getting cold as well, and the fells was iced o'er. One day there was a lot of snow and Michael said that would help – we'd soon spot a hoof-track on snowy ground – so we scraffled up right high and waited long intut night. We raked around and dint see no tracks but we heard bleating. Right up there in the crags. We came back down sharpish cos of the cold, and next day we set off again up the fell. This time twas a bright, bonny day and all't snow'd melted away.

'When we got tut fell top, we made our way to an edge that looks straight down a drop of crags. We saw a ledge Michael knew had got yowes in trouble over't years – some falling to their deaths. We followed a yard-wide track down tut ledge and saw footprints. Men's footprints. And they looked new. I says to Michael, "Mebby we should go back and get a gun?" He turned to me. "Nae!" says he, "we have to face whatever it is now, Jack." He was a brave man.

'The futher we went the louder the bleating got. Then the track turned all of a sudden tut right, and we saw a hole in the crags and down on a ledge, trapped on three sides by't crags and on tudder by a low wall, was eight yowes. We groped our way down and stood there with 'em, all bleating loud with panic. After a few minutes loose slates and stones started falling. Some bugger was climbing down intut hole by a rope. He hadn't seen us, mind, and when he landed we rushed him two genst one, and the sheep ran about bleating their heads off while we collared him tut ground. The yowes went into a right flap and bashed intut wall, breaking through it, and then they went – every last one toppled down't crags, fifty feet or more, smashing themselves to bits.

'Then the rope started tugging from above. The sheep-stealer's mates were trying to pull him up again, but the rope had snagged, and after a while the tugging stopped. We yanked the bugger back down. Michael, well, he were in a right rage, and without a second to think about the rightness of it, he pushed the villain through't broken wall the way the yowes had gone, and he fell the same fifty feet or so, and was bashed to bits just like our Herdwicks. When we got down to Grasmere we told folk we'd got our man but he'd fallen in a struggle, and none doubted it. But I knew he hadn't, God fugive me, and by yeck ole Michael knew he hadn't. So you see, Luke, there's guilt and shame runs along every man's heart if you cut deep enough.'

The blizzard had tired of waiting, and the farmhouse door blew open with a devilish howl. Forbidden the time to stand around shocked to the core at what he'd just heard about Michael, Luke announced his abrupt exit, the same way he had when Jack had given the abridged version of Michael and Isabel's demise. He hurled Jack's hodden grey fleece over his own fustian frock coat, donned the statesman's rabbit-skin hat whether he permitted it or not, threw some brusque words over his shoulder about when he'd be back and slammed the blizzard-blown door behind him.

The heat of his emotions could have boiled and then reduced an entire pan of pickled plums. He had to calm down, not think about his paragon of a father ending up a miserable killer just like his son had, and imagine he was a distraught mother of six, desperate to find her husband in the fells. Which way would Elizabeth Cragg have gone? After much lip-chewing, he decided he had no idea. He was keener to die alone in a blizzard himself than go into Grasmere and seek help, thereby letting Vipond know he was abroad. But he couldn't let those girls go motherless as well as fatherless. And what to do with Jem?

It was still well before noon when he reached the Swan and spotted the scarlet tentacles of its fire. Inside, as he warmed his hands and wondered who on earth he could persuade to run with him up onto Helvellyn in thick snow, a voice he knew well rang out.

'Chief!'

Gass was sitting at a table, just like the first time Luke had seen him, and next to him sat Weightman. Vipond had starved the two wallers so thin he imagined their bony arms chafing against the cold rock as they toiled, but their hearts were stout and they needed asking only once to help with the search. The three comrades stuck together for the six-mile walk to Wythburn, agreeing to split up once they were through the Swirls and at the start of the wall.

'It was bitter, chief, bitter,' said Gass as they marched up Dunmail Raise. 'We only came down last week.'

'Last week?' said Luke. 'It's winter! Who was in charge of the walling?'

'Yer man himself,' said Gass. 'Bet you can't believe it.'

'Unthank?'

'Not him, he's down in London. Vipond. He had to, there's so few of us left. Mind you, see young Weightman here going at it with those big through-stones,' he cried, patting Weightman on the back and drawing a rare smile from the farm-hand. 'But Vipond's like he's got something more to live for these days.' Luke worried that the something more to live for wore hair of Titian red.

The long drag to the top edge of the Swirls brought them to the first rood they'd done half a year earlier. The wind howled through the wall, lichens had laid their green felt over the stones, and mosses that fed ivy and ferns had made home in the cracks.

Higher uphill it had become a shelter not only for sheep, but for birds and squirrels. Rabbits scampered in and out of the gaps, toying with the departed Cragg's derelict traps.

The three men spread out, and Luke warned his fellow rescuers to take care scouring the blades of crag that looked deceptively benign beneath the whiteout. Half an hour later a shout echoed out from Weightman, who was waving his arms over on the screes below Swirl Crags.

'Over here!'

Luke made his way across, and as he approached Weightman and Gass he could make out a shape in their midst, a ghostly mound of snow that looked like a human figure hunched on its knees on the ground, back arched and hands clasped before it in prayer. Luke wiped the snow off the top of the mound, which revealed a human head and frozen long brown hair. He looked in awe at the snow-sculpted spire of clasped hands and imagined the prayer she might have uttered. That God might have her children looked after, fed, loved. That their estranged father might return home, so long overdue. That she be granted a miracle and allowed to survive, purely for the children's sake. He covered the body with Jack's hodden grey fleece.

Gass and Weightman set off back down for a sled on which to carry the body, and Luke made for Easedale, wondering what to say to the girls, whether his own mother had died that way, and why in God's name Jack had hidden so much from him? It had stopped snowing by the time he reached Goody Bridge, and the mid-afternoon sun was melting the ground. He squinted up at Churnmilk Force, glittering like tinsel, and he could hear it bickering down the valley into the beck. At Cragg's cottage the door was swinging open. The wind must have done it again. Why on earth didn't Jem close it, he thought crossly. Wild and bad men were known to pass through the vale, and those icy gusts would put out the fire Jem had promised to keep alight. He'd have to bar the door firmly on the inside, take charge again. He stamped through the doorway, slapped the snow off his shoulders and headed for the fire. It was out. He looked round. They were gone.

# 24

## Genesis

He ran back out of Cragg's cottage, leaving the door swinging open, and headed back through Grasmere towards Nettleslack Farm. He dared not imagine what had happened to them, but Sally would know what to do. At best, Jem had taken them out to play in the snow as a treat. At worst, no, he couldn't bear to consider it. He blamed himself, for trusting him, and for thinking he could act more grown up than he was.

Unmelted snow stuck to the iron caulkers nailed to the soles of his clogs, turning his feet into snow-clad sleds and making the mile and a bit across from Easedale to Nettleslack Farm last twice as long, and feature slips, slides, skids and stumbles that bruised both knees and both buttocks. Blessed relief came, however, on sight of Nettleslack Farm, garlanded in the twilight with seven giggling children running round the yard playing tig. Jem stood among them, looking like a happy little lad for the first time.

'Jem!' he hallooed, trying to sound cheerful despite his anger, frustration and considerable bruising. A pout usurped Jem's smile.

'Dint you trust me to tek care of them, then?'

'Of course I...' he couldn't finish the lie. 'Why did you bring them here?'

'Miss Sally came and got us. Whydyer think? Said we'd be better off with her. Said her fadder wanted to hear't noise of bairns about the place again one last time.'

Luke smiled. 'Well, you carry on, and make as much racket as you want.'

Inside, all was mysteriously quiet. Luke creaked open the door to Jack's room and Sally intercepted him on her way out. Before he'd had the chance to upbraid her for giving him the fright of his life by kidnapping the Cragg girls, Sally dealt him a look that he'd not seen on that particular face before, even though he'd seen it many times on others, particularly at Alexandria. A look of death. He was pleased. Not for Sally, or for Jack, but that the event had at last come. He hadn't wished anyone would drop down dead – apart from William Wordsworth, and Vipond, of course, and, the more he thought about it, many, many others who'd thwarted him over the years, but otherwise nobody – yet if they were going to do it, then they should get on with it. A death should be allowed to enact its life-changing dramas.

Luke reflected – as he and Sally covered the corpse with Dr Lea's dead wife's shawl and Jack's hat, the second corpse he'd covered that day – on Isabel's madness after the death of that sinner, officially not beatified after all. He wondered whether Sally might also be showing signs of a grief-induced madness. She looked straight through him, her ears were deaf to him, and such was her wistfulness – in which she poeticised the life of

Jack through misty eyes and tear-swollen lips – that she risked infecting the dead statesman with a mild form of apotheosis.

'He were a quiet, thinkin' type,' she snuffled. 'Man of God. I remember many a Sabbath he'd lie in the meadows and hark at the church bells, look out on the woods and vales, not saying owt – he wasn't much of a talker was Fadder – but he'd be thumbin' through his Bible. "I walk with my dog and I walk with my God," he used to say.'

The Jack Nettleslack of an hour after his death bore no relation beyond the name, as far as Luke could tell, to the one of an hour beforehand. She said he was a powerful singer as well as a devout man, which was the first Luke had heard of it, and that he might well have become a great psalmist if he'd lived longer and his talents had been recognised by the church establishment. On closer scrutiny of his Bible studies, Luke identified from Sally that Jack wasn't a Bible-thumber in the zealous sense, otherwise he would have been nodding over his Bible in church rather than lying in the meadows on the Sabbath. But he used to list on blank pages at the end of Genesis the names and ages of his own forebears, going back certainly as far as the flood – not Noah's Flood, Sally pointed out, but Greet-Greet-Greet Grandad Jack's night of diluvian rainfall back in the Seventeenundreds, which famously penetrated the farm's roof and ruined all the Nettleslack wrestling belts.

'Here, tek a look,' said Sally, holding out the very pages proudly. Sure enough, Jack had written, with what looked like a leaden sheep-marking stick, a parallel Genesis along the margins of his King James: '… These be the genrations of Lanslot: Lanslot were anundred year old, and begat Lanslot two year after't flood: And Lanslot lived after he begat Lanslot five and eighty year, and begat sons and dotters …' and so on. Only when Luke got to the end of the long line, into the generation of the present 'Lancelot (Jack) Nettleslack' – who was now, Luke remembered, in the past himself – did a word catch his eye. It stood faintly alongside Jack's. The word was 'in'.

That night Jack, Sally, Luke and Nance slept soundly. Jack, of course, was dead in his bed, and Nance had lost the will to live at the end of it. Sally was temporarily mad, and so exhausted that she was also dead to the world. As for Luke, it was the first time he'd slept in the grainstore in many a month, and the mattress Sally had once plucked a hen to make for him felt voluptuous. The only other guests, Cragg's six children and Jem, continued to do just as Luke had suggested they do when he arrived, make as much racket as they wanted. No one cared – the rest of the house was either permanently asleep or temporarily deceased.

Luke woke up thinking about Jack. Sadness had entered the grainstore and cuddled up to his heart while he was asleep. What would Sally do without the old man? They were both orphans now, just like the Cragg children and Jem, except not so young and so tragically orphaned as them. He remembered that they still didn't know about either parent's fate, and he dreaded having to break it to them. He picked up Jack's Bible, which he'd been flicking through in bed. He returned to the Nettleslack Genesis, and to that mysterious word 'in'. He made a decision.

He quit the grainstore and crossed the farmhouse threshold. Sally was feeding the girls turnip bread. She seemed cheerful, and Luke wondered whether she'd already reached a new stage of her grief, the first sighs of sorrow being tempered with the first sighs of relief.

'I'm going to fetch the parson,' Luke said, fantasising that Sally's turnip bread was roast goose in gooseberry sauce. Sally looked round wide-eyed at him, as though in terror. It was better than looking straight through him, but he wondered if she was still showing the madness of grief. 'For Jack,' he said, adding in a whisper, 'and for Elizabeth Cragg. You did well to bring them here,' he continued, having changed his tune, 'but they can't stay, especially now Jack is—'

'Dead?' she suggested, her face quivering.

*To Wendy,*

"A rich, humorous and refreshingly individual novel in the sublime Lakeland setting that inspired a generation of British poets. A terrific read!"

"The struggling rural poor, the still-feudal lords, the power of past quarrels – all are vivid and haunting."

"A lovely novel with a beautiful setting and lots of energy."

"I loved the grotesque characters and the language. It reminded me by turns of Dickens and *Cold Comfort Farm*."

"Hugely enjoyable. The author clearly loves language and delights in inventive, playful and clever use of it. The book is charming, witty and sensitive."

"Couldn't put it down! It has a real touch of Dickens and Balzac but reminds me too of Rohinton Mistry's books."

"A highly sympathetic portrayal of the epic day-to-day struggle of the almost-destitute ... and a stunning knowledge of nature and the Lakes. Wonderful!"

*Best wishes,*

*Matthew*

# 2

# Pagan Goddess

He opened his eyes and staggered to his feet. Beyond Airey
Force, across Lakeland's vales, beneath a sky bruised with
rainclouds, new-born lambs bullied the milk out of Herdwicks
in the vernal pastures, while buzzards menaced overhead. To
the south-west he noticed Helvellyn brooding behind its mists.
He stepped dizzily downhill to the lake. As he approached, the
wind sent waves like swords across Ullswater's surface, straining
the birches almost out of their roots. Brambles, primroses and
celandines clawed at his ankles.

All at once, a turnpike road-full of pretty lasses in yellow
smocks and white-gold bonnets appeared in front of him,
laughing at the wind, tumbling and reeling beneath hawthorn,
hazel and holly. Some paddled into the lake itself while others

you're away. Let it keep you from fear – and from temptation.'
Luke knelt down and placed the cornerstone. Father and son
embraced each other through tears. The following morning, by
sunrise, he'd left for London.

The fells of Fairfield, Great Rigg and Seat Sandal slung their
shadows across the vale as Luke looked out over his small
ancestral patch of ground. A gated stone wall caged it in, the
fields were full of what looked like larch saplings placed in
straight rows, and his birthplace, the Evening Star, was gone.
He placed his arms on the top of the gate; a wooden sign
shouting 'Keep Out' was fixed on it. He looked into the fields
and recognised the clipping tree standing tall among the yellow
seedlings. He climbed over the gate.

Further uphill beyond the larches Michael's sheepfold
remained, but less than half-built and shaped like a heart
unequally divided. The ground looked sunken. He imagined
his forebears stacked beneath, their skulls grinning scornfully
– shouting 'too late! too late!' – at the thump of his feet on the
earth above. He grasped the cornerstone and with a heave lugged
it over to the edge of Greenhead Ghyll. He launched it into the
water with a howl and lay down by the ruined sheepfold where
the cornerstone had been. He clutched a thick, fresh clump of
lamb's wool, turned on his side to face the ghyll and muttered
through bitter, tear-salted lips, 'Now I'm home.'

'Not good,' he replied. 'Weaker by't day, red in the face wit coughin', blue in the face wit choking.'

Jack nodded, and fell into pursed-lipped silence, then he leant forward and put his hand on Goan's lower arm, which was pouring ale into a jug, pressing it so hard that he spilt it over the sides, and fixed his eyes on him. 'Poor bonny lass. Have you tried passin' her under a donkey? Worked a treat with my missus – for a time, like.'

'Ay, tried that one, Jack.'

'It's a bastud intit, eh? A bastud!'

As Jack uttered the word a second time a customer swept through the door in a gust of wind. He was short and skinny, with thick, slaked-back raven hair and flabby, versatile lips. Blue worms for veins wriggled under the skin of his hand as he snapped his fingers for a beer. The two men at the table stared up at him like collies hoping for a bone but expecting a good beating first.

'A mug of ale for these lads!' he called out to Goan. 'I need some fine, young workers,' he announced and turned to face the men. 'Know anyone?' he added, his pint-pot frothing with sarcasm.

'Depends, chief,' answered one of the men, a long, thin and washed-out shadow of an Irishman, after which there was a long pause while all waited to find out what it depended on. 'What's the wage?' he added, at which point his tablemate, a young farm-hand, retreated into his mug of ale.

'Two shillings a week,' spat the thin man through his punctured plum lips. At the bar Jack spluttered into his ale. 'I'm after ten strong men to build me a fence,' the man continued.

'What kind of fence?' Jack called out.

'Boundry wall. Over't fells.'

'Which fells?' Jack persisted.

'Elvellyn,' the man snapped back. 'Now who's in?'

'El-bloody-vellyn?' Jack muttered. 'Presarve us O!' The man ignored him.

'Tuesday morning. Early. Outside the inn.' He slurped once

stone to inch the wall uphill. While Gass, the gypsies, Jem's mother and sister continued to fetch, fetch, fetch every shape and size of stone, Jem scampered around collecting small, sharp fragments on Cragg's instructions, to plug the gap between rows of footings. 'These are called hearting stones,' he told the boy, holding one of them up, and Jem ran off singing 'hartinstones, hartinstones' to himself. He turned out to be a prolific hearter, racing back to Cragg with splintered bits of rock, delighted with himself as he delivered them with cold, cut hands. 'Good lad,' Cragg said with a paternal smile, rubbing the lad's sore palms. 'Me, Luke and Weightman'll pack these dry and tight so they keep out the wind and rain. Off you go, now.'

Cragg turned to Weightman. 'Now for the next course. Every stone sits on two below. Then we put more heartins between.' After a long silence between them as they built up the course, Cragg suddenly stopped and, looking aggravated, turned to Weightman. 'So what about you, then, Weightman?' he asked. 'What d'you want outta life, eh?'

Weightman shrugged.

'Mus' be summut, son,' he said impatiently. 'All your days ahead of you.'

Weightman shrugged again. Cragg shook his head and carried on his work in brooding silence. Some twenty minutes later, out of nowhere, Luke and Cragg were stopped in their tracks by the sound of Weightman's voice.

'Lef' home at fourteen, went tut hiring fair and stuck a straw in me gob. Got work as a live-in for three year and built myself a bit of a dream.'

'Dream?' said Cragg, his ears all but pricking up. 'What kinda dream?'

'Y'know, find a wife, rent a cottage of me own one day, tuft of peat moss and garden to boot, mebby. Wife could spin while I work on the land, mek ourselves a home, be happy. That kinda dream. Bairns of our own, even, if the guineas drop under't bed. Who knows?'

Short nights had been stubbing out long days as Lakeland hurtled towards summer. It was dusk on Helvellyn as Luke, sitting resting for the first time that day, watched a lamb-fattened flock bleating a path to its birthplace near the felltops.

'What's bin filling tha yed these past weeks, eh, Luke?' said Cragg, sitting down beside him with a stiff grunt. 'Not a lass is it? Steer clear lad.'

'You married one, didn't you?'

'Ay,' Cragg replied sullenly. 'I wed a lass. But wimmin's wimmin. Melt yeh heart like wax, they do, then burn it tut wick. These skies, these rocks, they don't change and fade and set their face against you. Old Elvellyn won't never turn his back on you like a wummun.'

'One week!' Vipond announced, making the two men jump to their feet. 'Mek sure you're back next Saturday first thing. Well, what yeh waiting for?'

The gang, apart from Luke and Cragg, immediately began staggering downhill in dizzy disbelief, bags over shoulders, rubbing hands, wiping brows and shaking their heads with exhaustion. Vipond followed at a distance, pursing his lips to an indeterminate tune that was more breathy wheeze than whistle.

'Seems a shame to drop downt vale,' said Cragg as he and Luke watched them go. 'It'll be like standing on top of evan withem views ont summit. Almost too good to miss is old Elvellyn on an evening like this.'

'Thought you'd be pleased to see the wife and children again, Isaac,' said Luke, confused by his reluctance.

'Oh ay, course I am. Course. Yuh coming then?'

'I'll catch you up.'

Luke hadn't been near Town End in nearly two months, but he, too, was compelled by a strange urge not to go back down to Grasmere. His mind had been impregnated with thoughts of one person all the time during these hard weeks at the wall-face. Her image, robed in fetching grey moonlight, had lain in his head like a sculpted saint quickening on a stone slab. If he'd

'Yes, I went, to London,' he said, sitting up. He paused, then stood up and made his way to the edge of Churnmilk Force. He looked down the valley into Easedale. Dorothy followed and stood beside him.

'Those daffodils,' he said, 'the thousands we saw – imagine them all tumbling over these rocks and being carried away downstream by the current.'

Dorothy remained silent.

'If only,' he said, turning to her, 'I could let my past spill away like water.'

She looked into his eyes but again didn't speak.

'At first,' he continued after a pause, 'I earned a good wage and wrote home, telling them I'd return as soon as I could. But over time ... I ... changed.'

She looked round at him quizzically.

He looked away. 'You wouldn't understand.'

'Are you so sure?' she said.

He sat down, placed his elbows on his knees and cradled his head in his hands. 'I grew up to the ... temptations ... of London. Ones I wouldn't have imagined here. And with money in my pocket, my ... natural passions you could say ... turned into unnatural ones.'

'What are you trying to tell me?' she asked.

He sighed, dropped his shoulders and abandoned the effort to conceal the truth any longer. 'I lived my whole life in the ale-houses and brothels, gorging myself on the pleasures they provided for me. I can't lie; it became an addiction, seeking out the furthest, darkest corners of gratification. The life I led was like a demon growing inside me, eating away at me, turning fat on my beautiful, young flesh, and on my soul.' He stopped, in realisation. 'But it was me. I was devouring myself. My own ... despicable ... self.' He thumped the left side of his chest in disgust. 'This proud ... young ... beautiful man I was,' he snarled. 'You know, I used to gaze and gaze ... at this ... devil ... in the glass. I feasted on my own youth and beauty, and I went. The browning crusts of wild roses hung off the hedgerows and ragged clusters of harebells assembled by the roadside to watch her. No bird sang, and a blasé grey cat padded across her path with a fledgling robin in its mouth. Near the edge of the lake she heard the sound of splashing, as though a child were paddling in the water, and out of nowhere a lamb appeared in front of her, and stood a long time examining her, then it sauntered away. By the time she'd reached the place where she and Luke had sat, she had an armful of flowers, bursting with colour, all caught like fish in her white net bag. She thrust the petals under her nose and sniffed, sucking in their eye-watering sweet perfumes. She tore off her yellow poke bonnet and tied it round the white and yellow wild roses, kissing them so hard that their protecting thorns cut her lip. She shook her hair loose and wild, scraped her fingers through its knots, and felt the locks tickle her neck like the brush of butterflies.

She stood in the lake at Dolly's View and let the water pet the tips of her slippers. An old mahogany and oak skiff was tied up round a rock nearby, dangling in a reedy pool. She'd never noticed it before. She saw the name 'Georgie' on its side in worn-gold lettering. 'If I dared, Georgie,' she said, extemporising the way William did, only in prose, and vowing to write the words in her own journal later, for her own pleasure, and maybe even turn them into a poem of her own at some point, 'I would set you free from the cord that chokes you, and together we would sail through the lake at the whim of the wind. We would circle the island once, maybe twice, and sing and dance through the water. Then, when our time was at an end, we would yield to the prison of your moorings and I would tiptoe away like a guilty thing. But we would have been filled with gladness, at least for a short while.'

She entered the reedy pool, flicked open the knot round the rock and began wading out into the deeper water, gasping with the cold, pulling Georgie with one hand and holding the white net bag of flowers high above her head with the other. When following him uphill, a huge man with black, wavy hair and on the swarthy geography of whose face grew a colossal black moustache. The man lumbered forward.

'I'll tek care of this one,' said Vipond, grabbing him.

'Mind you do,' said the baronet. 'My prize possession ... You!' he shouted at the bald-headed man in the wings. 'Keep an eye on him,' he said, pointing at his hirsute companion. 'Understand?' The bald man nodded. The baronet turned, signalled to the parson and the two of them sallied downhill.

Vipond led the new wallers over to the gang, where Cragg was kneeling at the wall-face adjusting a hogg-hole. He crouched down, coughed a lungful of ropy spit all over the ground and said in a hoarse voice.

'Work this one hard. I'll see thee right.'

'I'll do no dirty work for thee,' said Cragg.

A glint of malice flashed through the clouds of Vipond's eyes. 'Tha'll be fit for nowt else but dirty work in the pasture after this, ole man.'

Cragg said nothing, but tested the weight in his hand of a rounded stone, as if sorely tempted. He stood up and gestured to the giant new waller to follow him. His instructions were received with mute, low-eyed compliance. Gass and the moustachioed mute scrutinised each other as if in recognition. Vipond turned to the bald man; he recalled seeing him at the Merry Neet sniffing round meat that wasn't his.

'What's tha name?'

'Tindle.'

Vipond gave him as much menace in his look as he could manage and beat a retreat.

'Now lads,' he heard Cragg bark in the background, 'half the country is dead on the battlefield, tuther half is dying of hunger. Let's not do each other in and save the powers that bluddy-be a job, eh? Stick together. What was it they went about shoutin' in Paris a few year back? "Liberteh, equaliteh, fraterniteh ... or death"!'

moonlight. Like the book of William's poems, it had suffered a terrible drowning in the lake and had dried up all raggedy, but both volumes were still just about legible. For the first time since the day he'd stolen it from Dorothy – that rose whose thorns turned out to have been dewed with blood – he turned over the ink-run pages. By chance he came upon an entry that appeared to describe the spot on which he was sitting, with the author's vantage point the eastern shore of the lake, not far below Dove Cottage.

*... as I climbed Moss the moon came out from behind a mountain mass of black clouds – O the unutterable darkness of the sky & the earth below the moon! & the glorious brightness of the moon itself! There was a vivid sparkling streak of light at this end of Rydale water but the rest was very dark & Loughrigg fell & Silver How were white & bright as if they were covered with hoar frost. The moon retired again and appeared and disappeared several times before I reached home. Once there was no moonlight to be seen but upon the Island house & the promontory of the Island where it stands ... I had many exquisite feelings when I saw this lowly building in the waters among the dark & lofty hills, with that bright soft light upon it – it made me more than half a poet.*

She'd written the words more than six months before, and yet it was as if she were calling out to him now through her bedroom window. He stared hard across the lake and thought he could see Dove Cottage, with a lamplight in a window. The feelings her words aroused, and the longing. There she was! There! Across that same dark sky, like an evening star, holding a bright, soft lantern for him.

He awoke to the suspicious whistle of an owl, not the usual screech. He shuffled down to the lake and looked across in the direction it had come from. On the western shore, shin-deep in water, stood a child. With hands cupped, the diminutive figure was mimicking the hooting of an owl so skilfully that any genuine owl nearby must have been humbugged. It was

# 22

# Whisper

It was reassuring for Luke that he could draw on ancient Greenhead skills in an emergency. Armed with a blunt stone from a wall he began seeking out, isolating and stalking a lamb the way he used to with Michael when one of the flock needed help. Only now he needed the lamb on a cottage table at Goody Bridge, cooed over by six famished females. The lamb, coming up to a yearling, had other ideas and gave chase in a playful, leaping, lamb-like way. He cornered it a last, with bloody-minded willpower and a dash of guile, and proceeded to demonstrate that its life wasn't all fun and games by mashing its brains with his stone, in a manner not unlike the finale between the English and French in the last brutal hours at Alexandria.

'Yes.'

'They're better off with me. Where can they go?'

'You can't fill seven hungry mouths. I'll ask in the village. Someone will take them in.'

Sally looked at him with glassy eyes. 'What they've got to face, poor chicks, makes me bear me own feelings a bit better. I want them with me,' she rasped. 'I'll not have them tekken away. I'll be a good mudder to them for now.'

'No! You can't do it on your own.'

'I won't be on me own.'

'Who else is going to help you?'

She didn't respond, but he knew who she meant.

'Don't you fret about the parson neither,' Sally said. 'I'll sort that.'

Luke couldn't help himself. 'If I come back and find him offering you a shoulder!'

'Well don't come back!' she thundered. Sally had clearly reached the next stage of grief – tempestuous anger, and it was highly infectious.

'Are you insane?' he roared. 'Don't you know what he's like?'

'Who?' she screamed, sending the youngest of the Cragg children into sobs.

'Don't shout attim like that!' cried Jem.

'Keep out of this!' Sally snapped. Jem backed away but his eyes had that defiance.

'I'll tell you,' Luke said. 'He's worked us half to death, starved us, lied to us, killed one of us. Yes, he pushed Cragg, the best of the lot of us. Know who I'm talking about yet?'

'I want me Mudder,' began a chorus. Luke realised he'd told Cragg's girls the news. Only Jem looked unmoved, as if he'd known it all along. Sally, puce with rage, turned on him.

'That's not what I heard. Lance told me another man killed him, whose name I best not say here. That's what I heard. Sounds like the pot's calling the kettle black.'

There was a general consolidation of tears among the children.

'If you can see me doing that,' growled Luke through bared

teeth, 'then you're not who I thought you were.'

'Mebby you aren't who I thought you were, neither,' Sally replied in a similar gnashing fashion.

Luke went to the children, the eldest of whom flinched away. He crouched down to the younger ones, and held them. 'Don't listen,' he soothed. 'Jem, take care of them for a while, will you? I'm going out. I won't be long.' Jem corralled the children and steered them away from Sally.

Sally stood weeping in the porch recess as Luke brushed past her. She shouted to him, then ran up to him and grasped his shoulder from behind.

'Don't go see't parson. Please!'

Luke shook her off. 'I'm doing it for Jack,' he muttered, walking away.

'Luke!' she yelled. He didn't look round. 'Luke, listen to me. Fadder said summut at the end.' Luke stopped, but didn't turn round. 'His last words was, "tell Luke, over my dead body will I have that swine do my funeral".'

# 25

# Swine

Upon hearing Sally's last words quoting Jack's, Luke's walking rhythm modulated from a steady tread to something more akin to the scamper of a trail-hound. It wasn't the first time he'd visualised Noble Snaile's Christian name bejewelled in irony, and he couldn't see any way round his visit to St Oswald's being transfigured into a stained-glass defenestration of the parson.

As for Sally, the latest stage of her grief as far as Luke was concerned was that he'd lost patience with it. And then there was Vipond. How could she fall for that man? Her judgement wasn't questionable, it was insane.

No one was home when he entered St Oswald's, so he made his way to the rectory and stuck his head through the hedge. Parson Snaile was in his garden at that very moment, his language in flower.

'Ah, winter,' he rhapsodised, hands aloft. 'Those dryads' crowns upon the oak branches, those rose-red necklaces upon the holly. The gold of the larch, the fire of the rowans, and the emerald of the alder. Oh, grant me the naked hazel, the defoliated ash!' He stood suddenly still, as though feeling with epiphanic lucidity that he'd missed his true vocation as a poet. Luke considered the quickest means by which he might steer the conversation round to the persecution of his mother, and decided to sling an accusatory hint over the hedge.

'How was Isabel Greenhead when you last saw her, Vicar?'

The parson lowered his arms from the sky in the manner of one who'd just completed the symbolic release of a dove. 'Who speaks?'

'Her only son.'

'Show yourself.'

Luke walked round the hedge and opened the rectory gate. He felt like a baited bull, and by the way Parson Snaile reacted he must have looked like one as well.

'Ah!' said the parson, backing away. 'How antagonistic you look, my son. Did I not see you on Helvellyn, on your knees, shoving stones into an un-mortared wall?'

'You did, Vicar,' Luke replied, advancing.

'And did I not see you on Rushbearing Day, again on your knees, digging up the earth in the church more earnestly than the sexton?'

'Yes.'

'Yet rarely, if ever, do I see you on your knees in church, am I right?' he dared.

'Right again, Vicar.'

'And here you are now.'

'Here I am now,' Luke repeated, closing in on the parson, who'd retreated through his arcadia of a garden and reached the door of his opulent home.

'Yet not this time on your knees,' said the parson in a surprisingly combative tone, maybe feeling protected by his sizeable house, or his sizeable God. 'Are you not a humble penitent?'

'Are you, Vicar?' Luke enquired, with violent emphasis on the 'you'.

'May I urgently remind you,' Parson Snaile gulped, 'that to love God is to love thy neighbour.'

Luke could never love this neighbour ... but nor could he wreak revenge on him for some reason. The parson seemed to sense this, and sighed with relief, even dared to approach his assailant, put his hand on his shoulder and usher him inside. 'Come, my son,' he said, almost the way a gentle, loving priest might, 'take tea with me.'

Luke felt he could develop quite a taste for this – not just the superb tea, but the general luxury of the rectory. He was seduced, to the extent that he almost forgot why he was there, until the parson – after intoxicating him with a tour of his rich fabrics and costly curios, glass and china, silver and gold, pictures and books, antlers and peacock feathers – reminded him.

'Now, what did you want to talk about?' Parson Snaile asked with tender condescension.

Luke had his tough speech off pat, and though he felt he should now clothe it a little more warmly, he ended up leaving the original text stark naked. 'Isabel Greenhead lived in a cottage called the Evening Star, on a small plot of land on the forest side of Grasmere. When Michael Greenhead passed on her mind went with him. You took her in, used her, humiliated her, forced her to work as a slave and rook-scarer here in your garden. She ran away, hasn't been seen since and is presumed dead. I'm told you even sold the Evening Star, my birthplace, and the land on which it stood, my birthright, as though both had been yours to sell.'

Judging by the parson's alarmed frown and the erasure of his superior smile the story had rung a bell. 'And you say you are

Isabel's only son?' he asked.

'Yes, Vicar, she was my dear mother, and one only gets one of those in life, I believe.'

With the exquisite languor of a sentencing judge – knowing necks hung on his response – Parson Snaile sipped his tea. Luke clenched his wrists tight and tried not to think about the parson's neck.

'Well what do you say, Vicar?'

'Nothing.'

'Nothing?'

'Nothing of what you have said is true. I can understand why you might feel aggrieved, but I am aggrieved, deeply so, that anyone should utter such wicked lies, about me of all people. Do you know I have relinquished all chances of becoming a bishop by insisting on staying close to the lower levels of society? Not for me the decadent life of the seigneur and libertine, a life that has brought France to its knees. Every bone in my body is gentle and noble – an aristocrat first and a Christian second, as the saying goes – but I see my mission with common men such as you, which is why you will find me in the ale-house on occasion. But does the common man want to walk with me? No, he regards me with hatred in his eyes. Oh, the monstrously ungrateful poor. That is my cross to bear. But no, as for this vile slander, I say nothing. In fact, I forgive the sinner who committed it, whoever that might be.'

'So you never even knew my mother?' Luke blurted in disbelief.

'I did not say that. I did know her.'

'Well what happened to her?' Luke exploded, rising to his feet and knocking his teacup to the ground. 'What is the truth of it?

'Mr Greenhead,' the parson replied, calmly sipping his own un-spilt tea, 'I get accused of many things, and it causes me considerable anguish. But on this charge I am entirely innocent. If I suffer for it at your hands or those of any other man, I will be a martyr to the truth, and martyrdom is the greatest secret wish of any man of the cloth, if he and the cloth be of good quality, that is.'

Luke wiped the tea off his knee and sighed. 'Please tell me what you know of Isabel.'

Parson Snaile gestured to him to sit down. 'Isabel, your mother, became desperate after your father died, alone at the mercy of her increasingly fragile mind, her memory gone and living in fear and confusion. She became a laughing stock. She wouldn't have lasted long where she was. I would see her wandering round the village, in and out of the inns. She didn't know what she was doing. Some teased, others gave sympathy, but few helped. I took her in, and cared for her. Her wits and her dignity might have gone but some strange family pride lingered – she wouldn't let the Overseer of the Poor near her.

'Isabel pleaded to earn her keep at the rectory, saying she'd worked all her life and it was the only thing she knew. She used to sit and watch me gardening, and though her memory was gone and often she had no idea where she was, or who she was, or who I was, and this caused her great fear, we became friends and companions. She was a good woman. Perhaps I will confess, in the humility that goes with my calling, that it was not untainted altruism that prompted my charity towards your mother. Perhaps I was looking for my own mother in her – I never knew her; we met once only, as I was making my entry into the world and she was making her exit.' The parson looked out of the window at his vibrant flower beds as if they had become swamps thick with grief.

'When Isabel saw how the birds went at the seeds in my vegetable garden,' he continued in the wake of a deep sigh, 'she would shoo them away – and I have to say, she shooed very effectively. That was how she ended up working as the rook-scarer – not because I forced her, because she wanted to. It kept her going for a while, but it didn't surprise me to wake up one morning and find her gone. My housekeeper told me Isabel had said quite simply that morning that she must get going, and had left. I heard she ended up in Kendal, in the workhouse, but I never spoke to anyone who saw her after she'd left here.'

The Kendal workhouse, Luke thought. Was that the Kendal poorhouse, and wasn't it called the madhouse?

Perhaps after somehow reading Luke's tortured mind, Parson Snaile steered to another subject. 'The cottage and land that you were born upon defaulted to their original owner, the Lord of the Manor, Sir Edward Unthank, and he had the Evening Star demolished and the fields planted with larches.' He paused. 'So you have no idea when she passed away?' he resumed, changing the subject again.

'Or if she passed away,' Luke said, barely able to speak for sorrow.

'Indeed,' said Parson Snaile with a slow, lofty nod. Luke then caught the parson glancing out of the window, and realised that however much Isabel had meant to him, the grounds of his estate would always mean more.

'If there is anything else I can help you with, my son,' Parson Snaile said by way of rounding things off in a civilised manner.

'There is one thing, Vicar,' Luke said, looking him straight in the eye. 'I don't suppose you excommunicated my father, did you?'

Parson Snaile puffed up his chest. 'If I did, sir, he will have deserved it. But I didn't. People may find my castigations wounding, but they will know that I lack the kill. It is my greatest failing as a churchman. If your father was excommunicated, it will have been the work of my predecessor, a rigorous catechist who has now passed on himself. Personally, I care more about getting Grasmere's sinners inside the church than casting them out.'

'I can't find his grave, though,' said Luke, frustrated, 'and he didn't die a pauper.'

'Well, I suppose he might have been buried up on the fells somewhere if he was excommunicated.'

On the fells somewhere didn't narrow things down that

much, but it was the best he was going to get without risking excommunication himself. He thanked the parson, apologised for almost killing him, and set off back through the ornate gardens imagining his mother shooing away rooks. Then he remembered the original point of his visit, on behalf of a man who had lied through his residual teeth, yet again. He fantasised that Vipond's 'comeuppance' epitaph might inspire the mason of Jack's gravestone. He stopped and turned to the parson, who was creeping up behind him to see him off the premises. 'There is one other thing, Vicar.'

Parson Snaile's shoulders wilted at the prospect of another accusation. 'Yes?'

'Jack Nettleslack is dead,' Luke said. 'His last words were that even though he wasn't a regular churchgoer, he was an honest man of faith, and he very much hoped that when the time came you might do the honours and bury him for good.'

# 26

# Touching the Corpse

Back at Nettleslack Farm Sally was nursing not only her own grief but six inconsolable girls, who now knew they'd lost a father but still knew nothing of their mother. Luke only just managed to convince her, before he set off for Goody Bridge with Nance trotting alongside him, that Parson Snaile had absolutely insisted on conducting Jack's funeral, despite Jack having specified the exact opposite. Luke had told her, rather cruelly she felt, that her mouldering statesman of a father needed to snuggle under the sod as soon as humanly possible.

Word got round that old Nettleslack was a goner, and the word was fleshed out by the rumour that he'd left a daughter and seven grand-daughters without a farthing. Refreshments began to appear in the porch, along with a black-painted casket for the deceased, which sobered heightened appetites within the house. Two mornings later, the funeral party of a baker's dozen stood around in the fire-house eating bread and cheese, and drinking ale. One mourner who'd never known the Nettleslacks, but enjoyed mourning, pointed out that mirrors must be covered because it was bad luck to see the reflection of the corpse in glass. Sally pointed out, in return, that there had never been a mirror at Nettleslack Farm and there never would be, implying that dishevelment was a proud family tradition. Jack was laid out and mourners were invited, in keeping with another tradition, to touch the corpse to see if it bled, in which case the toucher would be branded a murderer, after which tea would be sipped.

Jack's procession slid inexorably towards St Oswald's as the mourners carried the coffin downhill to Grasmere singing psalms. The black casket was thrown into sharp relief against a cloud-blurred sky. Along the way, Sally, by giving the time of day to a young woman travelling with her ass, enjoyed the guilty comfort of hearing about a tragedy worse than her own.

'You've had it right lucky, you have,' the woman said, giving Sally the begging cant and whine of self-sorrow, tugging her arm on the offbeat as they advanced to the rhythm of an imaginary funeral drum. 'I buried me yusband and three bairns in eighteen month over in Manchester. All in one grave. Levenansix it cost me each time I put another one in. You're a lucky divel, you are!'

Sally didn't feel like a lucky devil, and not only because her dearly loved father had died. The night before, as she'd snubbed out her candle, she'd thought about the two remaining men in her life. One was suspected of murder, while the other was also suspected of murder. She'd weighed up both, and concluded she'd rather cavort down the aisle with Billy Tindle after all than consort with either of these two damfools. Then there'd been that knock.

Wind and rain were thrashing the farm, rattling and tapping at the windows trying to find their way in, and Sally woke up thinking she'd dreamt about the knock on the door. Then it came again, knock, knock, knock, knock. Much too regular for nature's wild burglary, and with a kind of bloodless urgency that made her think of a starving pauper. She climbed out of bed and threw her shawl over her shoulders. She opened the door and was assaulted by the elements, which raced through the house upsetting everything in their path, triggering a plague of goosepimples inside her bedgown that made her clutch the shawl even tighter. Pacing the porch was a pathetic, wraithlike figure, little more than a perambulating wet skeleton in clothes, spluttering onto the back of its hand.

'Lance!' she gasped. 'Get inside, it's hossing it down out there.' She pulled him by the arm to the inglenook and all but shoved him into the ashes of the fire. 'It's the middle of the neet!' she scolded. 'The bairns are fast asleep. Jack's in that casket over yonder, what the bluddyell are you doing here?'

They crouched beside each other shivering among utensils that clanged like ships' bells in high seas. He looked across at the black casket, then turned to her. 'Is he dead?'

'Course he is. Haven't yeh heard?'

Vipond shook his head and erupted with a meaty cough, which he had at least the courtesy not to send sizzling into the warm ashes, but which he retained in his mouth and chewed on like cud while he looked round for a receptacle. Sally nodded to the peat spit and he obliged.

'You all reet?' said Sally noticing the myriad colours of the bile.

'I remember when me own fadder died,' said Vipond peering again at Jack's casket.

'Where were you?'

'Workhouse, where else? Spent twenty years there, teasing bloody wool to make sacks. With a big patch on me sleeve saying 'P' – for pauper. Four of us to a bed. Beatings every day for nowt. Fever, toil, hunger day and night. Had to fight for scraps of food even before me milk-teeth had dropped out. He wasn't me proper fadder, mind, old Tom Vipond, but he looked after me a bit and let me call him fadder cos he felt sorry for me, so I took his second name when he passed on cos I didn't have one of me own.'

'Who was yer real fadder?'

'Who knows. Any road, I've come to see you, Sally,' he said, taking her hand in his.

'Ay, I can see that,' she said, looking him in the eye suspiciously.

'Not because your fadder's dead.'

'Oh,' said Sally. 'Reet kind, Lance.'

'Nay, I've come with an offer.'

'What kind of offer?'

'Ee, Sally lass, do I need to spell it out?'

'Ay, Lance, you do. Spit it out or I'm off back to bed and you're off back out that door intut rain.'

Vipond spat it out, in all its sinewy detail, and then left her to sleep on it. Sally had ended up lying in bed not sleeping, but going over and over his words, weighing them up and still not sleeping, dumbfounded by his strange nocturnal offer, and tempted.

The mourners approached St Oswald's mumbling the words and melody of a psalm none of them knew, and Parson Snaile greeted them at the church door. A fair crowd had gathered. It turned out that the parson had double-booked. Isaac Cragg's body had finally been recovered from Red Tarn and he was to be buried at the same time as Jack.

'We brought nothing into this world,' Parson Snaile said addressing Jack's casket personally. 'Neither may we carry anything out.'

Luke and Nance had arrived earlier after two nights at Goody Bridge, and they'd merged into the crowd. Luke's head hung low among the mourners at Jack's graveside, more out of discretion than piety, but when he sneaked a look behind him he saw a face that made him gasp with surprise, crouch down out of sight and pat Nance with unusual fervour, as if she needed consoling without delay. Nance wagged her tail unlike a dog wracked with grief. She seemed genuinely taken aback at the sudden battery of stroking, after all those years of false dawns of affection, all those raised hopes and bursts of tail-frenzy. All that wasted energy, all that anticipation that had come to nothing. No patting, no bone, no fetch of a stick in a beck, no race across the fields, no good hard stroke and tickle. Chronic disappointment had even led, Luke suspected, to a sardonic over-wagging he'd noticed more than once. But this particular session he was giving was the real thing, and judging by her smile and the verticality of her head, and the serpentine sweep of her tail along the churchyard grass, Nance was in heaven.

When Luke stood up again the only thing he dared lift his own head to look at was Sally's rear view, a few rows in front. Venting his second gasp in as many minutes he watched a figure hook an arm inside hers. It was a short, raven-haired man.

'... Man that is borne of a woman,' droned the parson, 'hath but a short time to live and is full of misery. He cometh up and is cut down like a flower. He flieth as it were a shadow...'

Sally cast earth on the casket and wept like a child. Luke was so moved by the sight of her that he wanted to push through the ranks of mourners and hold her hand. But the snake had got there first and this was no time for Grasmere wrestling.

'... We therefore commit his body to the ground, earth to earth, ashes to ashes, dust to dust, in sure and certain hope of resurrection to eternal life, through our Lord Jesus Christ, who shall change our vile body that it may be like to his glorious body ...'

The casket was lowered.

'We give thee hearty thanks, for that it hath pleased thee to deliver this Lancelot Nettleslack out of the miseries of this sinful world: beseeching thee, that we with this our brother, and all other departed, may have our perfect consummation and bliss, both in body and soul, in thy eternal and everlasting glory. Amen.'

As the crowd began to disperse, Luke steered clear of the grave. Vipond was standing over it, his arm tightly linked to Sally, and Luke was sorely tempted to push him in and smite two birds with one stone. He crept over to another grave nearby, where the ground was raised and the flowers still fresh, and where the Cragg girls stood weeping. He thought about Grasmere island, and his strange ritual of burying the daffodil bulbs like tiny coffins on the edge of the lake.

After the tears, the girls began to wander, in that way of children, appearing to recover from inconsolable sorrow at the snap of a finger, and before long they were round the other side of the church playing games. Luke stood alone at Cragg's grave, closed his eyes and promised to do what he could to help his friend's orphaned daughters. He sensed a presence, not divine but human. He turned, and was faced with a grey stuff jacket inhabited by all-too-human Dorothy Wordsworth.

'Luke!' Sally shouted before words had time to pass between himself and Dorothy. 'Where are the bairns?' Sally's Viking eyes were aflame round the edges with grief but they'd lost their piercing blueness and her hair looked diluted. Luke caught the mean round eyes of her companion and wondered when the snake was going to bite. He remembered Jack's words – even though Jack's every syllable was now discredited if the parson was to be believed – not to let Vipond chase him to the gallows, but to chase him back.

'Other side of the church,' he shouted. 'I think they're dancing on the graves.' Sally disappeared round the church, with Vipond attached as though in a three-legged race.

'Good day to you,' said Dorothy, not in the half-hysterical stammer of a few months before, but softly and slowly. Hurt, anger, shame, pretty much everything scattered through Luke's heart. She looked as lean as a lath and her eyes had lost their sparkle and speed, their intensity – their passion. It couldn't be more than three months but ten years might have elapsed. Standing there in her sober, grey habit she could have passed, in everything but wimple and veil, for a shrunken old nun.

'You're ... back,' he stuttered.

'Last month,' she said gently, but she left it at that. No nervous blubbering. 'I hear you've been helping the children of this poor man,' she continued, pointing at Cragg's grave. 'To think of them all alone in that house with both parents gone. It tears me apart. And how did they find out about the mother's dreadful death?'

'They haven't, yet,' said Luke with an anxious look around him. Dorothy's face screwed up with pain. She paused, then her voice burst out at its old speed and nervous energy, and her wild eyes shot round the churchyard.

'Let me tell them. I so much want to help. I'll think about how I can find them new homes, and I will break it to them all, gently and separately, about their poor mother.'

Luke was reassured to behold the same fervid Dorothy in there after all. He remembered the kindness she'd shown for beggars and paupers, distressed swallows, even flowers, and he was touched by the munificence of her heart. He recalled, too, how she'd dropped him without mercy and vanished abroad on an extended tour of Europe with her brother.

'These girls can't be abandoned again,' he said ill-temperedly. 'They're depending on me and Sally.'

'But they can depend on me instead,' Dorothy whipped back, sounding almost selfish. 'I have a secure home, standing.'

Which implied that he and Sally lacked them, which he found insulting, even though it was the case. 'These children need their own kind!' he snapped, knowing at least that Dorothy could never offer them the grubby virtues of the peasantry.

'Luke, let me help you,' she said, putting her hand on his arm. 'I owe it to you.'

He hesitated. His own circumstances were indeed unsteady, and Sally couldn't possibly cope on her own. 'You don't owe me a thing,' he said. Then he realised she did. An explanation.

'Why did you say nothing about your trip to France?'

Dorothy flicked her head round conspiratorially. 'Can we sit down? Over here.' They sat on a bench underneath the yews at the back of the churchyard, listening to the children's echoes and watching the rooks defecate on the gravestones. 'I wanted to tell you, but you never came that day, and then I had to go. I waited, but, oh, it was a terrible time. I had an accident, and then before I knew it we were on the road south. But I am sorry.'

'So am I,' he said, alluding to the theft of her journal but hoping to avoid specifying the transgression. She'd cottoned on, however.

'Molly told me she gave you my gift.'

'The poems? Yes.'

'Did you read them?'

'No. I preferred your words to his.'

She treated his remark with the embarrassment it deserved by ignoring it and blushing slightly. 'So will you let me help you?'

He chose to ignore her question. 'I'll return your journal to you as soon as I can now you're back, but at least I know now you're much more than half a writer.'

Dorothy went vermilion. 'Maybe I was once, but .... you will let me help you, won't you? I'll speak to everyone I can, and tell them of the awful happenings. There are so many kind-hearted people in Grasmere, and I shall run the campaign personally. And one more thing,' she said as they walked together round the other side of the church. 'You told me you hadn't found your parents' graves. I'd like to pay for a memorial stone for them, if I may. In fact, I've already asked William to write an inscription, if you will agree to it.'

It was just the same Dorothy: she couldn't go a heartbeat without mentioning William. 'That would be kind,' he said – and her eyes lit up – 'but I'd prefer not' – and her eyes went out again. 'The sheepfold up by Greenhead Ghyll,' he explained, 'is to be their grave. I need to get the cornerstone out of the ghyll.

That will be the headstone.'

'Why there? Oh, of course, I should have realised. The ghyll is named after your ancient family. William dreams of waging war on the larch planters up by there – there's a wood full of larch saplings in ghastly straight lines.'

'I know,' said Luke impatiently.

'Well let me know how else I might support you, Luke.'

She seemed fanatical in her need to philanthropise. 'I do need to go to Kendal,' he said, testing out her charitable boundaries.

'Why, then, I will pay for a horse,' she said cheerily.

'That would be kind,' he replied, and this time he genuinely meant it.

The Cragg girls were desecrating the graves with sheep pellets by the time they reached them. Sally and Vipond had wheeled round the other side, which was just as well, because he didn't want her and Dorothy fighting over the children. He left Dorothy trying to coax the girls off the tombstones.

As he walked towards Sally, who was now standing at Cragg's grave, he saw that her hair had regained its bracken gold, and her eyes their varnished blue. No doubt the light had been poor earlier. He noticed for the first time that her ears pointed endearingly north-west and north-east. He'd come to feel such a fondness for her – a kind of explosive kinship – that he feared the way he'd just been looking at her might have seemed quite admiring from her perspective. And sometimes when she looked at *him*, and the azure icebergs of disapproval melted from her eyes, it seemed from his perspective that she was gazing at him with a molten form of affection, and that disturbed him.

'The fat's in the fire now, Greenhead,' snarled Lance. 'I'd go while tha still can.'

'Lance!' Sally cried. It was one thing to be ill-tempered, disrespectful and downright rude – in fact it was very much a Nettleslack custom – but this tone of voice was altogether more fiendish. And he'd now completely lost his genteel accent, which had been unravelling all over the place the past few times she'd seen him. Clearly he wasn't the man she thought he was, just as Luke hadn't been.

'You're a dead man,' said Luke in an equally fiendish voice. 'Your master will see to that when he knows the truth.'

'Heh heh! Truth. What d'ye know about that? Cragg dint like what I was telling him about his missus, he dint, and about all them strong young lads up on the fells he favoured instead. But we both know who pushed him.'

Luke clenched his fists. 'How can you stand over Cragg's grave and say that. You go bad-mouthing him with his bairns running round the place and I'll save the hangman a job.'

'Luke!' cried Sally.

'Nae, nae, lettim,' said Lance. 'Heh heh heh! There we 'ave it, my dearest. Won't be't first time will it, eh?' Sally looked round at Lance in horror. He seemed to have changed, not only in accent and behaviour, both of which had taken a decided turn for the worse, but in body. His lips and cheeks were as white as milk, he looked as if his skeleton was trying to break out of him, and he could hardly speak without spitting some foul, sticky and wool-like mass onto the ground.

Lance grabbed her wrist in a way that gave her no option but to hand it over. Luke moved towards him. Lance threw Sally's wrist down again and squared up to Luke, even though he was only two-thirds of his height and seemed to Sally to be shrinking by the day.

'I'm not gunta chase thee tut gibbet after all, Greenhead, don't fret. But I'll say this right clear.' He leaned forward and stared Luke in the face. 'Your luck's run out round here. I know what you did. You aren't gunta go near Unthank, nor her nae more. Yeh see, me and Sal's getting wed. But not till you're gone. Back down London way where you came from. Get running, Greenhead!'

# 27

## House of Correction Hill

It seemed years since Luke had felt the thump and tingle of a mare between his legs. He pounded and splashed through the crusty November puddles of Rydale, Ambleside and Winandermere thinking about Sally and Vipond. The more he considered the union, the better suited he felt they were. He enjoyed picturing Vipond smashing the bridecake over Sally's head – as custom had it, of course – and then bellowed into the horse-breath mist, 'Damn them both!', which made his transportation rear its neck abruptly as though struck by lightning.

Dorothy had touched his heart again, touched in the sense of re-conquering, he feared, and God only knew how he was going to deal with that on his return from Kendal – if he did return from Kendal, that was. It felt quite good to have Grasmere behind him again, all told. As the horse traced the final bends of the River Kent into Kendal, his thoughts turned to his mother, and House of Correction Hill appeared ahead at last.

Inside the workhouse, as he peered into all the poor, shattered faces in the hope that he might recognise one, or one might recognise him, he felt like taking the coarse sacks they were all employed in making, sticking them over their heads, and shortening their mortal misery. And yet no one – amid all those fetid vapours and the doleful hum of looms, the groans and cackles of pauper lunatics and broken matrons, the wails of forsaken children and laments of lame and dejected widows – had ever seen or heard of his mother. Apart from one. Possibly.

'Greenodd, you say?' roared a deaf old crone with both hands cupping her ears to hear him, making her look as if she was imitating a hare.

'Isabel Greenhead,' Luke bellowed gently in response.

'Cicely Greenodd? Ay, I 'member her.' Before Luke had a chance to shout, 'No! Not Cicely Greenodd. Isabel Greenhead!' the drivelling old dame had set in motion her reminiscences of the wrong person, and Luke could almost see cobwebbed memories vibrating in her ancient head. He began edging away, lest he get cornered for hours humouring her with nods. But when he heard the words 'Grasmere' and ''usband by't name of Michael', he stopped. Could Cicely Greenodd be from Grasmere, too, and have a husband called Michael? Or was Cicely Greenodd how 'Isabel Greenhead' sounded to a deaf crone lip-reading an insane and toothless widow?

Another thing that struck him was her use of 'is' instead of 'was' – as in, 'she's a good worker our Cis,' or 'daft as a lamb, she is, mind'. It was impossible to ask her questions, not only because she was deaf but because she'd become as unstoppable as a new-fangled thrashing machine in her recollections. It was also a racing certainty that the only letter she'd ever read or written in her life was the generic 'X', which meant he couldn't write her a note. He just had to wait, until her memory oozed enough for there to be something to go on. Then it came.

'Ay, eh? Pfoooph. I don't right … Nae, dost thee? Dayleet broke and Cis were off, sayin' work were warse than nowt and she mun get back rook-scarin, and that were it. Gone.'

'Gone, you say?' pressed Luke. 'Where gone?'

'Eh? Wigton?' she roared, hands on ears. 'Nae. Farm down't road, not Wigton.'

At the farm down the road Luke began to steer his mind, along with the horse, for the first time towards the unthinkable.

'Isabel Greenhead,' he told the farmer in his field. 'She'd be near threescore and ten by now.'

'Nae, never heard of her,' he grunted.

That was that. The scent was lost forever. Luke thanked him and turned to go.

'Mind you,' the farmer added, 'we did have an aal one out of the madhouse, four or five year back, come wanting work scarin birds. But Cis were't name. Dint want to send her packing but she was too worn out to set in the fields. Said she'd do it for nowt, mind, so I stood her in the turnip field yonder. Decked her out in an ole hat and coat fastened with cord, give her a rusty ole gun that dint work. Happy as a clam at high tide she was, poor beggar. Nice ole dam. Dint know what she was doing, mind, but best rook-scarer I've ever had. And not a bad guard to boot. One day when't wife and me was out haymaking, two tramps turned up at the house beggin vittals. Cis was in on her tod. They tried to get in but she wunt have none of it. Told them to stay outside while she brought summut out for them. A minute later she stuck the muzzle of her gun in their faces and said she was mad enough to shoot. Poor fools thought she was a maniac and took to their heels. Ay, quite a character is Cis.'

Luke was amazed now to find out that not only was his father a killer but his gentle mother had become a gun-wielding maniac – if Cis was indeed Isabel. It was reassuring to know he wasn't such a black sheep after all. 'Do you know where she is now?' he asked.

'Now? Why course I do. Up there,' he said. The farmer pointed heavenwards. 'Or should I say down there,' he added with a wry smile, pointing earthwards. 'Went some years back, poor ole dam. Rooks were flying low one day, I found her on the soil. Paid for her gravestone out of me own pocket I was that fond of her.'

Luke stood outside Kendal's mediaeval parish church. The farmer had directed him there and informed him that Cis was in good company, because it had once been attended by Katherine Parr, Henry the Eighth's sixth wife – the one the king hadn't beheaded. Luke felt relief to know that, however hard his mother's life had been, at least times were no longer so violent and barbaric. At that moment a vast and high-spirited crowd passed by, pursuing the town flogger as he whipped out of Kendal a sailor. The unfortunate was fastened by two ropes round his blue jacket and white waistcoat, one rope held in front, the other behind. Luke crept through the graveyard hoping he wouldn't be mistaken for a grave-robber in this violent town. Among the gravestones he vowed to himself, as he fingered the mossy letterings, that it was the last time he would go grave-fingering that year.

As he'd predicted, he couldn't find the grave. He sat and recalled what the farmer had said when he'd revealed himself to be Isabel's – or Cis's – only son. The farmer had said that Cis mentioned a son from time to time, and her husband, and brother, and even her own parents. If she'd been confused enough to think she'd had a brother, he realised, she probably wouldn't have recognised her only son anyway, so it was just as well she'd passed away.

Long after the whipping frenzy had dispersed and dark had set in the Kendal sky he stumbled on it at last – a grave bearing enough biographical niceties to suggest it was hers. It was a sad, stark stone but so much better than the ghastly intimacy of a pauper's grave.

*Here lies Cis*

*Died 1798*
*Wife of Michael of Grasmere*
*Mother of Luke ...*

Even if her name was wrong, it was comforting finally to see her gravestone, and he felt close to her. It was also consoling to see his father's name. It gave him a sense of peace. As for his own name, it was rather disturbing to see that on a gravestone so soon; he may as well have been born straight into the coffin-trench for the speed life passed by – it would certainly have caused his mother a lot less bother. He sat and wept for them, and stroked the letters and numbers. It was, after all his searching, something at least, and that was surprisingly better than nothing. As the tears dried into the skin on his cheekbones he wondered if maybe now he could stop running away, or to, or just running. He lay down by the grave, and remembered the touch and smell of his mother. He wished she was still alive – but only how she was at the beginning, or even the middle, but not at the end.

It was too cold to lie all night next to the grave, not to mention macabre, and even dangerous considering Kendal's mob mentality. He stood up, pilfered fresh flowers from a grave nearby and placed them beneath his mother's headstone. He read again the words 'Mother of Luke'. It was then that he noticed the stick of a letter on another line beneath, peeping out amid the subsiding ground. He scraped around it and revealed the letter to be a 'D'. Once unearthed, the letter revealed others, forming the word 'Daughter'. This then revealed another word, 'of', which led to several others, and even several more lines of writing below. A few minutes later, feeling a deep sense of shock as well as what he imagined to be the rare satisfaction of an archaeologist, he read out loud the whole inscription on the grave.

*Here lies Cis*
*Died 1798*
*Wife of Michael of Grasmere*

*Mother of Luke*
*Daughter of Lancelot*
*and Sarah Nettleslack of Grasmere*
*RIP*

He stood up, having now seen enough, and walked away.

Back on horseback, straddling a bridge over the Kent which coursed below in the darkness, Luke surveyed the roads north and south. He couldn't face Grasmere now. So south, then, back to London, into the arms of the Bow Street Runners? No, he couldn't face that either. If he galloped far west he'd be in the sea before daylight and a seafarer's life wasn't for him after what he'd seen in Kendal. East meant Yorkshire. No, they were even more barbaric than the Scotch. One thing he knew was that he couldn't sit around on horseback too much longer lest he be mistaken for a highwayman and thrashed out of town. He galloped off northwards, telling himself that at the very least courtesy required that he return Dorothy her mare.

# 28

## Leech

---

Only when that Wudswuth lady had gone and the house was fearfully empty – apart from Jem and Nance, the dog having been abandoned at the churchyard by her new master – did Sally realise what she'd done. Mothering bairns had felt so much more natural than mothering her own father, but Wudswuth had persuaded her that they'd be better off going with her, and that if their long-term welfare was what Sally wanted above all else, then she must let go now before they got too attached to her. It had caught Sally off guard, and in the end – in fact almost straightaway – the peasantry had, in time-honoured fashion, curtseyed to the gentry.

'If there's one thing,' she grumbled to Jem as they tidied the house for the first time since the girls' – and Jack's – departure, 'one thing that's kept me going since Fadder died, it's you bairns. As if I wunt make a good mudder to you all!' she said, flexing the child-bearing hips and oaken forearms of a classic Grasmere matriarch.

Jem nodded grimly in sympathy even though Sally could tell by his co-operativeness with the chores that, now his rivals for her love had been dispatched, his dream of having a gentle and attentive 'mother' all to himself was at last coming true.

'I know I'm poor as a pauper's cat,' Sally moaned on. 'But who does that scraggy little hen think she is telling me them orphans have to go with her? See how the poor bairns clung to me apron so hard? Damn pinny's ruined! And who the divel is she to talk about Luke like she knows him better than me? Saying when she came to kidnap the bairns that he's gone to Kendal to find his mudder – as if I dint already know.'

'But you dint, did you?' interjected Jem.

'That's not the point! I might want to tell her a few things myself about Luke, like who she thinks cooked and cleaned for him every time he dropped down off Helvellyn. And who brought him back to life when he turned up full of a fever all them months ago. Ay, I know right well she swept him off his feet, but who's bin't mug sweeping under them all year long? But don't fret, lad,' she said, seeing Jem's eyes sense another storm brewing, 'I'm not gunta get all het up. Not my way. But I'll get them lasses back under this roof even if I tear them out of Dorutheh-bluddy-Wudswuth's skinny hands meself.'

Nance raised her head off the floor, stared at the door and started wagging her tail. Someone was coming. Jem and Sally looked round. 'Please don't be him,' said Sally under her breath. She couldn't face him today. Sharing his bed for the rest of her life would be punishment enough – and soon enough that the wedding guests would be throwing the stocking at some mutation going by the name of Sally Vipond before the year was out.

Such was her relief not to see Lance barge through the door but Luke, that she could have thrown her arms around him and kissed the life out of him if it wasn't for the fact that they'd parted on worse terms than ever at the churchyard.

'Sally,' Luke said, appearing to have rehearsed that bit, but then he fell silent. She looked at him in surprise, detecting what she interpreted to be a new expression of affection.

'Dearest Sally,' Luke began again. That sounded even more promising.

'I found Isabel's grave,' Luke said.

'Oh, I'm right glad – I mean, I'm right sorry,' she replied, more than mildly disappointed that yet again another woman was on his mind, even if it was his departed mother. 'When did she die?'

'Four years ago.'

Luke paused, went dry-lipped and anxious-looking. 'Sally,' he said, taking her hand considerably more respectfully than was Lance's way, 'I don't know how to say this.'

Nance wagged her tail, and Sally would have if she could, because she was beginning to believe this might be her second proposal in a week, and this time without any arm-twisting.

'Sally, if she was his daughter then that might explain why she told the farmer in Kendal she had a brother, because, even though her mind had gone, she did. It might also explain why Jack wrote 'in' in the Genesis.'

'I don't have the first or faintest bloody clue what the divel you're blabbing on about,' replied Sally, incipiently crestfallen.

'Sally, don't you see? Isabel Greenhead used to be Isabel Nettleslack – 'I.N.' When I found the headstone it read "Here lies Cis, Died 1798, Wife of Michael of Grasmere, Mother of Luke". But then at the bottom,' he continued breathlessly, 'I discovered the words "and daughter of Lancelot and Sarah Nettleslack of Grasmere. RIP." That Jack Nettleslack was your grandfather. Your father and my mother were brother and sister.'

Sally's mouth stood agape.

'Sally,' Luke declared with arms outstretched on her shoulders, 'you're my cousin.'

Sally shut her mouth and swallowed hard. Her lips stuck together. She felt feint. 'Who's Cis?' she asked dizzily.

She stood over the oat-dusted oaken table, poured a jug of water into a bowl of buttered oatmeal – conscious that Lance's money had provided that oatmeal – and kneaded it as if it were Dorothy's neck, stretching the dough and identifying two ends. On one end, this news from Luke changed everything, and on the other, it changed nothing. The dough became a rigid, flat paste after she'd squeezed and massaged it, her mouth imitating the contortions of the dough. She rolled it out and plastered it onto the iron girdle plate, her forehead grooved with perplexity. She turned to Luke, who was eyeing the raw haverbread.

'I don't believe it,' she said, knowing that even the haverbread would be easier to digest than the news.

'I can hardly either,' he said. 'And they're all dead, so who knows how we'll clear it up.'

'No one said a word,' she muttered as she hung the girdle plate over the fire. 'It can't be true.'

Luke put his hand on her shoulder the way an affectionate cousin might. Sally hated the feeling and shook free, withdrawing into dark silence. She wondered who might know the truth. There must be a brace of shepherds who knew something, but shepherds were a close, secretive lot. They all knew who the rabbit-poachers were among them, but none said a word – not unless to one of their own, in a loud gale on a fell, through a wind-blown smock-frock. She thought back to Jack's last few hours and tried to imagine what he would have said if she'd probed him for deathbed secrets.

Something she'd forgotten he'd said came back to her. She'd thought it strange at the time, and what had happened next, but had put it down to the delirium of dying and the longer-term damage of senility. 'I've bin thinking about summut odd,' she said to Luke through teeth that gnawed on her fingers, not the actual nails but the skin contiguous to them, which bore the texture of over-worked leather.

Luke was at the doorstep looking out on the fells. He turned round.

'What?'

'When Fadder was dying and I was standing over him close up, he said, "Don't you say nowt now!" So I says, "Nowt about what, Fadder?", but his eyes went right through me, like he was gawping at someone else behind me. I can see now who it was, cos that same someone sneaked out of the chamber straight after.'

'Jinnyspinner?'

'Ay.'

Luke found Jinnyspinner stooping over the edge of Rydale lake, and tried to lure him to Nettleslack Farm by requesting fresh leeches for an improvised ailment of Sally's, something to do with indigestion. Jinnyspinner warned that his bloodsuckers were in ever higher demand because of their increasing rarity, and he doubted that Luke or Sally could afford them in their present circumstances, reminding Luke that Sally hadn't yet paid for Jack's final bloodletting binge. Luke tried to tempt him with the offer of fresh haverbread, but that didn't work, so he mentioned the possibility of half a dram of Quaker's Black Drop – the opium, wine, spices and quince tincture that had worked a treat on Jack, giving him a steady blush of pleasure, even though he'd died afterwards. Jinnyspinner remained under-tempted. Luke's final offer, therefore, was a taste of some of the ale in the barrel left over from Jack's post-mortem but pre-funeral refreshments. That did the trick.

When they got back to the farm Sally was gone. Luke planted Jinnyspinner in Jack's armchair and noted how at home he looked in it, despite the length of his legs, which led almost to the main door and across the threshold. Surely, Luke thought with a shudder, Jinnyspinner wasn't part of the Nettleslack-Greenhead dynasty as well?

Aglow with the haverbread and the Black Drop, which Jinnyspinner had decided he might as well taste after all now that he was here, he began to open up, his fiery eyes flashing. 'I've had my little suckers on every chest in the vale, and some of the yansomest bosoms in the district an all,' he glinted. 'Int nowt I don't know about bloodlettin' round Grasmere. War wounds, sores, cuts, slashes, gashes, I've seen 'em all. Nosebleeds, piles, fevers, headaches, bouts of poetical melancholiflower, the lot. My bonny babes, once they're suckling, can gulp a spoonful of bad blood in ten minutes flat. Splash of vinegar and you're good as new.'

The only way Luke could unclamp Jinnyspinner from the subject of leeches and onto Jack Nettleslack was to ask him about leeches in relation to Jack Nettleslack.

'I got to know Wile Jack well over't years,' he said, sounding sozzled by the Black Drop. 'Brought leeches here dozens of times – but not for cuts, gashes, fevers and the like.'

'Chilblains?' Luke guessed.

'Nae. For his temper.'

Luke had seen a little of this in Jack, but Sally had reminisced after her father's death about his choleric temperament, which she confirmed to have been a chronic ailment while she was growing up. She'd made it sound like part of the family heritage, as was the farm, and had even appeared to cherish the memory of her Grandad Jack's filthy temper.

'Ay, he had a divel of a head on him, did Jack,' Jinnyspinner elaborated. 'One time I had to leech him for his bad 'oomer after he'd come back from a bull-baiting in Keswick. He used to love watching them dogs goin' at the bulls' legs, making them bellow and foam before they was slaughtered. Said twas good for the beef – made it taste better, but really he just liked the sport of it, all that rowdy cruel stuff. That and quaffing, and gambling with his pals on market day, cheering and betting on the cocks. Hated losing, mind. But twas days like that he used to go home in a right foul one. A neudled, over-excited sore-loser. That's where Wile Jack got his temper. That and other things.'

'What other things?'

'Nae, I don't know I should be telling all this,' he said, peering up at him expectantly from Jack's armchair. The haverbread was gone, as was the Black Drop, so Luke reached for the dregs of the ale barrel. Jinnyspinner swigged a mugful and with a bellicose cough cleared his throat. 'Nah then, where do I start? Well, when he was a moonin' yoof he was kind, was Jack – wid Keswick lasses, like. Use to buy them things, vichals for their bairns and that. So he could, you know, keepum quiet. And not just the Keswick lasses.'

'Who else?'

'Eh? Nae, couldn't say,' he said, addressing the ale barrel with his eyes. Luke obliged.

'Who?' Luke repeated.

'A fine lady. A right fine lady. Ee, Wile Jack were a ned-turner. Marvellous ansome. One summer's day, so he told me once – well, he told me more than once, he were that proud – he was slouching and swaggering down that main street in Keswick with his rabbit-skin hat flopping about his ears, trilling a song or two for the lasses, quaffin a beer or two. Folk stopped to admire him, he said, even a couple of gypsies standing in a doorway baiting some young lady. Jack got vexed with them, took the lady by the arm and led her away, just like that. Said she told him later it were his bewterful barn-owl heart-face that did it. Now I'm not saying no more than that even if you do drop more ale in this mug.'

Luke obliged.

'All I know,' Jinnyspinner continued, 'is he spent a lot of time – and money – up in Keswick, with his sports, and he were only a poor shepherd. And he got into quaffing reet bad an all.'

'Did his wife Sarah know about all this?'

'Nae, nae. Man's stuff isn't it,' he said, patting his nose with his finger. 'But Sarah knew fine well the king's shillins were leaking out somewhere, cos hard as she toiled in the fields and at the loom, she never saw owt for it. Jack said it was man's business to tek care of the money, and he was such a charmer – apart from that temper – that she awways backed down. Then she got ill. Ee, I tried with all me bonny babies but twas no good. Sweats, chills, coughing, wasting away.'

Luke tried to picture the Aunt Sarah he'd never known, not coughing and wasting away in ugly, emaciated death, but as a beautiful young woman, the mother of Sally. Not cheated on and lied to and bullied by her husband, but loved by him. Not full of sadness and regret, but happy. Not dying before her time but living well through it.

'They had debts, then, even when Sarah was alive?' Luke asked, trying to pin down the connection between the families.

'Ay, summut terrible. Improvidence was Jack's middle name. Had to get his sister to bail him out, he did.'

There it was at last! Jack and Isabel were siblings. At that moment Sally barged through the door and Luke immediately saw her father in her, but maybe also now his own mother – or was it himself? It was getting confusing. One other person who came to mind was William Wordsworth, and Luke understood how the love between brother and sister, cousin and cousin, might be woven with imperceptible threads of complicated, often contradictory and sometimes even dangerous signals.

'Well?' demanded Sally.

All Luke's instincts were to button everything up in front of the women-bodies – he was of course a product of that close-knit Grasmere shepherding fraternity himself. The strife this mess might cause in the shadows was far better than the harm it would do in the light of day. Jinnyspinner hoisted his left leg up from Jack's armchair and tried to sidle out of the door.

'So what did he say?' stamped Sally.

'Not much,' Luke lied. 'Where've you been?'

'Seein' to a few things,' she said, and swung round to pin down Jinnyspinner with her eyes. 'Nowt about what?'

'Eh? What? Who?' said Jinnyspinner, looking like the beleaguered daddy-long-legs he was.

'Fadder! When he told you not to say nowt, what did he mean? Nowt about what?'

Luke had to be straight with her. 'Sally, Jack was a gambler, womaniser, drinker. He ran up terrible debts.'

Sally laughed scornfully. 'Is that it? I thought you was trying to find out if we're cousins? D'you think I dint know what he was like? He wunt no angel, he was a man. Just like you.'

'Good,' said Luke, nettled sufficiently by her scorn to say something he might regret. 'So you know he wasn't a saint. Do you know whose life that worthless rat wrecked because of it?'

'Don't you talk about Fadder that way!'

'The bastard forced Michael and Isabel to pay off his debts, and they had to sacrifice me because of him, by sending me away. That's how much of a man Jack was.'

'Sacrifice? Don't you go playing the victim, now. What kinda man are you, cousin Luke? You fooked up your own life – you dint need no Nettleslack to help you. I'll tell you one more thing an all,' she yelled. 'And you won't like this one bit.'

Luke braced himself. 'What then?'

'Michael weren't no angel, neither.'

Jinnyspinner flinched in the shadows.

'Leave him out of this,' growled Luke. 'He was a good man, and loyal. He loved his family, and worked hard all his life. If it wasn't for him you Nettleslacks would have been paupers long before now. Keep Michael out of this.'

Sally couldn't. 'Fadder told me what he'd said to you about Michael. Told me all about the sheep-stealer. I asked him to. I saw you two whisperin' away behind me back. Michael was a murd—'

'—I know!' roared Luke, jangling his fists. 'I know what he did, and he'll have suffered the agony of it. But I'm his son, and

I forgive him, even if he didn't live to forgive me.'

Sally went quiet, and wept. Jinnyspinner, instead of seizing his moment to flee, followed Luke outside and put a hand on his shoulder. To Luke it felt like Michael's hand, and it made him sob internally. Jinnyspinner turned to Sally, who was in the porch blotting the tears from her eyes with her apron.

'Luke,' Sally said in an ominously muffled voice through the sniffs she was wiping on her sleeve. Luke looked round. 'I saw Lance. He says he's got summat proper on yeh now. Said you should've gone while you could. Says he's out for your blood.'

Luke shrugged and shook his head, then began walking away from the farm, but he was near enough to catch what Jinnyspinner said to Sally.

'Sally, lass,' the old man mumbled, 'Jack lied to thee. It was him as pushed the sheep-stealer off the crag, not Michael. He told me himself. He could be a cruel man when't mood took it, and a coward and cheat an all. Ay, he knew that right enough.'

# 29

# The Source

Luke had stayed alone at Goody Bridge that night. He'd wished he could turn round, go back and face Sally, but he couldn't stop walking away. Anyhow, for all he knew, Wild Jack's daughter would have greeted him with the girdle plate if he had gone back, or set the dog on him, not that a wrestle with Nance would draw much of a crowd – the only wrestle they knew about was a roll on the floor together and a tickle of the belly. If only it could be the same with Sally, he sighed.

He set out early in the morning to the Forest side. On the rising ground by Greenhead Ghyll, beyond the old oak that had been Michael's clipping tree, he noticed the clump of lamb's wool he'd seen the night he'd slept at the sheepfold. The wool was greyed and stiffened, presumably rejected by the tarry woo men – over-thrifty shepherds who collected every last scrap of wool off ground and gate. He looked down at the broken-heart-shaped sheepfold. Michael had worked, sat, and died here – if he was to believe anything of what that rascal Jack had said. At least he could believe now that Michael hadn't killed the sheep-stealer after all. He'd kept his faith in his father anyway, whatever he had or hadn't done. Perhaps Michael had had faith in him, too, till the end, however much he'd messed things up. He crouched down on the sunken ground by the fold, and lifted a stone. 'This land,' he said to himself, 'will always be Greenhead deep down. That will outlive the ploughshares of strangers.'

Why had the ground subsided so much, he wondered, and he recalled Parson Snaile's remark that Michael might have been buried up on the fells somewhere. He had a sudden thought. If Michael had been excommunicated by the previous parson and buried here, could the whole Greenhead clan have been excommunicated before him? There were no family graves in Grasmere – was he part of a rich heritage of excommunication for poor attendance at church: the Greenhead Nonconformists of Grasmere? It explained, perhaps, why his mother had been taught her letters by Quakers. He could hardly believe it. All this time looking, and they were right here under his nose.

He ran to the edge of Greenhead Ghyll to retrieve the cornerstone that would now grace Greenhead hallowed ground. He knelt down, plunged his arms into the ice-cold water and swished around to find it, but it didn't appear to be there. It was too heavy to have been dislodged by the current. He squatted on the bank in puzzlement.

What was that? The grass crunching behind him? He suddenly remembered what Sally had said about Lance being after his blood. For what? Cragg's murder? Sally sounded as if there were something else. He didn't dare think Vipond knew about London. But it might as well have been anything now that the terror was upon him. The guilt of all the world, every crime, every sin, all his fault. That was how the terror worked, how it tightened.

There was nothing to stay around for anyway. He knew now where his parents lay, even if it wasn't quiet in the earth. And there'd be no work for him in Grasmere again even if he did slip through Vipond's bony fingers. Cragg was dead, not to mention Jack. And Sally? … Well, she was lost to him now.

It was settled. He'd set off south for the Kirkstone Pass before the day was out. Except …

… No. He had to see her one last time. He'd go and get her journal from Grasmere island as he'd promised and give it to her on his way out of town.

The grass definitely crunched behind him this time. He jumped up and swung round to defend himself from Vipond.

'Dorothy!'

'I hoped I'd find you up here,' she said, out of breath, feeling about as terrified as he looked. She'd run all the way from the village after hearing the news, and was most upset to feel so churned-up again about him after having tried so hard not to be. He'd bitten her heart once and she knew to be absolutely twice shy with that particular organ in relation to him. She was sick and fed up of being barricaded in by sorrow over men all the time. But this was different.

This was someone who needed rescuing, and, along with the Cragg orphans, that was her other new vocation. The first was to be a loving sister and aunt at Dove Cottage; the second to be a charitable rescuer of humanity in general. Armed with renewed strength of mind following the collapse after William's wedding, she'd woken up one morning a new woman. 'Dorothy Wordsworth,' she'd told the ageing maid looking at her in the glass – and it wasn't Molly this time, 'has officially completed her youth and begun her later life.' She now faced the world not as a young daffodil dancing in the breeze but as a dutiful spinster, an oak of solidity at Dove Cottage. And as for that other vocation, being the naturally zealous type, she would not commit her wilful acts of charity with the usual glassy condescension of a genteel do-gooder, but with an almost military compassion.

Without a minute's delay, therefore, she'd begun her mission to find the Cragg girls suitable temporary parents while donations were gathered for more permanent ones. She'd collected the girls from Nettleslack Farm within twenty-four hours of the funeral and broadcast them like seeds round Grasmere, each to a different plot. That little beggar Jem was a special case in that he'd refused to the point of bloodshed to move from Sally's side and accept the wrench of philanthropy, insisting with strange logic that Sally and … Luke, of all people, would make a perfectly suitable mother and father for him.

It was all going so well, and then she heard Luke's name mentioned in the village, and that a group of men were out looking for him, and now here she was, in thick black cloak and spenser, panting like an old deer under the gun and all a-blubber again with nerves.

'I think they're coming,' she gasped.

'Who?'

'Some men.' The gap opening between his top and bottom lips told her he was thinking the worst.

'Who is it, Luke? What have you done?' she asked, shaking his arm hard.

He said nothing, but stared into Greenhead Ghyll.

'Luke,' she said, this time more gently, 'what is it that you've done?

He rounded on her. 'Nothing.'

'You must have! Why are they coming after you?'

'Whatever I've done – and you, of all people, know the things I've done – I've been dragged to hell for it already.'

'Well then we must stay calm,' she panicked, 'and trust … in your innocence.'

'Innocence? I've been tortured by guilt ever since I left childhood.'

'You must reclaim your innocence, then. Proclaim it even.'

'I'm innocent!' he cried mockingly into the water beneath their feet. They both stared into the ghyll.

Dorothy crouched down, hurt by his scorn, and dipped a few random fingers in the water. 'I'm trying to help you,' she said.

'I know you are, and I'm grateful, but you can't stand before Lance Vipond and a gang of men and say "He's innocent." They'll laugh in your face.'

'So you know who's coming after you?'

'I think so, but not why.'

Dorothy continued to let her fingers drift in the river, and began to feel soothed and strengthened by it. 'So this,' she said quite calmly, 'is the wellspring of the Greenheads?'

Luke didn't reply.

'Where is the source, do you know? How high in the fells?'

'I don't know,' he said tartly. 'Right up there.' He pointed to the crest of Fairfield ridge. 'Past Stone Arthur. Michael used to tell me the ghyll sprang out of the ground as if by magic but he never took me there to see it.'

'I'd like to see it.'

'Shepherds don't usually venture that high. There's hardly any good grass for the sheep. Only desperate ones and stragglers will bite into the tufts of moss wedged in those rocks.'

'You've never been?'

'One time I got quite near, but… I got into danger up by there and never went back.'

Dorothy turned to him excitedly. 'Show me!'

Luke looked around as if expecting Vipond to attack at any moment.

'What?'

'The source of the ghyll. Let's hunt it down.'

'Aren't I the one being hunted?'

'Well they won't find you up there.'

He hesitated. 'It's a steep climb. Are you—'

'More than sure.'

He assented with a solemn nod. She smiled and wove her arm inside his as they began the ascent. The November nip in the air bit harder the higher they climbed, but Dorothy, who adored the bracing cold, knew it would have to be little short of arctic for her to turn back. In fact, as they grappled with the gradient she felt sweat trickling down her thighs beneath all those silly, unnecessary layers of clothing women had to wear. She secretly wished she could just strip the whole lot off and run naked in the fells.

Luke looked withdrawn and fretful as they made their way uphill by the ghyll.

'Tell me what happened,' Dorothy said, panting, 'the time you got into danger.'

It seemed to bring him out of himself.

'I was about fourteen. We'd gone up after a storm in search of a ram, a straggler in the flock. But though we searched, we couldn't find it anywhere. After walking right along the ridge past Great Rigg and Seat Sandal towards Grisedale Tarn I suddenly remembered something Michael had told me, about Herdwicks returning by instinct to their heaf, the place where they were born and pastured at their mother's side, even if they're driven many miles away by a storm.

'"I know where we'll find him!" I cried. "Let me go straightaway to the heaf, father."

'"Take care then, lad," he warned me.

'I went all the way back to the flock's ancient pasture by Greenhead Ghyll. The flood rain had come on hard again as I searched, and the hours passed by. Finally, just as I was about to give up hope I spotted the straggler on a grassy island in the centre of Greenhead Ghyll. It was dangerous but I leapt over the water to the little patch of ground halfway across. But as is the way with them, the ram jumped away from me as soon as I got near it, and fell into the flood-water rushing downhill. I watched the poor beast sucked away to its death. The water had become even fiercer and I knew I'd be swept downstream myself if I jumped back the way I'd come. What chance was there of my father finding me, in the middle of Greenhead Ghyll? I was trapped, and thought I'd soon be drowned, and called out for Michael.

'He was so worried not to find me home that he'd already set out again. He struggled in the dark and storm all the way uphill along the ghyllside. Finally he heard my cries and followed them to the point where he could see me quivering on my little island. "Hold on, son, don't let go!" he shouted, crouching down and stretching his staff as far into the water as he could without falling in. "When you can, when you think you're ready to do it, jump. With all thy heart and might, Luke, jump to the staff and grab it. I won't let go of thee whatever happens, that I promise."

'I stood paralysed in fear, but the torrent was close to sweeping me away. I looked over at Michael, watching me silently and seeking for the courage I had in myself and the trust I needed in him. I jumped, and just about managed to catch hold of the staff. He held me tight in his arms long after that. "I'll never let go of thee, Luke," he said. "Never."'

They stopped not far below the ridge and, out of breath, Luke pointed into the ghyll. 'There,' he puffed. 'That's where I got stranded.'

Dorothy put her hands on her tired hips and her eyes followed the journey of the tumultuous brook downhill. She imagined the ram falling to its death, and Luke leaping into his father's tender clutches. She turned and watched him lie down wearily on the ground and close his eyes. He was close enough to the water for little droplets to come to rest on his face, and she imagined him as a young shepherd boy, not rescuing a ram but lazing by the water's edge. She was amused, and touched, and sat down beside him. She allowed herself, perhaps for the first time, not to gaze at him, but to gaze into him, feeling for his essence, so that she might capture it – but not so that she could put it in her journal and William might one day put it in a poem. Luke had been her spring daffodil, one she'd enjoyed watching grow, wondering how it might change through the seasons. But the ground in which it had taken root, she now saw clearly, was her heart.

She yearned to get closer to him, to lie down next to him and talk about ... everything! She'd start by telling him that she and William also loved to lie down next to each other and pretend that they were lying in their graves. On second thoughts, maybe that wasn't such a good idea – she didn't want to spoil the moment by talking about death, or William for that matter. She didn't need William's presence, in person or in mind, for this to be the most affecting moment.

For almost the first time in her life ... no, genuinely for the first time, she corrected her inner voice ... she was gazing upon a man lying on the ground beside her in her beloved Grasmere who wasn't William, and whom she consciously didn't want to be William. It was a liberating, thrilling feeling, and she almost did lie down, but being at the matronly age of thirty and no spring flower anymore she stood up instead, and gazed down over Grasmere into glittering sunlight that made the ghyll's spray look like ten thousand stars in the Milky Way.

'A rainbow!' she shrieked. 'Luke, over Grasmere. Come and look!'

He jumped just like a shepherd-boy caught napping and planted himself beside her.

'Oh, Luke, will you let me relate a poem William wrote just a few months ago? It seems so perfect for now. So perfect for you.' She knew she was all but risking her life mentioning William again so she placed a pacifying hand on his chest. 'Now,' she said with her usual hurry of enthusiasm, 'before the rainbow disappears?'

'Let me hear it,' he said, his voice gruff and resentful.

'He wrote it in March,' she trilled, 'and as with all his poems they come at the most humdrum times. I think we were spreading dung all over the garden that day or the next. But anyway,' she babbled on, all the while checking the rainbow was still there, 'I happened to be climbing into bed when he composed it. So here it is...

*My heart leaps up when I behold*
*A rainbow in the sky:*
*So was it when my life began;*
*So is it now I am a man;*
*So be it when I shall grow old,*
*Or let me die!*
*The Child is father of the Man;*
*And I could wish my days to be*
*Bound each to each by natural piety.*

'Did I tell you you make me think of a chaffinch?' he said.

It felt as if he'd spread dung all over the poem by his response, but she wouldn't take it personally – her brother was big enough to be offended on his own account. Anyhow, it had to be maddening hearing William's name at every turn. It maddened her!

'They call them skobbies round here, don't they?' she fired back.

'Come along, then, Miss Skobby, there's no safe path from here to the source of the ghyll – I think it's just over there – so let's stick to this track up to the ridge, shall we, and take a walk along?

Once on top they turned round briefly and took in the views down west across Grasmere vale as the glimmering hearths of eventide began to illuminate dwellings. When a wintry wind droned to the north over Fairfield's horseshoe-shaped range Luke thought he could hear the distant rumble of bagpipes, and imagined Vipond had assembled a whole clan of pillaging Scots to bring him in.

They pushed on headlong into the wind along the side of the Horseshoe beyond Great Rigg and Fairfield Brow. A bright light shone on the stones beneath their feet. Above them, a radiant moon was hoisting itself above a dripping sea of vapours. The North and Irish seas were dim pools on the horizon. They dropped downhill and arrived at the waveless shore of Grisedale Tarn. There they knelt down and rolled the cold water through their fingers and gulped it from cupped hands.

Luke saw something in the water and gasped at its beauty. It wasn't his own reflection but a radiant red sky.

'A foxfire sunset! Michael used to say it was like looking into the fires of Heaven ... or should that be Hell? He wasn't much of a church-goer.'

Dorothy giggled.

Luke jumped up. 'What are you waiting for?' he cackled, flinging off his smock-frock, breeches and gaiters and wading into the tarn, whooping as the icy water curled up his bare body.

Dorothy roared with laughter. 'I told you the child was father of the man,' she yelled.

'What did you say?' he called back, having heard her perfectly well. 'I can't hear you, you'll have to come in.' He dived under and the freezing water gave his head such an agonizing ache that when he re-emerged he emitted a long lupine howl that resounded over several ranges of fells and might well have been heard by the imagined bagpipers approaching from Scotland.

To his joy and surprise, Dorothy had taken off cloak, spenser, petticoats, in fact everything apart from that shift she'd been mending on the wall back in May, and was wading into the tarn. The exact moment she started swimming – she didn't swim as such, but whirled around in small circles shrieking, her shift billowing like a Montgolfier balloon – her cries were broadcast over the fells like a she-wolf answering his howl.

'Dip your head under!' he shouted. 'It's worth the pain. You'll never get toothache again.'

'No,' she screeched, 'I couldn't do that. I really could not.'

'You can!' he laughed.

Her facial muscles scrunched. She submerged her head and

reappeared no more than a second later screeching out like a wild cat, not a she-wolf.

'Your childhood,' she gasped, treading water frenziedly, 'and your home in nature ... must be a source of ... p-pleasure to you again, Luke, not pain.'

'Forget my childhood!' he snapped. 'And nature ... and poetry ... and me!'

She turned to him in what looked like mortal fear. He launched his mouth at hers with such passion that when they released their lips not more than ten seconds later there was blood on them. They put their fingers to their mouths to feel whose it was.

'It's me,' he said, licking his lips and tasting a quaint Lakeland concoction of blood, tarn-water and Dorothy Wordsworth.

Dorothy was shivering and pale as ashes. 'I'm getting out before I perish with the cold,' she rattled through her teeth, dragging herself from the tarn, the baggy outlines of her legs revealing themselves through her shift to Luke's ravenous eyes. 'Mercy upon us!' she gasped again. 'What have you done to me?'

Luke climbed out and stood dripping wet before her. If only he could see through all those layers of skin into where that naked heart was beating.

Was it for this? Was this the moment to bellow his feelings off the felltops in the knowledge that on Lakeland's mountains echoes of declared love never died away but rebounded between the rocks forever? Dorothy had taken her eyes elsewhere, wringing the water out of her shift and reaching for the remainder of her clothes.

Luke took what felt like the deepest breath of his life, but not so that he could swim underwater. 'I ...' he roared, 'want to dance ... with the daffodils!' The final word rang out, and echoed, on and on, not fading but gaining, seeming to stretch into the past, back into the present, and into the future.

They made their way back up to Fairfield Ridge, judging it safer to make their descent the way they'd come, via the Greenhead Ghyll path. In the far sky over the North Sea to the east a dark mass was moving slowly westwards towards them. A giant black mist was approaching fast from the east. It perched above the ridge, then fractured and stole away. The clear dye of the Indian-ink sky broke up the grey and uniform deadness of the night landscape. Dorothy moved at speed; Luke worried that she was running away from him. Two cold, wet silhouettes headed back along the ridge beneath a million pinhead stars, and reached what they judged to be the point above Greenhead Ghyll.

'Listen,' whispered Dorothy. 'Can you hear water?'

'Yes,' he murmured back. 'The source must be just below us.'

A short but blind scramble on unreliable grass and unpredictable stone led them to what they expected to be a tiny spring seeping out of a stony gully in the fellside. But the sound of water had fallen silent, and there was no source to be seen.

'It must be further along,' said Luke. 'Let's forget it and try and make our way down from here.'

They started to scramble down further, and in the confusion and darkness they found themselves on rock, groping around with their feet for invisible footholds below. Luke felt his foot touch a ledge the distance beneath of about six feet. He lowered himself and then dropped down onto a second ledge, letting out a gasp of relief as he steadied himself. 'It's a dry waterfall,' he called back up. Under that ledge lay another, but at much more of a distance, and he had to hang by his fingertips, drop and hope for the best. He looked up beyond Dorothy into menacing black crags protruding like bulls' brows. He surveyed below. Ledge after ledge, the distance growing between each.

'There's no way back up,' shouted Dorothy.

'I'll watch out for you,' he called back, and she began climbing down the same way, hanging from her fingertips and hoping for the best.

She arrived safely by his side, but as they looked below they saw a drop of maybe twelve feet or more.

'We can't do that,' she said.

He shook his head. 'We'll have to stay here till it's light.'

They huddled close on the ledge, shivering and afraid, with Dorothy's cloak pulled round them both and their knees up to their chins.

'Now I know how those swallows on my window ledge felt,' said Dorothy with a smile. Luke cast his mind back to that fragrant day in the summer. They were in a real fix now, but at least they were together, and he clasped her tight while he still could.

Many sleepless hours later they watched the setting moon hang itself like a lantern on the Langdale Pikes. They caught the first blinks of waking day and, although they couldn't see to the east from their ledge, they knew the red-bronze orb of sunrise would be mounting the firmament over Ullswater where their daffodils had once been.

It was light enough to see below, and the view was as bleak as they'd feared. The long drop was to a ledge so narrow that if they stumbled they'd topple backwards to certain death. But the gaps between ledges narrowed from then on, so if they got down this one alive they'd be safe.

'I'll go first,' Luke said grimly, peering down at a distance twice his own height. Dorothy nodded. She looked too cold and distressed to protest. He crouched, turned and faced the rock, lowered himself leg by leg, arm by arm, until he was holding on by fingertips like icicles. He looked up into the anxious but ardent eyes of Dorothy, and let go.

# 30

# Tally Ho!

Sally looked desiccated by tears when he paid her a farewell visit at the Farm. She was too preoccupied with herself to notice the derelict state he was in after his near-death night on the fells with Dorothy, and the volcanic wrath was gone from her voice.

'I know now,' she said numbly, serving him up poddish but not looking him in the face. 'Jinnyspinner told me all about it. Looks like the Nettleslacks are reet divels and your lot are the saints in all this.'

'They weren't saints.'

'They'd always known about Fadder's bad ways, but never said nowt. Fadder got worse and worse, flandering, boozing, betting, and bullying – shouting at Mudder, really shouting, when he was neudled. I remember that bit. I used to run out of the house so I couldn't hear it. She shouted back. That was how it was. But they loved each other. Michael was an honourable man, paid off Fadder's debts, but his heart was broke when you had to leave, and he never forgave Fadder for that. They were loyal to him, though, and kept his secrets.'

Luke wanted to comfort his cousin, but didn't know how – her beloved father had turned out to be a charlatan and a murderer. 'Michael couldn't forgive Jack. What kind of a man can't forgive?' It didn't sound convincing.

'Ay, that's true,' said Sally, picking up on Luke's mild paternal denigration a little too keenly for his liking. 'Jinnyspinner said Michael dint want none of you nowhere near Fadder, so he kept you away, from all of us. That was right hard for Isabel, Jinnyspinner said, cos she loved Fadder 'spite everything.'

'Well what did he tell you about the debts?' asked Luke, reversing now into protection of the Greenhead name.

'The Nettleslacks and Greenheads made a pact one day, when you and me was still bairns, that if wust came to wust and Fadder got us so far in debt we'd have to sell the farm, Michael would pay them off. When't wust happened, and as you know Michael sent you away to London, Fadder sent Jackie to sea to earn his fortune, and the split got wider between us all. Isabel and Sarah never spake again. I never knew owt about you lot, they kept it all so hushed up. Then Mudder died.'

'And died knowing we were strangers to each other,' said Luke. 'I wish she could see us now.'

Sally smiled sadly. 'Only time Fadder and Michael's paths crossed again,' she continued, 'was when't sheep were disappearing. They worked together to hunt down the sheep-stealer – they had to, or both flocks woulda bin lost. And that was when Fadder showed his true colours. Yours was a better man, a truer one. He kept his silence for the rest of his days about what Fadder did. After Michael died I remember Fadder did try and talk to Isabel – not that I knew she was me auntie, mind – but he dint get any sense out of her and gave up after a while.'

'That must have been when Parson Snaile took Isabel in. Why did Jack lie about all that?'

'Jinnyspinner says the parson's never had a good wud to say about Fadder cos he knew all about his past and cos he never went to church to make amends. He says Parson Snaile got some right good stuff for his sermons knowing all about Fadder's sins, and there was a big grudge twain't two of them about some little bairn an all.

'Fadder dint have the guts to admit his mistakes, no doubt about that. He never owned up to Mudder or me about all sorts of things. Mebby he thought he could get away with murder after Michael died. But you know,' she said, turning to him with tearful eyes, 'he wasn't a stone-hearted man all his life. He took you in, dint he, even learnt to love you as one of his own this past year. He knew he'd done wrong, mind, and knew he had a wild side but that caught up with him.

'The other thing you need to know about Fadder – and Jinnyspinner dint tell me this cos I've known it myself for years – was that his mind was going an all. He dint know what the truth was half the time. What d'you think all that stuff was about cragfast sheep and ploughs and thrashing machines? We haven't had sheep in these fields since last year, and we haven't had hay and grain in the store neither. It was all a game to keep Fadder going. I knew he wunt last long if he realised the farm was ruined. I just had to keep telling him tales cos I couldn't face telling him the truth. His mind was too fragile.'

'We're all as bad as each other,' sighed Luke.

Sally turned her gaze away from him. 'I went to see Lance,' she muttered. 'Told him to go tut divel.'

Luke's eyes brightened. 'How did he take it?'

'Said he'd get me in the end. I don't know if that means he'll dance me down the aisle or do a jig on me grave.'

Luke smiled. 'Sally, I need to get something from that hut on Grasmere island before I go. Come out on the lake with me. We could take that skiff.'

'Go?' she said, her all-cried-out eyes reddening for a few dry teardrops.

He turned to her, wanting to tell her how much like family she felt now that they'd been jarring and tearing each other's throats out; and how desperate he was to see her happy, and happily married, and the happy mother of six children, at the bare minimum ... not one of them Vipond's, mind. And how he'd realised on the island – and this was very difficult for him to say face to face – that she might have been thinking that he could learn to love her in a certain way, but that he couldn't; but he could and did love her in another way – the right way, if that didn't sound too convoluted; and how he hoped that she loved him in the right way, because that would make things so much easier. And that he was sorry, sorry for having buggered up her year, if not her life, and sorry that, despite his long history of not doing things the right way, he couldn't bring himself to love her in the wrong way just when he suspected she might want him to. Yes, this was the perfect moment to say it all, but, in the emotionally primitive and inarticulate way the Lakeland male of the species had evolved, he didn't say any of it.

'What'll you do?' grunted the caveman.

'Don't know,' she said flatly. 'I can't keep the farm on any road. Go into service or summut. Mebby get work int wool mill in Ambleside, or one of them big noisy ones in Manchester.'

'Sally—'

'Come on,' she said. 'Tek me out on the lake before I change me mind.'

She led him to the place he and Dorothy knew as Dolly's View. The trees on the far side of the water were yellow-brown but Grasmere island was as green as spring. Luke took the oars and rowed out while Sally watched the water slide past. Luke studied her. She seemed as fluid as the Grasmere air itself, composed of its bold colours and myriad intermediate shades. She might have been pretending not to notice him but she didn't show it with those half-closed blue almonds for eyes, their abstracted limpidity, their languid roll over the lakewater as it danced past the boat. There was an ease, a grace as she sifted the water with her freckle-drenched arm. Of course she was a beauty, and if things had turned out differently ... but now they were blood cousins, practically brother and sister, and besides, much as he'd learnt to love Sally, he really wanted to be sailing through Grasmere Lake with an entirely different woman. Out of the two women he was clearly fated never to marry, Sally wasn't the one for him.

'Luke,' Sally said, turning and catching his eye, 'did you ever see me when we were bairns?'

'I don't remember,' he said, 'and I'm sure I would have, dearest cousin Sally.' He allowed the skiff to drift, and placed a tender hand on hers, not the one hanging languidly over the side of the boat swishing through the water, but the one whose fingers received his within its folds.

'Did you ever see her?' she asked.

'Who?' he said, taking the oars again.

'Dorothy.'

'No. She only came to live in Grasmere a few years ago.'

'Will you see her again?'

He shook his head.

'What about feelins?'

He started rowing again, aiming for the island. 'No feelings,' he replied, focusing his mendacious eyes on the island rather than her, and centring his ears on a distant and simultaneous howl; it was as though an animal somewhere far off had felt the injury of his lie. He looked round at Sally, and as he did so Helm Crag echoed to a canine chorale of trail-hounds throwing their tongues.

The huntsman of the Grasmere pack had always wondered what it must be like leading a battle charge against the French. He speculated, as he galloped along salivating more than the dogs at his feet and expectorating red curd to both sides of him, that he might have made a good officer, a general even. He suspected that the nearest he'd get to that feeling of the imperial bloodletter was the Grasmere Hunt. The hunters followed the horn across the fells, the only lady among them having taken knives to her petticoats and partitioned her skirt so as not to be slowed down in the chase. Amid the cries and howls among the crags, the huntsman caught sight of his quarry before the dogs had, and with a tallyho he tumbled downhill to the lake with the scent of blood in his nostrils. It would be a perfect end, the huntsman thought – a kill then a round of roast beef and plum pudding in the Swan, if only he could face eating something and then keep it down.

'That's him!' cried the lady, her eyes looking greedy to sling the fox on a pole. The lake surface was unsettled by the pawing of hounds on the western shore. They all stood watching – the huntsman, the lady, an official-looking man in conversation with the huntsman, and a miscellany of men fitting the general description of local ne'er-do-well. When the huntsman took off his hat and pasted his black hair back, Sally sighed, but not this time with ease and grace.

'It's Lance!' she cried.

'And Tindle, too,' said Luke with weary resignation.

'I think that's the constable an all,' said Sally. 'What's he doing there?'

'He can smell blood.'

'Get away while you can, Luke! They've got you.'

'For what?'

'Quick! Drop me off at the island then row tut far shore and run for it.'

Luke hesitated.

'Luke! What can you do against all that lot? Go! If you don't now you won't be able teh.'

Luke rowed hard, and they scraped aground at the island. He stood up in the beached boat, paused, and the little pinnace wobbled, nearly tipping him and Sally headfirst onto the muddy shore. He hopped out of it and scampered up the little hill past the hut to the knoll shouting for Sally to follow.

'What are you doing?' protested Sally as she scrambled after him. 'Lance'll be here any minute.'

Luke sat where he had so often during his time on the island. With Sally beside him he looked out at the lake, with the village he so loved behind it, and watched breezes whisper across the water. It was time to set things straight.

'Sally,' he said, turning to her, 'I—'

'I meant to give this back,' she interrupted, handing him the *Lyrical Ballads* she'd had secreted about her apron. 'And there was another book – a diary or summut – but it's back at the farm.'

'It doesn't matter now.'

Sally looked into his eyes expectantly.

'Here they are!' came a roar. Vipond materialised, flanked by the constable, the several ne'er-do-wells captained by Tindle, and a lady Luke recognised but couldn't put his finger on. Luke and Sally stood up.

'Well?' said Vipond to the lady.

'Yes.'

The constable stepped forward. 'Luke Greenhead?'

Luke gave him one of Jem's defiant looks.

The constable placed a hand on his shoulder without a trace of sympathy. 'You're under arrest.'

# 31

## Assize

On the hoar-frosted upper fells the rooks had lost their clamour, no sheep bleated, and runlets had frozen silent. Down in the vale the wind had stripped the remaining Grasmere leafage and brought unaccommodated winter. Grasmere's farmers strayed from their fields, the ground too sticky with winter frosts, and gave the hedges over to the robins to feed on the berries. Clotted oak leaves carpeted the ground under the gaunt versions of Sally, Jem and Nance's feet as they trod the lakeshore. The water stretched out corpse-like beneath the woods, and torpid trout lay in the icy shallows. Coot and widgeon alone cried fowl among the grey reed-beds, rehearsing the new season's alarm call in advance of the sportsman's gun.

They passed through Grasmere and Rydale and arrived at the Ambleside hiring fair. While Jem and Nance loitered nearby, Sally stood among others at a stand ticketed 'women-bodies' while farmers came and went, looking her over, checking her teeth. She reflected, as she stood selling herself, on the sale of the farm's furniture. It had been hard getting rid of Jack's armchair, especially when it didn't fetch much, but it had all been for the best. That and the sale of the cow and hens had been enough to keep them going, for a while at least. Farmers continued to come, examine and go, and they tended to go to a stand ticketed 'girls' where the stock was fresher and overall better value for money. At the end of an unsuccessful day they made their way back to Grasmere, Sally debating in her mind whether she was too proud to beg vittals on everyone's behalf. The answer, she concluded, was that it depended on the folk she was begging from. On their way back through Rydale between Ambleside and Grasmere she decided to try her hand, encouraging Jem, who boasted of many years perfecting begging, to go first and show her the ropes. They stopped at a cluster of cottages beyond Rydale lake at Town End in Grasmere, several of which didn't even bother to answer the door to them. Then they tried the door of a very pretty place.

'It's Sally isn't it?' called a voice from the doorstep over to Sally out on the road, after Jem had first been met by the eldest Cragg girl, who'd greeted him with a superior air, and then by ... her!

There was nowhere to hide. 'Yes, ma'am,' Sally muttered, mortified and once and for all put in her place. Dorothy disappeared inside and returned with a few pennies for Jem, whose begging instincts told him to whine for more as a matter of course, but Sally – who was trying to get away as fast as she could but not so fast as to forfeit the money – cut in before he opened his mouth. 'Thankee, ma'am.'

Only when they'd walked away did Sally suddenly remember something and stop in her tracks.

'What nah, Mudder?' whinged Jem.

'I'm not tha mudder, lad,' she blasted, the sharp scolds of harried motherhood already raining on the head of her adopted son. 'Don't call me that. Not fit to be anyone's mudder, me. I'm just a beggar, an ugly old spinster.'

She turned back and rapped on the door.

Dorothy reappeared.

'This is yours,' said Sally.

Dorothy took back her own very confidential journal. 'How did you—?'

''Twas Luke. He took it.'

'Yes but how did you get it? ... And where is he now?'

'Jail.'

Dorothy cast a horrified look. 'Where? What for?'

'Appleby. Dunno. Could be murder. Could be sheep-stealing.'

'Mercy upon us!'

'What is it, sister?' came a voice from within the cottage.

'Oh, nothing, Mary, nothing at all.'

'Beggars again?' called Mary.

'Yes, yes. I'm coming in now.' Dorothy stepped up close to Sally. 'Communicate my deepest sympathy to Luke,' she whispered.

'Ay, ma'am, if I get to see him again before it's too ... well, before.'

Jem tugged on Sally's apron and Nance raised her ancient frame off the ground. It was a good a time to move on, as beggars did. Sally left Dorothy on the doorstep. A brooding set of male eyes prowled behind her in the cottage's shadows. She set off walking again, her mood suddenly changing and her lips posting a pyrrhic smile to have come to the decision that she would, by hook or by crook, get those lasses back home with her, even the stroppy eldest one. Half a dozen bereft orphans God-knows-where and likely to be recaptured only through violent kidnap – it couldn't be that hard could it?

Jail. The very word was a funeral bell. Dorothy retired forthwith to her chamber and fell on her bed. She clasped the redeemed and much-missed journal to her breast. She couldn't help fearing the worst, that Luke was a condemned man, whatever his crime. It was an extreme reaction, she admitted to herself, but she'd heard rumours when she'd returned from France that he'd been implicated in the death of the Cragg fellow, and now this. Surely he wasn't the type to do something like that. But then again, she knew all about his London past. Could his concern for Cragg's children be no more than guilt? She prayed not, and thought about that swim in the tarn and that magical night cuddled up to him on the ledge below Fairfield. She held the journal ever tighter to herself, fondling the pages round the edges. She opened it up and thumbed the folios back and forth so fast their breeze made her eyelashes flicker, with growing amazement to think that she was the person who'd written it. She certainly couldn't now. She had absolutely nothing to write about in the replacement journal she'd bought in Calais. She might be as chatty as a sparrow in a hedgerow with everyone else, but with herself it was as if she'd simply lost her voice – her inward voice.

Something else disturbed her. The violation of her privacy – not necessarily by Luke, although it was unforgivable what she'd forgiven him for, but by this Sally woman. Had she read it, too? But what did it matter if she had? Who was Sally to her? And then the answer came to her. Sally was in love with Luke. How dare she, the little …!

But to be fair, didn't she, soon-to-be Aunt Dorothy the hardy perennial spinster, have to let him go again? How could she be so selfish as to detest the idea of him loving and being loved by someone else? Could she not let those unique sensations, that life-enhancing bitter-sweetness ('Oh just say it, Dolly,' she self-scolded, 'the *love*!') flutter and dance in the breeze like the daffodils, and then die away? Was her new life as loyal sister and philanthropist, maiden aunt and housekeeper, nothing more than a despicable charade?

Having been intimate with connoisseurs of the art in London, Luke thought he knew all there was to know about jail-languishing, but the sojourn at Appleby was something else, with its filthy cells, jail fever and prohibition of basic human needs that fell just short of requiring him to lick the walls for moisture. At first he'd shared his cell with a conscienceless brute by the name of Soulby who boasted that he'd casually murdered his sweetheart, despite denying it at his trial. To cheer Luke up in the cold, dark evenings that came at the end of the cold, dark days, Soulby had entertained him with macabre tales of death, full of gut-churning detail.

'There was a highwayman from round these parts,' Soulby had whispered one night, 'who terrorised Lakeland so bad no one dared go abroad at night. One day he shot some poor soul in the back and was seen doing it. Gibbeted him alive, they did. Stripped him, dipped him in hot tar and fixed an oak-and-iron cage round him. Hung him from't gallows and left him there. Swinging for days on end, he was, cryin' out in misery, till some kind-hearted passer-by couldn't bear the howling and shot him. The stiff was left up there on the gibbet as a warning, for a whole twelvemonth till it was half-rotted and scoffed by birds.

'Now remember,' Soulby said with a sparkle in his eye, 'there isn't no going to heaven without a body, so when another kind passer-by saw the gibbet blown down with fleshy skeleton still on it, he gathered the highwayman's bones, folded 'em in a sheet and buried them. And the lucky divel probably went to heaven after all. So there you go,' the cut-throat grinned in triumph. 'An 'appy ending. Sleep tight my friend.'

Luke had dozed off that night after his bedtime story feeling that a man's optimism, once he was down on his luck, had the capacity to plummet ever lower given the right conditions. Sure enough, the months went by and the prison set about breaking his independence of spirit, with mindless rock-splitting, corn-grinding fuelled with gruel, and total isolation in his cell punctuated only by the human contact brought by gratuitous beatings. He gradually came to reminisce about the Soulby cell-share as a time of commodious warmth and shared humanity.

The solitude of his confinement – designed by some or other enlightened Christian not only to punish the felon but to give him the time and space to submit an application for divine forgiveness – served as an inescapable opportunity for Luke to examine the one thing he'd managed to secrete about his smock-frock upon arrest. He sat on the floor of his cell reading by moonlight his secret copy of Wordsworth's *Lyrical Ballads*.

It wasn't easy at first, partly because he'd flicked through the book's preface but failed to heed its advice to bestow much time and 'severe thought' upon the poems lest he end up making the rash decision that they were a dreadful enemy to pleasure. Instead, he'd skimmed desultorily through and been left confused and unmoved. But poetry, he reminded himself, wasn't written for men like him anyway, it was for gentlemen, and noblemen, and churchmen, and every man apart from the ignorant common variety that made up the major part of the population and kept the cannons of war fed. The *Lyrical Ballads* didn't see the light of day for a month of nights. Then he tried again.

He spent much time thinking severely about what severe thought meant, and when he noticed that it was an approach that brought on a headache in its pursuit, he began to realise why Dorothy was always complaining of them, and conjectured further that the whole laudanum and opium trade – even the leeching profession – was built around the injurious consequences of severe thought. After a while he started reading through some of the poems again, and came upon one called *The Idiot Boy*, a strange, childlike tale about a simpleton sent out on a pony at night by his mother to fetch a doctor. The boy failed to return and the mother feared the worst, that her idiot son had got lost pursuing the moon in a brook or trying to catch a star out of the sky. Luke was moved by Wordsworth's sympathy for the poor mother, and her joy on finding her precious son safe. Such compassion for ordinary people and their hard, unnoticed lives was not what he'd expected from Wordsworth.

The last lines in the book Wordsworth declared to have composed several miles above an abbey by a stream. Unlike *The Idiot Boy* they were a rhymeless and tough read, demanding the severest of thought, manufactured to guarantee a thumping headache, and he had no tinctures of opium as a salve. But this final poem – a eulogy to youth, a vision of new hope in the maturity of years, to be glimpsed in nature, in the light of setting suns, and in humanity – gave voice to the longings of Luke's own spirit. He put the book down and closed his eyes.

He then realised he'd recognised one of the lines in the poem – Dorothy had recited it to him by Easedale Beck and he'd been furious with her for mentioning William. 'Nature never did betray the heart that loved her'. He re-read the poem, and saw something else he recognised. William had addressed his verse to a person whose identity was unmistakable for the shooting lights of her wild eyes, in whose youthful passion he beheld the child he once was.

It was as if William and Dorothy were feeding off each other's senses, as if they *were* each other, these two inmates of nature. There couldn't be a William without a Dorothy, it was plain to see. What worried Luke was that there couldn't be a Luke without a Dorothy either, so they were bound up together, all three of them, like triplets in the womb. How could he possibly hate William – his brother! – now?

No! She'd thrown a harness and reins over her heart and was resolved not to submit to it. It was a wrathfully bitter January morning when Dorothy set out on horseback from Grasmere, intending to go the whole way on nothing but moral fibre, potted beef and sweet cake. She'd inaugurated her second mission while ice-skating on Grasmere lake on Christmas Day, which was also her birthday, her charitable imagination skating ahead in much the same way William was inspired to poetry when his legs were in motion.

The first mission, to re-house the Cragg girls in Grasmere, had been a success, she told herself as she cantered up Dunmail Raise. Not an unqualified one, however: the poor things had howled like puppies torn from the teat when she'd taken them from each other's clasped hands and given them to local farm folk. And that eldest Cragg girl – by far the most surly, having entered that totally unmanageable phase of adolescence which required everyone and everything to be scowled at as a matter of basic bodily function – had, as bad luck would have it, been the only one housed at Dove Cottage. The girl's manifold defects of character had tested Dorothy's kindness to the limit, but she'd been resolute that their tiny, quiet Dove Cottage would become the tragic orphan's long-term home ... despite the fact that it was now also home to William's new wife, Mary, William and Mary's as-yet unborn child, as-yet unnamed, as well as the inevitable Molly for much of the time, and, of course, Dorothy and William themselves.

Dear Mary was indeed with child and was due the following June, a fact which overjoyed and desolated Dorothy in the same emotional breath, reminding her that the only clock ticking within her own body was that of maiden aunt-hood, and that nurturing her mind as consolation for the sacrifice of skipping motherhood was hardly likely to happen either. The domestic toil of keeping house at Dove Cottage would see to that. But her thirty-first-birthday epiphany came when, in an accidental spin on the ice which had turned into a rather maladroit pirouette ending in a bruised hip, she suddenly realised that although she couldn't have the only man who'd ever kissed her in *that* way, she might at least be able to help him, or – dare she hope? – even save him from the gallows.

She trotted the forty-mile journey north past Keswick and westwards to Penrith feeling comforted to know that her second mission was finally under way. In fact, that comfort was already easing the discomfort she'd been suffering over Luke, which had manifested itself specifically in toothache. Her plan, which she went through in her mind as her mare headed south-east from Penrith in the direction of Appleby, was first of all to get to see the prisoner and drench him with the festive offerings she'd gathered over the Christmas season, such as ale, bread and prayer-books. That, she hoped, would help ease his hardships. If she was by good fortune allowed to visit the accused on a more regular basis then she would importune the local gentry for charitable donations and quill pleading letters to the Magistrate, not that she expected anything on that score, the man being an uncharitable charlatan.

She arrived in Appleby and found her way to the jail, and – through obscure genteel connections with the Hereditary High Sheriff of Lakeland – in the jail she sniffed out the cell where Luke was purported to be languishing.

Indeed, there he was, barbed beyond belief and cheeks as hollow as shells, looking peaceful but frail, and certainly looking pardonable for whatever he'd done. A faraway look sat in his eyes which puzzled her, then she saw William's *Lyrical Ballads* in his hands. She took one of the hands, and said, in tones she was determined would not sound patronising, that she would do all she humanly could to enhance his comfort and secure his release.

'I'm so happy,' she added, 'to see that you've been reading William's poetry. You, Luke, are a true child of nature, the kind of person William wants every man to be. Thank you.'

'For what?' he asked.

'I don't know.' She did, she just couldn't say it, unable despite everything to break free of the straitjacketing discretion of the fair sex and unfair class. It was for turning her life upside down and insisting that she half-fall in love – not with a flower, or a swallow, or a poem, but with him. And for their brief but exhilarating season, when she'd felt more liberated than ever, however shallow and short-lived and ultimately doomed that emancipation had been.

'I have you to thank,' he said.

'Me?'

'For helping me on my way.'

'To jail?'

'Well, maybe via jail.'

'You perplex me just as much as ever,' she said with a smile and sideways nod.

'I'll never forget as long as I live,' he said – Dorothy suddenly frowning at the thought that that might yet prove a shorter time-span than he'd expected even though she still didn't know his crime – 'the final words my father said to me, the morning after I'd laid the cornerstone.'

'The cornerstone?' gulped Dorothy, beginning to shift around uneasily as if she'd gone numb beneath her skirts on the wooden plinth Luke had been using for a bed. 'The morning you left Grasmere, you mean?'

He nodded. 'That big stone was gone last time I looked. I thought it wouldn't shift in a thousand years.'

Dorothy shrugged as if to suggest it was a complete mystery to her as well. 'What were your father's parting words?' she asked.

'He told me there was a comfort in the strength of love; that it would make bearable things which otherwise would break the heart.'

Dorothy went silent.

'Love?' she checked.

'Yes,' he confirmed.

# 32

## Loved

'Hangum first and tryum afterwards!', was the impartial suggestion of the mob, and in their considerable wisdom the Justices of Assize of the Court of King's Bench, along with the Hereditary High Sheriff of Lakeland and the petty Magistrate – who didn't need to be there but wanted to for the sport – and various other most respectable gentlemen of the courts, all tended to agree. But irritatingly for them they had to go through the motions of weighing the crimes alongside the gamut of inhuman punishments. The clerk to the court administered oaths and read out the charges with unwavering clarity of voice and not a little drooling of mouth, the trials were conducted, and soon the grubby-fingernailed hack from the Lakeland Gazette was scribbling away all the eventualities for the titillation of his readers, mis-spelling names and other salient words in keeping with the newspaper's honourable tradition.

Mr Willaim [*sic*] Percivall, for stealing a game-cock – guilty – to be imprisoned for six moths [*sic*] and publicly whipt in Kendal. Miss Eleanor Mooney, for stealing a purse – guilty – to be transported. Mr Robbit [*sic*] Bird, for dishonesty at work – guilty – to be publicly whipt and sent to Liverpool. Mr Lancelot Varty, for hore-stealing [*sic*] – guilty – death. Mrs Jane Satterthwaite, for stealing wearing apparel to be transported [*sic*] – guilty – to be transported. Mr Anthony Soulby, for murdering his sweetheart and confessing it to a fellow prisoner – guilty – death (giblet) [*sic*]. Mr Luke Greenodd [*sic*], for sheep-stealing – guilty – death.

The first wave of springtide had strewn the ground with snowdrops and the skies with translucence. The snow turned out to be more than hinted at in the snowdrops, a heavy blizzard catching Grasmere by surprise in the middle of the month, and folk tramped back indoors, livid that winter was back, only to discover the sun was out again and the snow gone. Sally set off across the Kirkstone Pass with her four companions, one of whom pointed out at length, with constant reference to the great Abercromby, that the great British army had won the Battle of Alexandria two years before, almost to the day.

Not far from Patterdale, avoiding a place called Nell House whose landlady, so Sally heard, welcomed wind-stricken travellers but tended to overcharge them, the five companions stopped at a dim-windowed and weed-defaced cottage and placed themselves at the mercy of a woman suffering from the facial modifications of a broken heart. Over half-boiled water and pleasurelessly thin haverbread, a passing remark by Sally about the amount of snow and ice still around despite it being the eve of spring brought the woman to tears. With no encouragement the woman related the tale behind why her countenance betrayed such obdurate melancholy. It was a chilling story, about her two young sons who had fallen through the ice while skating on Broad Water on New Year's Day.

When Sally told the sniffing mother where the five companions were heading, and that they, too, had their own cause to be downhearted – confiding under her breath that it would be a long journey into the night and, when they arrived, no place for children – the woman suggested Jem and Nance could stay with her until Sally returned.

As they left, Sally glanced back and waved sadly to Jem, wondering if it would be the last time she ever saw him. The bereft mother's face looked modified into what Sally suspected was her first half-smile since her two sons had drowned. The three companions headed eastwards for Patterdale and Ullswater in the direction of Penrith.

Beyond Penrith on the outskirts of Appleby sunrise began to shed light on Gallows Hill the way a candle might illuminate a corpse. A group had gathered around a makeshift wooden creation. Some gentleman Sally assumed to be the Magistrate was there, talking to Lance, and Parson Snaile was there, as well as the Sheriff, Gass, Weightman and Sally herself. After a while a cart drew up and an emaciated, beaten beggar was turfed out of the back by two turnkeys. They led her Luke, hands tied in front of him with rope, to the wooden creation, where he stood and turned. Everyone was watching – apart from the Magistrate, who continued to bend Lance's ear. Sally caught Luke's eye. She wasn't one for tears, but she made an exception in this case as she moved to the front of the group to within leg-pulling distance.

The Sheriff nodded to the hangman, who nodded back. Sally backed away from Luke, and Luke backed away from Sally. Parson Snaile shuffled forward and muttered a prayer, and Luke turned his back on the group and climbed the steps. The group went silent. Even the Magistrate stopped nibbling Lance's ear, much to Lance's evident relief, and seemed to focus his eyes on the face of the condemned man for the first time. The hangman put a white hood over Luke and positioned him underneath the noose.

The rope tightened round Luke's neck and he closed his eyes. In the hell of his fear his mind fell upon the image of Alice Bell. He saw his parents, and was glad they didn't have to watch this. He opened his eyes and looked out to Sally, though all he could do now was visualise her. Her tearful, torn-apart face had killed him to see.

His memory was slung back to Greenhead Ghyll that day late the previous year when Dorothy recited the rainbow poem. 'The child is father of the man,' he muttered, and he could hear again her trilling 'so perfect for you.' He thought about Grasmere island, and staring into the lake at himself. He'd been looking for the man and had stumbled on the boy, father of the man he'd learnt to love again.

And he thought about what he might do if he was granted more life. Had some other goddess rocked his cradle apart from nature? All that anger at the unfairness of things. He wondered what England had been like in the past, when people had been free, and equal – long before the noblemen and the churchmen had stamped their indelible seal on everything. He wouldn't go standing in a mob brandishing a hatchet like Cragg had advocated, but his heart stood with the poor, over-exploited, underpaid and hungry people he'd been born amidst, worked with on the fells, fought with on the battlefield and festered among in London. Were they not worth living for? But it was too late now.

He reached out blindly to his heart's desire, and saw that his love for her wouldn't change with the weather – it was all weathers and all seasons; it would find its flower each spring, and be a warm shelter in winter; it would bound across meadows in summer, and weep for the beauty of autumn. Most comforting of all was the knowledge that it wouldn't need life in order to live. Like mother-love itself.

He closed his eyes again and didn't make the panicked request for a place in a realm anywhere more exalted than the earthy womb to which he now knew he would return. The last memory he had was of lying by the edge of Airey Force nearly a year before, listening to the waterfall thundering down from the wild fells of Lakeland. Upon his inward eye flashed the daffodils, and for a moment his heart filled with pleasure, and he danced with them. He could hear Airey Force, even taste the fresh, cool water. The jolt made him gasp, the thunder of the waterfall became a numb rumble, and he felt himself toppling over the edge, soon to be dashed against rocks and sucked into icy pools below.

# 33

# Struggle

Dorothy felt her neck crick as she crouched down at White Moss to smell the sweetness of the grass. She fingered her throat, wincing at the pain, and moved her head round like a slow owl to soothe it. As she stood up she remembered the moment she'd first come across White Moss and how her senses had been afire at its beauty. William had been with her then, of course. He might now be at Dove Cottage with Mary, but he was not with her. Their days were over; William's as a poet, hers as his muse. But the rips and tears of love which Luke had wrought on her and William; the anger and jealousy he'd stirred up, the half-destruction of them, well, maybe all that might have broken her brother's fall as a poet in some way, given him some gritty experience to write about when he wasn't penning love sonnets for Mary. The whole affair had, after all, brought herself and William, the poet and his muse, closer for a time – in France, a time when the love between them was fragmenting. Perhaps a line or two of verse might come out of all that. As for her, not only had she lost William, but Luke as well – in fact she'd lost herself again. The reinvention of her public persona since the wedding was as unnatural and wrong as the harem inside Dove Cottage.

She looked out on White Moss and remembered the words she'd first used to describe the glories of the scene before her in her journal. 'A place,' she recited aloud from memory, 'made for all kinds of beautiful works of art and nature, woods and valleys, fairy valleys and fairy tarns, miniature mountains, alps above alps.' She allowed herself poignant pleasure at the sound of her own words, and sighed to think that Luke would have delighted in them if he'd been there. She dreaded to think what had become of him, the man who'd so inspired her. Her plan to rescue him had failed, as had her courage to go to the hanging and see him one last time. He was as lifeless as she now felt in the depths of her own soul. Dead. Her inspiration.

'Oh God!' she called out and fell to her knees, horrified suddenly to think that she herself had killed the one she'd come to need and love the most. 'My muse,' she sobbed, and scraped her fingers through the soil beneath her hands. '*My* muse!'

Sir Edward Unthank Bart watched the prisoner's legs swinging comically at the gallows. One ignorant peasant the less, he muttered to himself as he dealt with the slight mental distraction of having recognised the prisoner from somewhere or other, just as the hangman was putting the hood on him. Oh well, it might come to him later. He wished, now that it had sprung to mind, he'd got to see that rascal of a highwayman drop and dangle as well, the one who'd held up the Flying Machine just outside London. Then he twigged.

'No!' he roared. Some fool of a milkmaid had raced up onto

the gallows and was giving the man's legs a good stretch to put him out of his misery. He ran up after her and wrestled her off. 'Stop, you maniac! Lift him up, cut him down, do something for God's sake!'

The turnkeys seized the dangling man and lifted him out of the air, grunting with the weight. 'Take the hood and noose off, you fools,' bawled Sir Edward. The hangman undid the noose and the turnkeys carried him down and placed him on the soft earth. The Sheriff marched up to Sir Edward while a group of onlookers ran to the prisoner and removed the hood.

'Sir Edward!' demanded the Sheriff deferentially. 'What are you doing?'

'This man saved my life,' he declared. 'It would be churlish not to save his. I didn't recognise him until now.'

Sally was kneeling down over Luke. One minute earlier she'd been hastening his death, now she needed to slow it down, but apart from stroking his face and searching for life in his eyes she didn't know how. And she worried that the more she touched him, and wept over him, and held his hand, and adhered herself, the more her love would set in. She leant over his face and let the auburn locks she knew he was rather fond of attempt to tickle the life back into his cheeks.

'Saved your life?' queried the Sheriff, who was standing with the Magistrate – who she now realised was Unthank, Lance's master – who'd called her a maniac purely for trying to kill the man she loved.

'Sir Edward,' the Sheriff continued, 'this man here stole and killed a Herdwick.'

'Which is unpardonable, I know,' said Sir Edward. 'But he fought off a highwayman who was about to blow my brains out, and who had already appropriated my favourite eighteen-carat timepiece. Which makes your crime pardonable, Mr – what's his name? – Greenodd?'

'Greenhead,' spat Sally. 'Old Grasmere family, sir. Older'n

yours I bet. All gone now. He wut last of the flock.'

Gass and Weightman had crouched down over Luke, next to Sally.

'Is he still alive?' asked Weightman.

'If he is,' chuckled Gass, 'he'll be white as milk from now on. He won't have no blood in his head.'

'Ay,' laughed Weightman, copying Gass's unexpected mirth, 'long neck an all.'

'He isn't a dyin' swan,' rasped Sally, her nose running all over Luke.

'Are you his friends?' Sir Edward asked Gass.

Gass nodded threateningly, as if protecting the blessed Abercromby from the final fatal blow.

'If Mr Greenodd – Greenhead – is indeed dead I will see to it that he is granted a posthumous pardon, and I will pay for a grave in Grasmere. I trust money is all you are after?' he said, addressing the top of Sally's head and dropping some coins down by her side.

'Well, sir,' said Sally, looking up at the baronet, 'first of all, he int dead. And third of all, I might not have no learnin', and I might be a woman-body, and I might look like a ninslent milkmaid, but I know what's right and what's not. You rich gentlefolks steal all't commons, wipe away centuries of blood lines from't face of the land, work half the poor folk to death – I reckon you wunt even dare set your cotton-picker negroes on that walling job on Helvellyn – then spill tuther half's blood fighting your wars.

'Any that's left, you hang the starving buggers for pilfering sheep. None of that blood is yours, mister, none of it. Nae, it's all the common red stuff you're draining away. You're killing off the villages and tearing the heart out of this land. This land is the likes of us, not the likes of thee. We're the ancient oaks, not you rich fowks. Nae, I'll sort him myself.'

'Well said, chief,' cried Gass.

'Very well,' snapped Sir Edward Unthank Bart straightening

up with indignation at the rant. 'But if your friend is still alive he cannot stay in Lakeland. He must never return to Grasmere. I'm sure the Sheriff will agree. We don't want to set a precedent – the man is a sheep-stealer, after all. Now if that is all, Good Day!'

He turned on his heel and began striding away.

'Good Day, sir,' said Sally calmly, adding, 'There is one thing.'

He stopped. 'What, dammit?'

'Get the Sheriff to arrest him,' she said, pointing a finger as sharp as a lance at Lance and making everyone crane their neck round, everyone apart from Luke. 'He pushed Mister Cragg off Helvellyn. He told me.'

'What are you talking about?' he shouted, even though Vipond, watching him from a few yards away, knew he knew. The Sheriff was watching, and if the Sheriff wasn't convinced by his performance, then the sacrifice would have to be made. They'd rehearsed just before the hanging, going over things, and now it was the time to sound spontaneously astonished and furiously indignant. He would mount an attacking defence, not only of his man, but of his own class, encompassing the enclosure of Helvellyn, the slaughter of inarticulate peasants in the war with France, and the slave trade. Yet his master was for once speechless.

Vipond looked on with mounting discomfort. Before the hanging he'd suffered a hateful voice drilling into his ear. 'You are a filthy peasant's bastard son,' Unthank had flattered him, 'the runt of an idle fornicator and adulterer. I knew the moment you were born you were worthless. I thought I might be rid of the stain of you forever when Parson Snaile in his kindness took you and delivered you to the Poor House. But you have pierced my side ever since. And then you kill the only craftsman on my wall, the only man who could do the job properly.

'Yet I will defend you should anyone accuse you. Not

because I care for you but to protect your detestable mother and condemn this foul secret to perdition forever. So let the blackguard who calls your name answer to me. I will do everything to shield from contamination the ancient and noble blood that comes down to me. And when this is over you will go back up Helvellyn, whitewash the whole wall so every man can see it is mine, and finish the job before this year is out, or you will be finished and I will have you on a pole like a fox before you know it. Do you understand?'

So why, wondered Vipond as the seconds pulsated by and he sweated, gurned, coughed, spat and scratched his head, was Unthank not defending him? He concluded that, although his master would dearly love to have him tried and hanged for Cragg's murder – whether he was guilty of it or not – there remained the risk that he might blurt out from the gibbet – and he certainly would – the name of a lady they both knew well and loved? His own mother, his master's wife.

They were all interrupted by Greenhead, who spluttered back to life in Sally's arms, to Vipond's profound disappointment.

'Come this way, my good sir,' Unthank beckoned to the Sheriff. 'I say, do you know Parson Noble Snaile?' He put one hand on the parson's shoulder and the other on the Sheriff's. 'I insist you both join me for lunch at Unthank Hall, gentlemen. And a spot of deer-hunting afterwards, what?'

The two wallers hoisted the hanged man up onto his feet and swung his arms over their shoulders. The four friends began descending Gallows Hill, Luke tottering palely in the middle as if he'd spent a week in the Swan in Grasmere. Sally walked a few paces behind, and slinking a few paces behind her – but catching up – was Vipond.

'Sally, lass!'

Sally ignored him.

'Sal. C'mon nah, I forgive thee.'

Sally stopped, but didn't turn round. He caught up. She

turned to face him. 'For what?'

'That nasty lie. I never said I pushed Cragg.'

'Who did then?' Sally hissed back.

Vipond lifted his scrawny arm into the air. 'The wind, I nearly fell off myself, but Cragg grabbed me so I took hold of him. I'm not a killer, Sal. He fell. It could've bin me who copped for it.'

Sally looked him straight in his little owlish eyes, and for the first time thought she recognised someone else. 'Let me go now.' She set off walking, and heard his voice calling after her.

'We'll set up away from all this. Ay, time to move on. Bairns, pounds in our pockets. Nice farm, land, corn, cattle, even get one of them thrashing machines.'

Sally carried on walking. Vipond strode so fast that he caught up with her. She turned to tell him once and for all to leave her alone but saw that he'd marched straight past her towards Gass and Weightman, who were shouldering the burden of the half-alive Luke.

'Yuv stuck by me all these months, lads, and now it's time for't reward,' he wheezed. 'Back to work again tomorra, eh, double the wages, double the vittals. Plenty to do now spring's here. Rood a day keeps the wukhouse away. We can start off by doing a nice bit of wall-whitewashing. Easy! Heh heh!'

Gass looked round at him with disdain. 'Ye don't look well enough to lean against a wall never mind build one.'

Vipond turned to Weightman.

'Don't even think about it, chief,' Gass snarled. 'He's with me.'

Sally walked past Vipond without looking round at him, and helped the others stumbling downhill bearing Luke by the armpits.

Vipond watched them disappear and soon found himself alone on Gallows Hill. What good would a wife be anyway, especially a potato-picking farm lass with no brain and no breeding, and she was probably too old to be a housewife and mother. He didn't need any of them; they could go and hang themselves. He'd managed just fine on his own. He set off alone down Gallows Hill with his hand over his mouth and his legs feeling utterly sapped of strength. He wasn't short of money, the farm was doing well, and he could probably buy Nettleslack Farm. That might teach Sally. Then again, he could sell up and move on; start again somewhere else. That would teach them all. A storm of blood-coughing passed upwards through him and out of his mouth. No. He'd see a doctor and get some rest, then think things through when he was feeling better, maybe when the summer had put some warmth and dryness back into the air.

Luke dropped insensible several times along the way, but somehow they got him to Penrith, where a few of the coins Unthank had tossed onto the ground at Gallows Hill bought them bread and ale enough to revive the body – and to a slight extent, the spirits – of the last of the Greenhead flock. When he had the strength for it, Luke croaked the answer to the question on everyone's lips.

'A terrible shock,' Luke whispered, 'then a flame, a light, which flashed right through me. After that no pain, no sensation. When they took me down and the blood came back into my head, the worst headache and shooting pains. I wished they'd left me up.'

'I'm right sorry I near killed thee,' said Sally.

Luke smiled. 'I would've done the same.'

Gass, looking uncomfortable to hear such tender talk, stood up to attention. 'Now you're on the mend, chief,' he announced, 'we're on our way.'

'Where?' asked Luke.

'Time to turn young Weightman here into a hero.'

Luke and Sally looked at Weightman. 'I'm gunta join the army, gettum back for Abacrombeh.'

'Said like a true Irish redcoat,' laughed Gass. 'And I'm coming with ye, Weightman. I'm ready for it. We've been lying next to a Froggeater for months and didn't know it. Hiding behind his big black moustache, he was. Worked harder than any of us, mind you. Likeable fella for sure. Never stopped. But a Froggeater's a Froggeater.'

'Ay,' echoed Weightman. 'Froggeater's a Froggeater.'

Sally and Luke watched sadly as the two comrades march away.

'I wonder,' said Luke as he and Sally began marching away in the opposite direction, 'how many Froggeaters they'll kill before it's their turn to chew the sod.'

When they got as far back west as the fork in the road by the Struggle, Luke stopped. The sun tussled with the clouds like an actor trapped behind curtains, and Sally and her cousin stood squinting at each other in the crystal air, shading their eyes with their hands as if in naval salute.

'Yeh not going back over to Grasmere, then?' said Sally.

'I'm a condemned man in Grasmere, don't forget,' he said. 'So I go this way.' He pointed back eastwards the way they'd just come, the way out of Lakeland. 'I wanted to see you this far and say goodbye.'

'Nae,' said Sally. 'I'm going with you.'

'You can't. What about Jem?'

'He'll be all right.'

'And Grasmere?'

'The only thing I might've stayed for was Fadder and them Cragg bairns, but they've all bin tekken away from me.' She hesitated. 'I only have you.'

The hand-loom weaver took the spinster by both hands. 'Sally, you know that even though I love you dearly, I—'

'—Don't love me. I know. Dyeh think I'm daft? You love her. Think I can't see?'

Sally waited for him to say something but soon felt she didn't need him to, and he seemed to diminish in front of her eyes. She saw him as who he'd always been, just a man, and she wasn't going to have no man wreck her life – she could do that perfectly well on her own. She turned to face the wind and felt, as if for the first time, the violence of nature, the endless fracas it had made of her life, splintering and snapping her off the ancient rockface, thrusting her downhill and tossing her about among the ghylls and becks.

'Sally!' he called out as she began walking away onto the Struggle. She could hear him, but she couldn't listen. She had other plans. She might follow up on her promise to make some gingerbread for Mr Lea. Maybe take him up on that idea he had for a little gingerbread shop next to the village school. 'Sally Nettleslack's Gingerbread'. Yes. But first, and most important of all, she'd get them damn lasses back. She'd bring Nettleslack Farm back to life somehow, by squeezing more money out of the bleeding hearts of those rich folk Lady Wudswuth went to in the first place. She'd get them fed and clothed and reared proper if it killed her. The maternal instinct was too impatient now to wait around for such a trifle as a man, especially one with a past as wild and chequered as a plaid shawl in a Skiddaw squall. The hen would do without the cocks chasing her round the farmyard and then clambering and stamping on her back, clawing out her hair, leaving her sore, raw and humiliated. She'd gather up those lost chicks and regrow her fine Nettleslack feathers in time for winter.

'Sally!' he called out again, but her name might as well have caught the wind and spiralled up like a lost kite into the sky over the fells for all the good it did in making her stop and turn back.

Luke watched her walk away and turn miniature in the distance. Eventually she fizzled to nothing on the horizon. He set off dejectedly towards Patterdale. How he'd let poor Sally down. He would miss her. He wished he didn't have to leave again, but he couldn't go back to Grasmere. As he passed along the edge of Ullswater he looked out on the lake and saw a tiny rocky promontory. He fancied that one day he'd return and make his home on the little island in Grasmere lake, turning the stone hut into a little croft, keeping watch on a small flock for some farmer.

Nice dream. No. He would make his way to Manchester and get work in that huge cotton mill again; get men to club together with him and maybe stand up for themselves a bit; try to change things, not by breaking machines or joining riots like others were doing, but somehow slowly just change things.

As he followed exactly the same path that had led him straight into a host of golden daffodils a year before, his thoughts turned to Dorothy, how she'd helped him to see that his soul wasn't soiled, but of the soil; and how they'd been levelled by their love. William might write poems about common people, but she was a true believer, in the freedom and equality of people. How he wished he could have had her for himself.

'Who else,' he cried out into the clouds 'will ever love Dorothy Wordsworth for *her*self?'

# 34

# Golden Daffodils

In grounds of ancient oak and ash near the foot of Rydale lake, in the State Bedroom of a large building whose walls were rashed with Unthank family coats of arms, Lance Vipond sat in an Elizabethan oak wainscot armchair with the back of his bony hand pressed against his mouth. He looked up at his nurse in her flimsy cotton dress and saw that her raven-coloured hair had gone grey. But her beauty, most striking in those dark eyes and deep red lips, remained. And her waist, short and slipped up to directly below her bosom, was as slender as he'd ever seen it. No wonder she'd turned so many heads in her time, he remarked to himself proudly.

She stood above him, the top of her right hand testing his brow, her left holding a silk handkerchief monogrammed with the letters E and U.

'Here,' she whispered, and he took the ornate handkerchief languidly and coughed a thick blood-streaked sphere into it. 'Lie down on the bed, now,' she said. 'This curse has done enough. Rest.'

'I can't rest, and I can't lie down,' he said. 'It makes the coughing even worse.'

'You must. You haven't the strength to sit in that chair any longer. If I turn my head for a minute you'll be sliding out onto the carpet.' With a sigh Vipond allowed her to take his arm and lift him to his feet.

'Wait a minute, I want one last look.'

'Where?'

'Out at the fells, from that big window.' He raised his right arm and she put it over her shoulder. They limped out of the bedroom and into the Great Dining Room. As they passed a giant oil-on-canvas picture of Sir Edward Unthank Bart and horse in the hunting field, Vipond looked round and into the eyes of the man in the painting and thought to himself that they were together at last, where they should be, where he should have been all his life. He noted how unlike his father he was, and then he remembered that of course the man in the portrait wasn't his father.

'There,' said Lady Unthank gently as they reached the big window. 'There's Helvellyn in the distance.'

He looked, and thought bitterly about all that the world had refused to grant him, and fell into another paroxysm of bloodletting into the Unthank heirloom. 'They'll need to buck their ideas up if they want that wall built,' he croaked, and turned away from the window. 'Tek me back to the bedroom. I want to lie down now.'

They returned to the State Bedroom and to the sumptuous four-poster bed with silk hangings where he presumed so many Unthanks — the vast majority of them legitimate — had taken their first breaths, and their last. His curdled spit was cherry red and his voice was a mere whisper, giving him an air of mildness that was, although a quality of his mother, categorically not him. Breaths became harder and harder won; sweat ran off him like April rain and his ashen eyes sank slowly beneath the rocks of his skullbones. His mother asked if she could take his shirt off him because he was perspiring so much, and as she did so he bent his head forward in a way that felt more comfortable to him, a way that slightly eased the pain of trying to breathe. He didn't move his head from that position, and while he watched her sniffing and touching her nose as she looked down on him, and while he wanted to reach up and kiss her, or at least receive his mother's kiss, his mind and vision began to loosen and he knew the time had come when he didn't need to carry on fighting them all.

Good air was the goal. The air was so crystalline that any conscientious picturesque painter – not just Noble Snaile – would be alarmed into rummaging around for easel and palette knowing such heavenly accidents of light and shade passed as quickly as life itself. The parson balanced easel, palette and glass in his arms and chewed on his pencil, and sighed that the name Snaile would never be uttered alongside Titian, Raphael or Claude. Perhaps 'fine landscape artist' in his *Times* obituary? He chuckled – he was at it again, writing his own obituary.

After an hour in the huddled confusion of thickets – where art required him to crowd and clump, exaggerate and distort, render unfaithful imitations of nature in search of opulence for the eye – he lost his patience. For his first time as an artist he headed for the fells. He'd heard the air was good up there, but he'd never dared go alone, not being the type to take liberties with points of the compass the way he did with art.

He retraced the exact footsteps of Sir Edward Unthank that day on Helvellyn, and some hours later ended up in a maze of disorientation in the foothills of the Swirls, leaning against the Unthank drystone wall. The air was indeed good, a happy blend of the endless dyes of yellow, red and blue, and the views magnificent. He could clump Helvellyn and Wythburn Water together, add a cow, a cloud, a rock and a human or two and have himself a delightful picture.

He set the easel down and held up the blackened, tinted mirror that would frame and colour the landscape in the style of Claude. He turned his back on the scene and looked into the mirror. 'Oh this is absurd,' he snapped. 'I shouldn't have to peer through a glass darkly. My eyes – my soul – should be free.' He thought of St Paul. "Now I know in part; then I shall know fully, even as I am fully known."

He looked up into a celestial azure sky and felt struck, not by an errant pebble or birdlime, but by something invisible, intangible, powerful. 'I believe,' he said, and concluded that this was the finest air he'd ever experienced. As he lowered his Claude glass he saw in it the face of a man not quite himself. He leapt with the shock.

'Forgive me, Vicar,' mumbled Sir Edward Unthank Bart, feeling, now that he'd mentioned it, genuinely in need of absolution. 'I've been following in your footsteps.'

'In *my* footsteps?'

Sir Edward realised by Parson Snaile's bamboozled visage that he'd taken him figuratively. 'You happened to be going where I was going – on my fell, to my wall.'

'I came to do some sketching,' said Parson Snaile defensively.

'Ah, another of your vocations? … Vicar, I was thinking of challenging you to a duel, but it's probably just a whim.'

'A… du … why on earth would you want a duel with me?' replied a tiny howl.

'Some silly idea I had that being shot to death in the name of compassion by a man of God might reduce my sentence.'

The parson offered a puckered brow. 'You're talking nonsense, Sir Edward.'

'Vicar,' said the baronet looking around him, 'can we speak confidentially?'

Parson Snaile looked embarrassed, but crouched on the ground and lowered his head. 'What is ... troubling you, my son?'

'My son,' said Sir Edward.

'Your son?'

'My ... wife's son,' he qualified. 'Haunting me. I think we both know who I mean, Vicar.'

'Yes, God rest his soul.'

'I spurned him, turned him away ... I'd do it again.'

'You gave him some kind of chance, did you not?'

'Only because his mother forced me to, threatening revelations.'

'Revelations?'

'Oh, the usual thing, whores and mistresses, nothing that weighs on my conscience whatsoever. But it is one thing to have the right to do as one likes, quite another for the world to know about it. My immoral wife nearly ruined the Unthank name. I was able – thanks to you, Vicar – to get the bastard whisked away the moment he was born. But he used his mother to wheedle his way back into my life, into my house and home. And now, he's on my ... my ... conscience.'

'Ah.'

'I'm too old to change, Vicar, it's too late.'

'Never too late, Sir Edward, never too late.'

Sir Edward crouched and looked out over the Lakeland landscape with defeated eyes. He knew, much to his vexation, that divine absolution was about the only thing he couldn't buy, and that this was his chance. 'There's one other ... little matter.'

The parson closed his eyes, possibly rolling them heavenwards, and bowed his head. 'Lay bare your conscience, Sir Edward,' he droned.

'It's about ... my son.'

The parson's nose twitched in irritation. 'Haven't we ... been here before?'

'No, my real son.'

'Your ... who is your real son?'

'I have wanted an heir all my life but my wife refused me

that one wish. For another man, however? A simpleton, a grimy crofter? Why by all means, she was more than happy to oblige.'

'Let go of the bitterness, Sir Edward.'

'By God I will,' he roared. 'I was at last blessed with a son of my own. Of course not a legitimate one, but how else is one supposed to manage it? I had a beautiful baby boy. But what did his wretched mother do? She ... she ... cast him away! My beloved son. Into the arms of thieves and murderers.'

Parson Snaile shifted around. 'Did you not see him again?'

'I never saw him at all. I never held him, not once. And then he was gone.' Sir Edward wiped his eyes and tried to regain a composure he hadn't had in the first place. 'How, Vicar, could I ever forgive his mother for that?'

The parson shook his head and grimaced.

'Well, I opted for revenge instead. I ... arranged it so that she was arrested ... and accused of the child's murder. As we both know, the ruling classes enjoy spilling the blood of a fallen woman, so it was easy. Before I knew it the whore was being tried and convicted ... and hanged.'

Parson Snaile gave him one of the grimmest, most disapproving looks he'd seen in years.

'Do not,' Sir Edward continued, 'underestimate a man's bitterness at being denied the thing he wants most in life.' He hung his head low. 'Nor his sorrow.'

Some moments of painful reflection, but not prayer, later, Sir Edward looked up into the eyes of Parson Noble Snaile, his vain, spineless, ridiculous pillar of Grasmere. 'God help me, Vicar,' he whimpered. 'I need you now.'

Parson Snaile spoke solemnly. 'You must pay your dues, my son. Tell me – tell God – how you intend to do that.'

'Pay my dues?' Sir Edward said the words several times and chewed them over. It came to him. 'I owe a debt, Vicar, a very large debt, to a respected Grasmere family. Could I could start paying my dues by ... paying them?'

'That would be a good start,' nodded the parson.

'But then again,' Sir Edward muttered, 'settling my debt to – ahem! – Mr Wordsworth would mean the end of my wall.'

Parson Snaile clasped his hands together. 'Let the wall go.'

'I … I couldn't, Vicar. Too big a sacrifice. Too big a dream.'

'You must, and find it in your heart to forgive your wife, and the son she bore. It may ease your conscience.'

Sir Edward had been looking down into his hands, and now he looked up into the sky. 'You know, Vicar,' he sighed, 'there's something about being up here, that gives a man …'

'Faith?' suggested the Parson, turning to him.

'Perspective.'

Sir Edward paused. 'It makes me feel …'

'Closer to God?' tried the Parson again.

'Humbled. And that things are possible.'

'I feel it too. The air is indeed good. Good for painting, good for the soul.'

'The soul?' Sir Edward hesitated. 'I haven't got it in me anymore.'

'An eternal soul? Why surely you—'

'—No, no, the will to get this wall built. You might be on to something, Vicar.'

*Friday, April 15th, 1803*

Dorothy Wordsworth strolled through the churchyard, stopped and looked down at an unusually large memorial stone with the names 'Michael and Isabel Greenhead' carved on it. She was astonished to think William had found the strength to lug it out of Greenhead Ghyll, and felt not a little guilty that she hadn't owned up to Luke about it when she'd visited him in jail. But her motivation had been honourable, she told herself as she knelt down and read the inscription William had composed at her request.

*There is a comfort in the strength of love;*
*'Twill make a thing endurable, which else*
*Would break the heart.*

Standing up again she noticed that fresh spring flowers had been planted at the foot of a freshly dug grave not far from Jack Nettleslack's. She was relieved to have heard that it wasn't Luke's grave – it was that awful man Vipond's, God spare him. Luke, her Luke, hadn't died after all but had left Lakeland for good.

Another spring had come around. 'What a year!' she sighed as she began making her way from the grave towards the lychgate. It was enough to send her round the bend. Everything had changed. Yet here she was, still living in Grasmere, still at little Dove Cottage despite the recent and imminent arrivals. But now she had money for the first time in her life. By some miracle the family's debts had been paid off. She almost didn't know what to do with her riches. Perhaps roast venison and goose a little more often than mutton chops and broth. She could buy herself a proper reticule, and some satin slippers to wear indoors. 'No,' she said, 'I am not the satin slippers type, at least I know that.' Besides, they weren't rich, merely not poor anymore, and the household was growing, and would grow bigger every year. 'So don't get too excited about your little vanities, Dolly!' she checked herself. It was enough to know that at the even-more-matronly age of thirty-one she still had her health, and that maybe in time she might be able to afford herself the luxury of a few porcelain teeth.

A breeze welled up purely out of mischief as she passed through the lychgate and she immediately thought about the daffodils at Ullswater. Of course! It was a year ago to the day since they'd seen them at Ullswater. How the meanest of flowers could inspire such deep feelings! She left the churchyard in a melancholy mood and began the walk home. On the way, though she'd promised she'd be home directly, she couldn't resist going via Dolly's View and having a glance across the lake to the island. It was her secret little mutiny against her destiny.

As she did so something caught her eye. There! On the little island, dancing in the breeze, a few even tiptoeing into the lake. Not a whole constellation of them like at Ullswater, but enough to gladden the saddest of hearts. She'd never noticed them there before. She vowed, this time solemnly, that the absolute moment she reached home she'd show William those few lines she'd written in her journal about the Ullswater daffodils. And then the thought struck her. 'Why,' she cried out into the Grasmere sky, 'should I require *William's* poetic alchemy to turn our little yellow daffodils into gold?' With that she turned to go, but again she caught the flash of something moving on the island, and not the daffodils this time. She screwed up her eyes to get a better view. A man! A big, foxfire-haired hulk of a shepherd in a smock-frock, fitting slates onto the roof of the stone hut. Her heart leapt up, and filled with the purest pleasure, to behold her muse.

THE END ...

*I wander'd lonely as a cloud*
*That floats on high o'er vales and hills,*
*When all at once I saw a crowd,*
*A host, of golden daffodils;*
*Beside the lake, beneath the trees,*
*Fluttering and dancing in the breeze.*

*Continuous as the stars that shine*
*And twinkle on the Milky Way,*
*They stretch'd in never-ending line*
*Along the margin of a bay:*
*Ten thousand saw I at a glance,*
*Tossing their heads in sprightly dance.*

*The waves beside them danced; but they*
*Out-did the sparkling waves in glee:*
*A poet could not but be gay,*
*In such a jocund company:*
*I gazed – and gazed – but little thought*
*What wealth the show to me had brought:*

*For oft, when on my couch I lie*
*In vacant or in pensive mood,*
*They flash upon that inward eye*
*Which is the bliss of solitude;*
*And then my heart with pleasure fills,*
*And dances with the daffodils.*

# Dances with the Daffodils

# Acknowledgements

Special thanks to:

Felicity Connolly; Eve White; Jane Bailey; Martin Medina; Stephen Guise; George Green; Andy Loudon; Ian Whyte; Marc Atkins; Alistair Sanderson; Wendy Toole; Helen Carter; Rachel O'Flanagan; Sally Edwards.

*The Grasmere Journals* by Pamela Woof (1993) 428 words from pages 81, 85, 87, 96, 115 and 117 by kind permission of Oxford University Press.

Poems by William Wordsworth and Dorothy Wordsworth reproduced by kind permission of The Wordsworth Trust, Dove Cottage, Cumbria.

# Acknowledgements